NOAH
CAN'T
EVEN

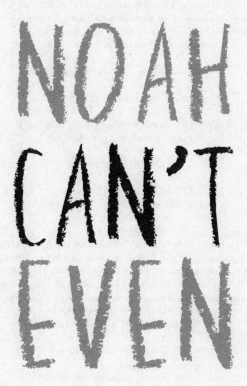

NOAH CAN'T EVEN

SIMON JAMES GREEN

Scholastic Children's Books
An imprint of Scholastic Ltd
Euston House, 24 Eversholt Street, London, NW1 1DB, UK
Registered office: Westfield Road, Southam, Warwickshire, CV47 0RA
SCHOLASTIC and associated logos are trademarks and/or
registered trademarks of Scholastic Inc.

First published in the UK by Scholastic Ltd, 2017

ISBN 978 1407 17994 0

A CIP catalogue record for this book
is available from the British Library.

Printed by CPI Group (UK) Ltd, Croydon, CR0 4YY

Papers used by Scholastic Children's Books are made
from wood grown in sustainable forests.

1 3 5 7 9 10 8 6 4 2

www.scholastic.co.uk

For Sarah

CHAPTER ONE

Noah clung on for dear life. One slip and that would be it. He wasn't sure how much longer his fingers could hold out. If he let go ... instant death! Maybe that would be the best option now. Was this how it would end? Three weeks before his sixteenth birthday. Had he achieved enough in his short life that there would be headlines in the papers? Sure, he had his spelling bee medal (second place, thanks to that villainous word *dodecahedron*), twelve Scout badges and a certificate for making the best apple crumble in Food Technology, but would it be enough for them to describe it as a "tragedy"? Would they print things like "He had so much to offer the world" and "His death is a huge loss not just to society, but mankind"?

He sighed. *Probably not.* Damn it, why hadn't he

donated his liver to a dying child or raised millions for blind, orphaned puppies in Peru? On the other hand, did he want a newspaper article at all? They would only go and illustrate it with a photo from his Facebook profile, and knowing his luck it would be the one of him crying at his thirteenth birthday party when his mum hired a stripper because she thought it would be funny. It wasn't at all funny. All he'd wanted was pizza, bowling and a sleepover with Harry. Instead, she'd invited a load of her *own* mates over, along with "Bambi Sugapops" and her terrifying, medically unfeasible breasts.

At least in his young death, there might be a certain kind of glory. At least he would be immortalized, never growing old, forever young and...

"Get the hell down, you skinny little runt!" shouted Ms O'Malley from the bottom of the climbing frame, blowing her whistle at him. "Now!"

Noah felt his knees weaken as he glanced down at her. Ms O'Malley had a hard, craggy face that had clearly never seen a drop of moisturizer, and a body so ravaged with physical exercise it was a solid, rectangular block of pure muscle. She wasn't just the PE teacher from hell; she was Satan in a tracksuit.

"I can't, I'm stuck!" Noah lied, readjusting the stupidly small shorts that his mum had bought him in Year Eight and had point-blank refused to upgrade ever since. If this debacle could just end swiftly and quietly, he would totally reconsider his atheism.

"If the Year Sevens can climb to the top, then so can you!"

"They're smaller. More nimble!" He shifted about, hoping a combination of *distance* and *angles* meant she couldn't see what he was hiding.

"Get down!"

Running out of options fast, he decided to play the health and safety card; having a kid die on school premises never looked good. "Miss, I am up here, *without the protection of a safety harness*, and I'm in grave danger of falling and sustaining a catastrophic injury."

"No one cares!" she yelled, because apparently student welfare was of no interest to PE teachers. She grabbed a medicine ball and hurled it at the base of the frame. "STRIKE!" she shouted, like she was playing some massive ten-pin bowling game. Then she strode off, probably to hang crosses upside down and sacrifice a goat.

Noah gritted his teeth and watched her go. It was only a strike if the pins were knocked down. He was still very much ... *up*.

He glanced despairingly across the expanse of the sports hall. The boys were in one half, engaged in an assortment of crap gymnastics; the girls were in the other half, enjoying the genteel and cultured pursuit of badminton. In the far corner, Eric Smith was secretly filming the girls on his phone from behind some crash mats, undoubtedly so he would have something to get off

3

to later. Eric looked up and, clearly startled to find Noah staring at him, dropped the phone into the pocket of his shorts and ambled towards the exit, flipping Noah off as he pushed through the double doors on his way out.

"Aww," Noah whimpered, as the frame rattled and his best mate started climbing up towards him. *This was all he needed.*

"I've been told to get you down," Harry explained, clambering up opposite him so their noses were almost touching.

Noah glanced down to see Jordan Scott, a brute of a boy who was six feet tall and nearly three feet wide, looking back up at him and saying "Dickhead!" whilst pretending to cough, much to the merriment of his assorted lackeys.

This had been an error of judgement. Noah'd created a spectacle, and he would never live down the now-inevitable finale. He would have to move schools. After this, it wouldn't be worth going on. "Just leave me here to die, Harry. Save yourself."

"Noah! Man up and stop being a wuss. You put one foot below the other. And repeat. I'll do it with you, take your mind off the height."

"That's not the problem!" he snapped, feeling his cheeks starting to glow bright red.

"Right, well, what is, then?"

Noah looked away, desperately willing himself to spontaneously combust.

"This is ridiculous. I'll have to perform a fireman's lift!" Harry said.

"Haz, no!"

"No choice," he said, trying to swing round, the frame lurching dangerously as he did so.

"A boy-type issue has come up!" Noah bleated, deftly avoiding Harry's grasp.

Harry looked at him blankly. "*What?*"

"A *boy-type* issue has come *up*," Noah repeated, "which makes it *hard* for me to come back down. Right? Very *hard.*"

A grin spread across Harry's face, and he looked down at Noah's shorts. "Oh yeah."

"There was no need to look."

"*Wowzer.*"

"Stop looking!"

"Well, what caused it?"

He felt his stomach flutter. "What?"

"Is it 'cause I'm looking *fine* in my new polo shirt?"

Noah rolled his eyes. "Shut up."

"Sophie!" Harry grinned, face lighting up with realization.

"No!"

"Yes! Oh, YES! I knew it! I knew—"

"Shut up! It's not!" Noah scowled at him. *One comment.* He'd made one stupid, ill-conceived comment in Year Nine. Loads of the boys had been talking at lunch about girls and boobs and sex and stuff. It had been awful because everyone else seemed to have watched loads of porn and knew all about different types of sex. And he'd never really ... he didn't think about that. He didn't know why, he just didn't. Probably it was because he was *nice* and *respectable* and not a *sex maniac* like everyone else. But, in any case, he'd confided in Harry, as they walked home that afternoon, that he'd thought Sophie had "a pleasant manner" and "good bone structure". That was all. And then it went:

> **HARRY:** Oh my God, you *lurrrrve* her!
>
> **NOAH:** No! I mean, she's nice, but—
>
> **HARRY:** She's *nice*! Oh my God! Coming from you, that's basically saying you want to do *bow chicka wah wah* all night long. *Yeah, baby, I lurrve your pleasant manner! Your pleasant manner is so hot! Pleasant manner, baby! Gimme your sexy, pleasant manner!*
>
> **NOAH:** Go home, Harry, you're drunk.

And, honestly, he really *had* just admired her polite tone and pleasing facial symmetry. Sophie was an amazing girl. She had this indie-cool thing going on, wearing stuff that she liked – not what the latest popular-culture craze was. She had awesome hair – or more specifically, shiny, bouncy black ringlets that cascaded down to her shoulders and smelt of peaches, or sometimes other nice fruits. She also had the most radiant golden-brown skin – either by good fortune, genetics or witchcraft, *she had never suffered from acne.* Yes, she really was perfect. But what Noah liked most was the fact she was intelligent and didn't try to hide it. If you're predicted good grades, it's normally best to keep a low profile because of the crap you get from other kids. But Sophie didn't care. She hung around with her small set of intelligent girls, reading books and having proper conversations that didn't include petty gossip or salacious rumours about who might be getting with whom. He'd walked past them once at lunch and distinctly heard "I *would* read Dostoyevsky, but the text just feels so dense, you know?" And Noah had sighed, and wished he could one day be considered for membership to their friendship group. That's all he wanted. A discussion about Russian authors over smoked salmon sandwiches and freshly squeezed juice. He didn't think about doing … *other stuff* with her. It wouldn't be right. She was too sophisticated, cultured and elegant. Something as base and animalistic as sex was surely beneath her.

"Noah, give it up," said Harry, shaking his head and readjusting his footing on the climbing frame. "She's entirely out of your league."

Noah huffed. "What's that supposed to mean?" Sure, he would never be considered the hottest boy in the school; that accolade would be given to Josh Lewis. (To be fair,

Josh had the unfair advantage of being *nineteen*, as the school had apparently asked him to stay on for an extra year to help out the sports teams. Noah had his doubts about the story, but a young man with such an athletic build and soulful eyes wouldn't be a liar, so it was probably true.) But Noah did have a number of points in his favour: good teeth, feet that didn't smell, and a relatively new pair of black-rimmed spectacles that definitely made him look like he worked in advertising in London. Yes, there was work to do. Other boys had more muscle tone and looked bigger, whereas he was skinny and a bit awkward. Other boys were more hairy in unexpected (and sometimes alarming) places, whereas he was quite ... well, *smooth*. And he was still shorter than most of the girls – with the exception of Maisie Andrews, who was currently in a wheelchair, having broken both her legs in a riding accident. But assuming she got better and could one day walk again, she'd be taller too. *But*, and this was his ace card, he was top set for *everything*.

He narrowed his eyes at Harry. *"What exactly do you mean?"*

"Let's put it this way: what are you wearing for Melissa's party tomorrow?"

"I'm not going to ... oh, *funny*. You're *funny*," Noah grimaced. OK, there might be some slight issue in the popularity department, but who cared? Even if he did want go to her stupid party for cool people, *which he didn't*, there wouldn't be anyone else going whom he liked. And even if he did want to go, *which he totally, one hundred per cent didn't,* he didn't have anything remotely suitable to wear. And even if he did want to go, *and he absolutely could not think of anything more vile than spending any time in Melissa's cursed company,* he would probably need to bring alcohol to get in and there's no way he could buy any because he still managed to look about twelve, even though he definitely wasn't. No, he would actually *prefer* to spend a night at home, munching his way through a family-sized bag of cheesy Wotsits. In fact he would *pay money* to do that.

"Some people like geeks!" he exclaimed. "Some people know it'll be us who will one day get the top jobs and the big salaries. We're good long-term bets!" Anyone with a bit of foresight would see that and date him now.

"It doesn't matter. We don't look like we'd be a good shag."

"Geeks can get a bit of *bow chicka wah wah* too. It's not unheard of!"

Harry screwed his face up. "Er, I think it is pretty unheard of. Anyway, if someone wants to do *bow chicka wah wah,* they'd probably want to do *bow chicka wah wah* with someone who does *bow chicka wah wah* really bloody well."

"What sort of person *is* good at *bow chicka wah wah?"* Because he had a nagging doubt it wouldn't be him. He'd seen diagrams in PSHE and it seemed unduly complicated.

"I dunno – maybe he has pecs and abs. Maybe he has a tattoo..."

"I'm not getting a tattoo. I'm not a manual labourer."

"These are the things people go for."

"Are *you* planning on getting a tattoo?"

"No. Maybe."

"What?" Noah squealed. "It's illegal until you're eighteen!"

"Rule breaking. It's very attractive. Everyone loves a bad boy."

"I'm telling your mum. You can't trust those places. They don't have medical training, you know? They stick all these dirty old needles in people and they haven't got so much as a first-aid badge from the Cubs. It's disgusting."

"Chill out, I'm not getting a tat."

"A tat? A *'tat'?"* What had Harry become? Why was he speaking in slang like some drug-dealing street urchin? "You can't become cool. If you become cool, I'll be the only uncool person left!"

Harry grinned. "There's no danger of me becoming cool, *innit?"*

"Don't push it. *Knob."*

"Speaking of which, how's yours?"

"It's worse than ever. If you have a ... *boy-type issue* for more than an hour you have to go to hospital. I read it on the internet. I can't be hospitalized with a boy-type issue! My mum would have a field day." He closed his eyes and pictured the scene: the doctors consoling his sobbing mother. *We're sorry, Mrs Grimes, there was nothing we could do... It just exploded. The operating theatre is carnage.*

"What's happening up there?" Ms O'Malley shouted up, rattling the frame again at its base. "This isn't a mothers' meeting! This is Year Eleven physical education! I don't see anything *physical* happening!"

"You would if I came down," Noah muttered, making Harry snigger.

"*Naomi* Grimes – get your bony little arse down here – NOW!" Ms O'Malley bellowed.

"My name's Noah!" he shouted down indignantly. "She knows damn well my name's Noah!" he hissed at Harry.

"I think it's clear she's taking the piss."

There was a sudden flurry of excitement at the entrance to the sports hall as Jess Jackson ran in, clutching a fistful of A5 pages in her hand.

"OH MY GOD YOU GOTTA SEE THIS!" she squealed. "YOU ARE GONNA PISS YOURSELVES!"

Noah watched as the entire class swarmed around Jess, grabbing papers from her like she was giving out free Starmix at a Year Seven disco.

"What the hell's going on?" Noah asked.

"Who cares? It's probably nothing."

"Why's everyone pointing at us?"

"Umm ... I think they're pointing at you."

It was then that Jordan Scott held one of the sheets

aloft, affording Noah a razor-sharp view, as the gym erupted in hysterical laughter and piss-taking cheering.

Noah swallowed hard. They were flyers. And he knew exactly what those flyers were. In fact, he had already destroyed a stack of them, hoping – he had even *prayed* – that they would never see the light of day.

CHAPTER TWO

Noah sat in the furthest corner of the classroom, watching a solitary fly repeatedly hurl itself at the window, and bravely ignoring the fact everyone was still looking at him like he'd accidentally come to school completely naked.

Seven years! He had kept this quiet for seven years! And then the stupid cow decided to "up the ante" (his mother's words) and get some flyers made. He had binned the ones he'd found in the house last week, but she must have made more. And now everyone knew; she might as well have just printed some little cards advertising *escort services* and Blu-Tacked them up in the phone box.

Officially his mum was on the dole. Unofficially, she toured pubs and clubs with her blisteringly shite act "Ruby Devine – A Tribute to Beyoncé". She wasn't actually called Ruby Devine. That was a stage name to "enhance the magic and glamour" (his mother's words), but also to put any investigators from the jobcentre off the scent. To date, her act had only been performed in larger nearby towns and a few coastal holiday camps, meaning the true horror of what she did remained a secret to the locals. But in a misguided attempt to break into the Little Fobbing market, she'd had ten thousand A5 flyers produced, and, for reasons known only to her idiotic self, had clearly left a bunch of them on reception at the front of the sports hall, most of which had now been stuck up all over the school. His mother, in a catastrophic Primark leotard, pouting at the camera like she actually thought she was an internationally acclaimed superstar. He might have got away with it, badly disguised as she was in false eyelashes and a wig, had it not been for the details in the bottom right:

"For bookings contact Lisa Grimes."

And the small personal biography she had added in an attempt to big herself up:

"Lisa has performed at many of the top and most glamorous establishments for over two decades. Proud mum of Noah, she splits her time between New York, LA and Little Fobbing."

None of this was remotely true. She'd never even been to LA or New York, plus *proud mum*?! Was she having a laugh? Noah clenched his fists, fingernails digging into his palms. Why did she have a complete inability to be a normal mum? Why couldn't she be a top lawyer or businesswoman or even just quietly accept dole money and lie low? At the very least, why couldn't she try, just once, *not* to totally embarrass him and ruin his already appalling life?

And the piss-taking at school had been on the level of:

"All right, Noah? How much would your mum charge for a *private* dance?"

And:

"Hey, Noah? Say my name! Go on, *say my name*!"

And even:

"Oi, Noah?! You got any *lemonade*? Yeah, I bet you do. I bet there's a lot of lemonade at your house!"

It had been the most humiliating day ever. Worse than the time his mum loudly accused him of "playing with himself" as they queued for chicken in a packed KFC, and he wasn't even— SOMETIMES THINGS JUST NEED READJUSTING, OK?! Things being as they were, Noah decided he was now ninety-eight per cent certain God didn't exist. God was supposed to reward the good and punish the bad; that's how Noah'd always understood it to work. But he hadn't been bad. Not bad in the sense of being an evil despot doing war crimes, anyway. The list of bad things he'd done was decidedly lame. In fact, the top three entries would be:

1) Pocketing a spare condom from a PSHE class, just in case he got lucky (obviously now well past its expiry date).

2) Sabotaging Penelope Carter's apple crumble in Food Technology by moving her oven dial when she wasn't looking, causing her crumble topping to burn and thereby securing his success in the Best Apple Crumble Contest in Year Eight.

3) Forging several excuse notes from his mum during football in the cold months (which was totally fair to do when the teacher was wearing ten layers of weatherproof, fur-lined survival kit you could climb Everest in, and you only had on thin nylon shorts and a threadbare T-shirt. It was a matter of *human rights*, right?!).

So not really all that bad in the scheme of things. Surely an all-powerful being would cut you a bit of slack at some point?

But apparently not.

"How ya' doin', No-ah?" came the mock-sultry voice.

Jess Jackson flicked back her dyed-blonde hair, smiled maliciously and eased herself into the empty seat next to him. Noah froze in horror. She was so close he could smell her fake tan and Justin Bieber perfume. All the lads fancied

Jess. Every inch of her was manicured, primped and preened, with dark, heavy eye make-up and scary, severe eyebrows. The other boys seemed to like that, but Noah just thought she looked like a demented clown from a horror film. With her above-the-knee skirt she also blatantly flouted the uniform rules in a completely unacceptable way. Jess was trouble. In Year Five she took the class hamster home for Easter – *and it came back dead*. In Year Seven she threw a KitKat at a swan on a geography field trip – *provoking it to attack a nearby toddler*. In Year Eight she clearly faked a seizure after an assembly about epilepsy but somehow managed to get off school anyway; Year Nine, stole a horse; Year Ten, threw a drumstick at Mrs Butcher and the police were called. And this was just the stuff Noah knew about.

"What do you want, Jess?" He stared down at his desk, doing his best to sound strong and in control.

"I was wondering, does your mum do other acts as well as Beyoncé?"

"No."

"Does she do Miley Cyrus?"

"No."

"Does she *twerk*, Noah? Does she *twerk it* all night long?"

"No, she does not."

Straight answers. Direct. Give her nothing.

"You've gone bright red. Is it because you're getting turned on, thinking about your twerking mum?"

He swallowed hard. *Ignore her. Don't rise to it.*

"Is everyone getting on with their work?" Miss Palmer said, looking over. "Jess?"

"I'm just *liaising* with Noah, miss, about one of the questions, but he doesn't know the answer! Are you sure he should be *top set* for everything?"

"*Piss off!*" Noah hissed. How dare this *utter clod* question his hard-won academic success!

"Ooh, Noah, look how mad you getting!"

He flinched. "It's *you're.* Look how mad *you're* getting!"

There was nothing more irritating to him than incorrect grammar, but Jess either didn't understand or was deliberately winding him up more. "Not me who is angry, Noah! You *crazy* man!"

"Shut up!"

"*You* so vexed!"

"YOU'RE!"

"*You* bitter! *You* salty! *You*—"

"Shut up, just SHUT UP!" he shouted.

Silence. The entire class stopped what they were doing and looked at him. Miss Palmer crossed her arms and gave him a disapproving stare.

He felt the blood drain from his cheeks. He'd let Jess get to him. You didn't answer back to people like her. Better just to take it and not give them bait. When would he learn?

"Wanker," Jess said, getting up abruptly so the chair fell backwards. "Nice boner."

On the bright side, having to see your own mum in a leotard did at least put a stop to any *boy-type issues.* "I haven't got..."

"You so have. Everyone! Noah's got a boner 'cause he's thinking about his pop star mum!" she shouted, to cheers from the rest of the class.

"Jess! Enough!" shouted Miss Palmer.

Jess sauntered off in the direction of her desk as the noise subsided. He clenched his jaw and seriously considered throwing his pencil down *really hard*, or maybe snapping it in half or something. Only it was a freshly sharpened Paper Mate Mirado Black Warrior with classic medium-firm lead and pressure-bonded cedar wood that encased the ultra-smooth core. He wasn't prepared to sacrifice premium stationery for her.

He sighed. He'd never done anything to Jess. Why couldn't she just get on with her own pointless life and he would get on with his? Why did the day have to get worse and worse? He snuck a look across the room to see if Sophie was also joining in the fun at his expense.

No.

Of course she wasn't. Because Sophie was lovely and all-round A-star fantastic and wouldn't do something like that. She was just quietly finishing her worksheet – with all the correct answers and with perfect handwriting, Noah guessed. Perfect Sophie. Perfect, intelligent, hard-working-but-still-popular-not-that-she-cared-about-popularity Sophie.

If only he could be just a bit more like her.

Why had he been dealt such bad cards?

Damn it. He was now ninety-eight-point-five per cent certain God didn't exist. Ninety-eight-point-five per cent certain there couldn't possibly be such a miserably vicious and malignant force at work. Life wasn't a miracle courtesy of some higher power; it was just bad luck.

And yet...

What if, in fact, his near-atheism had *angered* a very real and vengeful God, who was now determined to make life hell for this apostate? What then?

Well, God, if you do exist, he thought, *this is it. This is your final chance. You have a literally one-point-five per cent window in which to prove yourself to me. Make something good happen. Just one thing. Prove it. Prove it by the time the bell rings at the end of the lesson and I might reconsider.*

"Right, everyone!" Miss Palmer began, wearily moving to the front of the class.

Noah looked up, point-blank refusing to give his usual encouraging smile because Miss Palmer had completely failed to reprimand Jess in an acceptable way.

"Listen up; here's what I want you all to do over the weekend ready for Monday's lesson..."

"Monday?!" said Jess, looking up from where she was filing her nails.

"Yes, Monday. I'm going to put you in groups of three and assign you the roles of either being 'for' or 'against' the building of a new fictional supermarket in Little Fobbing. You're going to imagine that we're having a big town council meeting, and you've got to present your views. Everyone understand?"

There were general discontented murmurs from the cool kids, who didn't want their weekend of underage drinking and being popular to be put in jeopardy. Noah got his best fountain pen out and selected a fresh page of his homework journal, ready to make notes. There would be time for fun when he was a millionaire. And that would be fine. Really, it would.

"Right!" Miss Palmer surveyed the room, deciding on the groups. "Jess with Jordan and Tom... Ella and Louise with Eric..."

"Jesus Christ..." muttered Ella.

"Sophie, you can go with..."

Noah held his breath and looked up like an enthusiastic meerkat, hoping to catch Miss Palmer's eye and make her choose him. Being in a group with Sophie might solve everything! Thanks to his mum, his social status was in negative balance, but Sophie would help raise it back up again; her enigmatic coolness would rub off on him! Not only that, she was an intellectual match so she would play an equal part in the project and not make him do all the work whilst taking all the credit herself.

"You can be with Jon and Lauren..."

Noah sank back down. Ninety-nine-point-nine-four

per cent. What was the point? Things were terrible, and they were always going to be terrible. He wallowed in misery whilst Miss Palmer rattled through the rest of the class, the percentage points of his atheist certainty going up like the display on a stopwatch. Ninety-nine-point-nine-five per cent. Ninety-nine-point-ninety-six per cent. The All-Powerful Being just had the perfect opportunity to prove his existence and had blown it.

He realized only when Miss Palmer started recapping exactly what the exercise involved that he didn't have a group at all, never mind one with the best girl in the class in it. Noah panicked. Everyone else had a group. Why had he been left out? He raised his hand.

"I'll answer questions at the end, Noah."

Transparently, that would be too late. If it waited until the end, the bell would ring and everyone would be leaving the room, so he wouldn't be assigned to a group in time. He would have to do the exercise all by himself, with no help. That might mean he wouldn't get top marks. Intolerable! Ninety-nine-point-nine-seven per cent.

"Noah's still got his hand up!" Jess said, with relish.

"I will answer questions at the end!"

Ninety-nine-point-nine-eight per cent.

"Maybe he needs the toilet, miss," suggested Ella.

Oh, here we go! Noah thought, knowing damn well what was coming.

"He might piss himself again, miss, like he did on the Year Eight trip to the London Dungeon," Jess added.

"What is it, Noah?" Miss Palmer sighed.

Ninety-nine-point-nine-nine per cent. He lowered his arm. "I haven't got a group, miss," he muttered.

"Right. Well, why didn't you say?"

"Nobody's gonna want to go with *him*," Jess said.

The bell rang. That was it. The end of the lesson. The window of opportunity for the All-Powerful Being to prove himself had closed. A hundred per cent. It was over.

And then the clouds parted, angels sang, a blinding light shone down as the earth quaked and a million cherubs shot arrows of bliss into the joyful air ... and the miracle to end all miracles occurred.

CHAPTER THREE

"Actually, I'll go with Noah." It was Sophie. She had volunteered herself to work with him. But seriously, WHAT?!

"Great. This is for first band on Monday!" Miss Palmer shouted, barely audible above the din.

Noah stared down hard at his desk, unable to stop his right leg jiggling up and down. He didn't dare look at Sophie. He didn't dare do anything except sit there, motionless, in case it was all suddenly taken away from him, as quickly and easily as it had been given. This was crazy. Why would she want to work with him? Why would she put her coolness at risk by actually *offering* to work with him, rather than being reluctantly forced by the teacher?

"Hi, Noah."

It was her. It was Sophie. She was standing over him. Speaking words. Oh God.

"Do you want to arrange a time to meet, then?"

Noah looked at her blankly. "You want to meet up?"

"Yes."

"With me?"

"We're working together for the presentation."

"Right. Yes. Of course."

He couldn't believe it. She was asking to meet up with him. His mind spun: he'd wear his blue hoody, he looked OK in that. And he would lather himself in Lynx Africa. He had it on good authority that girls *loved* that smell. If his mum lent him some cash, he could take her to the cafe. Buy her a milkshake. That's what people did when they met up, wasn't it? He was pretty sure he'd seen that type of thing on the telly, before they...

"Shall we just go back to your place now and do it?" Sophie suggested.

He looked back at her, wide-eyed. Surely she didn't mean ... not *it*? Not that? Surely? Not so soon... He cleared his throat. "When you say *do it*, I mean... What do you mean?"

"Do the homework," she continued, patiently. "Then we don't have to worry about it all weekend."

"Yes, I see. Good." That was excellent news. He would hate to be rushed into some sort of sexual liaison. "But ... *now*, did you say?"

"Yes."

"At *my* house?"

"It's just my dad's in and he'll only be annoying. You know how it is with parents."

Did he ever. "Yeah..." He managed to nod. But *now*? Bloody *now*?! He was in his school uniform, the house was a tip, he knew there wasn't any Coke or anything nice to drink in the fridge and his room was littered with dirty pants and used tissues and other stuff he didn't want her to see. No. "Now" was not good. "Now" was a disaster. "Now" was...

"Now's cool," said Noah. "Now ... is *really* great."

She gave him a little smile. This was a good turn of events. He may still have been the butt of jokes, but as they walked along the corridor and out into the yard, at least nobody said anything to his face. They whispered. They may have stared for a bit too long. And yes, they may have performed an entire Beyoncé routine, which had clearly taken a considerable amount of time to put together, and included choreographed backing dancers from Year Seven, *but nobody said anything to his actual face.*

Harry was waiting as usual by the little wall near the gates, lazily chewing some gum whilst he watched Noah and Sophie approach.

"All right, Harry?" said Noah, doing his best to play things cool. "You know Sophie, right?"

"Yes, I can easily remember everyone we've grown up with. Hey, Soph. How you doing?"

"Good, thanks, Harry. Feel like we've never really hung out, have we?"

Harry shrugged. "We should fix that."

"We should."

How was Harry able to be all natural and flowing with his conversation? How did he suddenly manage to come across as some sort of all-American high school hero, all *cool* and good with the ladies, whilst Noah was clearly showing himself to be some sort of blabbering child?

He decided to take control. "Anyway ... Sophie and I are working on a project for geography, so we're going to my house now to finish it 'cause it's due on Monday, so..."

"So, you're blowing me off?" Harry said.

"I'm ... *what*? What am I doing to you?"

"Blowing me off."

Noah went red. It all sounded terribly sexual and awkward, but they *were* with Sophie, and she *was* cool and zeitgeisty and stuff, so he supposed he should indeed make an effort with modern Americanized language, even if it drove him completely crazy. "Erm – well, I do need to *blow you off*, if that's OK, Harry, because Sophie and I are just going home now to do this thing. But then we'll blow each other off, so after that maybe I'll see if you're about?"

"Whatever, that's cool."

Harry was being nonchalant about it all, but Noah

knew this was a major deal, and he felt terrible. This would be the first time they *hadn't* hung out after school together. First time since Year Seven. "I'll make it up to you, Harry."

"Look, *guys*," Sophie said, holding up her hands, "we could totally do this another time. I mean, *now* would have been good, but if you've already got plans..."

"No!" the boys chorused.

Sophie looked at Harry and then at Noah. "Right. *Fine.* Well, shall we all walk in the general direction together anyway?"

Noah locked eyes with Harry, sending an important subliminal message. A message that read *I am with Sophie. This is important. It's my chance to impress.*

"Actually, I gotta see some peeps," Harry said, breaking eye contact.

"OK, *great.*" Noah nodded. "Computer club?"

"No," said Harry.

"Oh? Then ... then *who*?"

"Noah, will you just, you know, *go*?" Harry suggested, popping another piece of gum in his mouth. *Now he was chewing two pieces of gum.* That was serious rebellion. Gum was not permitted on school premises. Harry stood up. "I'll catch you later. *Good luck!*" and he winked. Harry *winked.*

Noah looked at him aghast. "What do you mean?!" he squealed. "What do you mean, 'good luck'? Why would I need luck? Nothing's happening, everything's normal! It's not a date!" He turned to Sophie in an attempt at damage limitation. "It's not, Sophie, honest – I don't know what he's on about!"

"I think he just meant with the geography project," Sophie offered.

"What?"

Harry shrugged again. *He was shrugging a lot. And chewing gum a lot. What did this mean?* "Exactly. Good luck with the project. What did you think I meant?"

"But you winked when you said it, so it sounded like you meant..."

"Like I meant 'goodbye', maybe?"

"No, but winking can sometimes mean that the thing you're talking about is really, like ... sex ... stuff."

"WHAT?!" Harry and Sophie both chorused.

Noah gulped. He'd got it all badly wrong. He wanted to bang his head against the brick wall. *Why are you such a social disaster? Why are you not locked away to save everyone else's embarrassment?* He brazened it out, because he didn't want to draw any more attention to fact he was a TOTAL GORMLESS MUPPET. "Anyway. Good. I see what you meant now. Of course. That's fine. Good luck with the geography project. *Thank you.*"

Harry shook his head in disbelief. "Call me."

"I will. I'll call. I was already gonna anyway." He pressed a slightly furry Haribo from his pocket into Harry's hand, by way of an apology for not hanging out with him. "Get home safe."

Harry rolled his eyes. "It's literally five minutes away, so hopefully I'll avoid the kidnappers, terrorists and any rogue volcanoes. See you later, Soph." He smiled at her. He had a *very charming* smile, Noah considered. *Very charming* indeed. Was he secretly trying to charm Sophie with it? Was he trying to seduce her with his deep brown eyes you could get lost in? With the fact he had hair with a fringe that swept across perfectly, with no cowlicks, ever? Was he trying to beguile her with the fact he was a couple of inches taller than Noah, didn't have bags under his eyes and had a sweet little snub nose? Damn his perfect BMI and twenty-twenty vision! And he had the beginnings of proper arm muscles. Noah had noticed that in PE. Something else too … something potentially more alarming. Harry had suddenly started wearing Calvin Klein boxers. Underwear for people who were thinking about bewitching others into sexual activities, for sure! Why this sudden change? Until now, Harry had worn underwear from any normal high street chain store. Now, he was a designer underwear person. Noah hadn't commented on the development, but maybe it all made sense. Maybe Noah had competition for Sophie's attention.

Noah watched as Harry sauntered off, all aloof and mysterious. Aloof and mysterious and charming and cool and all-American high school hero with Calvin Klein boxers…

"*Please* can we go?" Sophie asked, breaking in on his thoughts.

"What? Oh, er, absolutely! Let's go, go, go!"

CHAPTER FOUR

If Little Fobbing had had a completely truthful Wikipedia entry, it would have read something like:

> Little Fobbing
> Little Fobbing is a crappy little town in the middle
> of nowhere, with absolutely nothing fun to do;
> filled mainly with people over the age of 130.
> Come here if you want to be an undertaker,
> otherwise don't bother. See also: Hell, Pit of
> Satan, The Abyss, Purgatory.

Noah's house was on a bland estate built from cheap brick in the eighties, during an apparent national shortage of architectural imagination. He took a deep breath and turned the key in the lock, showing Sophie in through the tiny hall and into the lounge, where he was mortified to discover his mum had erected a clothes horse proudly displaying an array of her ridiculous frilly knickers and horrific thongs.

"Oh, GOD!" he howled, throwing himself in front of the display in an attempt to hide it all. He manically concertinaed the contraption together and rushed it through the door into the kitchen-diner, out of sight.

"Not mine, obviously!" he laughed, attempting to make light of it but realizing immediately it sounded like they *were* indeed his, because why deny it otherwise?

"I mean, I don't wear women's knickers!"

No, that still sounded like he did.

"They're Mum's. Not mine. I wouldn't wear knickers. I hate them."

You hate them?!

"...Unless they're being worn by a girl I like..."

Oh, shut up, you utter fool, now you sound like a pervert.

"I don't wear knickers. Girls wear knickers. Knickers are fine on girls. But I don't think about it a lot."

He nodded. That was the best he could do.

"Wow," said Sophie, ignoring him and surveying the room.

"Yeah. Sorry," he said, casting his eyes over the faded, limp curtains, ramshackle sideboard and twenty-one-inch TV that wasn't even flatscreen. The reason he never wanted anyone to come back here? The embarrassment of living in this house. It screamed the fact they were totally broke.

"No. I like it."

"What?"

"It's got individuality."

"That's just a nice way of saying it's weird," Noah said, convinced that she was just being polite and was inwardly in hysterics at the crazy junk shop she'd just walked into.

"It's got history." Sophie smiled. "I like that. Like this sofa. It's got a soul."

Noah tried very hard not to gawp at her. A soul? The only thing that manky old sofa was likely to have was *fleas*. Certainly not a soul.

Why was she being so nice? Nobody in their right mind would be this nice, except Harry, of course. It felt like she was setting him up for a fall. Like she was actually just taking the piss, but in a really clever, cunning sort of way.

"This your mum, yeah?" she said, looking at a photo montage on the wall from gigs she had done.

"Yeah," he muttered, waiting for the barbed comment that would surely follow.

"Cool photo. Have you seen her show?"

"Couple of times." *Thirty-six and counting.*

"Any good?"

Noah shrugged. The show was probably the worst thing he had ever seen in his life, consisting of ramshackle choreography, piss-poor lip-syncing and a portable fog machine that frequently malfunctioned and pumped out thick smoke that nearly asphyxiated the audience. Bizarrely, people often clapped and cheered. Maybe they were mocking her? Maybe they thought his mother was on a "scheme" to help talentless people find jobs in the performing arts, and so they felt they should be encouraging? "I dunno, it's probably OK if you're drunk."

"I know what they've been saying at school about it," she said, glancing at him. "Although some of the boys definitely weren't complaining, if you know what I mean?"

"Oh, God! Really?"

"*Really.* The boys at our school are so pathetic and disrespectful. Present company excluded."

"Oh, yes, thank you," he said. "Compliment ... accepted. But I mean ... those stupid flyers she had done, though."

"But that's how performers get work. They have to advertise."

"Yeah, but in *that* outfit? Did you see them? Pouting and ... in a *leotard.*"

"Nothing wrong with a leotard."

"She's forty!"

"You'll be forty one day."

"Yeah, and when I am, I won't wear a leotard!"

Sophie laughed, and Noah relaxed and cracked a smile. She wasn't going to take the piss after all. Why would she? That sort of stuff was beneath her. Things were going OK, he supposed.

"What about your dad?"

Things were *not* going OK.

"What about him?" he said, pretending to be busy by pulling his stuff out of his school bag and slinging it on the end of the trampy old sofa. And, after all, what *could* he say about him? That he'd disappeared six years ago, whereabouts unknown? That he'd left Noah and his mum with nothing? So what could Noah tell her? *Dad's gone. I don't know where. I don't know why. He's screwed up our lives, but I still miss him. And I still love him. And I know that's mad, but everything would be better if he just came back.*

"Nothing. I just..." Sophie shrugged and looked away. "Nothing."

Noah looked down at the floor and wondered if he should say something. He knew what she was getting at. *Everyone* had heard the story. He'd only just turned ten when his dad vanished. When he asked his mum where he was, she just told him she didn't know. On the first night, the second night, the third week, the fourth month – she "didn't know". But then people starting saying things. Saying they hadn't seen his dad – where was he? So Noah made up little stories, because saying you didn't know sounded really weird. So he'd be "on holiday" or "visiting some friends" or "working away". But as time went on, people were more intrigued, especially because it transpired that he owed money to various people in the town. People started taking the piss: "Your dad still 'away on business', is he?" They taunted him and his mum was saying nothing – wouldn't even talk about it with him. He couldn't stand it. So he made up the mother of all stories: his dad was being held hostage by pirates. It was the perfect cover: it explained why his dad had vanished. It explained why they hadn't heard from him. And it would hopefully make people feel sorry for his dad too, even if he did owe them money.

The trouble was, no one believed him. *Fine*, he thought. *I'll prove it.* So, he constructed a ransom note, made to add credibility to the story. But then someone pointed out the note was composed of letters cut out from the primary school newsletter, even though the pirates were, according to Noah, from "Timbuktu" – which had been the first foreign-sounding place that had sprung to mind.

Fine, he thought. *I'll produce more proof.* So, in a final *coup de théâtre*, Noah produced and starred in a video purporting to be from the kidnappers. He'd heard about pirate attacks in the news, so he knew pirates were real, but it didn't occur to him they would be substantially different from the ones in books and films, except maybe they had modern weapons and communications technology. So he donned a skull-and-crossbones hat, eyepatch and ten of his mum's necklaces. He ran the footage through some software that made the image grainy and distorted and it was job done: a vicious piratical kidnapper telling the world that Noah's dad would "dance the hempen jig" or be made to "walk the plank". He finished it with a "Yo ho ho" and a "Shiver me timbers" to add authenticity to the piece. A couple of clicks, and the masterpiece was uploaded to YouTube.

And then ... *calamity!* Within hours it had amassed a ludicrous number of likes and gone viral. "Funniest shit ever!" one comment read. Or: "This kid is crazy!" Everyone laughed. Everyone thought he was a joke, and no one was going to let him live it down. And the whole pirate story was something that everyone still ridiculed him for to this day. No one, not for a second, cut him a little bit of slack for being a confused, frightened, heartbroken ten-year-old whose dad had vanished.

"It's just me and Mum now," he said, desperate to change the subject because he could feel the tears behind his eyes and he didn't want to cry in front of her. *Keep it together!* he told himself. *Keep it light. Keep it normal!* "Do you want a drink?"

"Cup of tea would be nice," she said, flopping down on the sofa.

"Tea? OK. Tea." That was fine, he could do that. Teabag, hot water, milk. But what if she wanted special tea? What if she wanted Earl Grey or Darjeeling or something? What if she wanted sugar? Did they have sugar?!

"Is that OK?" Sophie said.

WHAT IF SHE LIKED TO DRINK IT WITH SOMETHING WEIRD LIKE A SLICE OF LEMON?! "No, yeah. 'Course it is. I like tea too."

"Good."

"Tea's great," he nodded enthusiastically, trying to engage in harmless small talk like a normal person. "Tea's lovely. I love tea. Good old British tea!"

Sophie glanced up at him and raised an amused eyebrow. "Chill out, yeah?"

"Yeah," Noah agreed. "Yeah."

He sloped through to the bomb site of a kitchen, flicked the kettle on, took a couple of deep breaths and massaged his temples.

"OK, OK," he told himself, wishing he'd come back with Harry instead so they could just spend half an hour chilling out in front of the telly, watching stupid kids' programmes.

No. No, he must impress her. She must end up liking him enough that they could maybe become good friends and people might think he was just a normal, regular guy after all. This would be fine.

He rinsed a couple of dirty mugs under the tap and, in the absence of a washing-up brush, tried to scrub them clean with his fingers. What was she doing in there right now? Was she nosing around? What if she stumbled across the list of suggested dinner recipes he'd prepared for his mother, which she'd callously dismissed as "up-its-own-arse *MasterChef* crap"? A normal boy doesn't jot down ingredients for "duo of pork with potato and celeriac rosti, apple puree and roasted sage, followed by rose-petal panna cotta with damson and lavender Viennese shortbread". Oh God.

Tea.

He was looking in the cupboard for the tea. Where was it? A jar of Mellow Birds ... empty ... some sweeteners, a congealed jar of beef extract... Noah began to panic, flinging open random cupboards. Where the hell was the tea?

"You all right in there?" Sophie called through from the lounge.

"Er – yes!"

"Need some help?"

"No! No, it's under control."

He slammed the final cupboard shut, and it fell off its hinges and clattered on to the floor, scraping a good layer of skin off his shin on the way down. Noah writhed in silent agony, not wanting to alert Sophie to the mayhem that was unfurling just the other side of the wall. Defeated, he leaned weakly over the counter just as the kettle reached boiling point, forcing a jet of viciously hot steam into his face. "AAAARGH! SH— SHOOT! F— FLIPPIN' ... PANTS!" he screamed, desperately trying not to swear in front of her.

"Noah?!"

"NO! STAY THERE! DO NOT COME IN!" he squealed, fumbling around for the tap.

"What's happening?"

"STAY!" he shouted, splashing cold water on to his face.

He patted his face with a dirty tea towel and propped the stricken cupboard door back against the unit. He could feel the wetness of his bleeding shin against his trouser leg, but looking for a plaster was futile. His mother didn't even have any teabags; why would she have anything as opulent as basic first aid?

He considered whether using an old teabag out of the bin might be a viable option. It was gross, but the boiling water would kill off any bacteria so it would probably be OK. He gingerly poked through the fag ash and remains of his mother's Indian takeaway from last night, finally discovering a hard little bag covered in korma sauce. He fished it out and rinsed it under the tap. It wasn't ideal but it represented the best hope of success. He plonked it in the mug and poured the water over it, squashing the unyielding bag against the side of the cup in the hope of releasing a bit of tea flavour.

Nothing.

It was just a mug of hot water with a mouldy old teabag and a bit of scale from the kettle at the bottom. Maybe it needed time to brew. He poured in a little milk and a solid lump of what looked like cottage cheese fell into the mug. Noah closed his eyes and counted to five. He was determined not to let his mother and her piss-poor housekeeping ruin this for him. He calmly took the teaspoon and began to fish the cheesy bits out of the mug, piece by piece. There was loads of it. Millions of little specks, floating around in the pale white water. Satisfied he had removed the bulk of big lumps and deciding he could run the tea through a sieve prior to serving, he squeezed the bag again in the hope of at least making the water tea coloured.

But nothing happened.

He squeezed harder, aggressively pushing the spoon into the bag, which responded by splitting open, the pale water immediately filling with tiny flecks of tea leaves. All things considered, this had a high chance of being the worst cup of tea Sophie would ever have in her whole entire life. This was terrible. How would she ever see him as a possible friend, a person who could provide support and companionship, if he couldn't even provide a simple cup of tea? His mother, his bloody useless mother, through a total lack of grocery planning, had ruined everything.

"There's a problem with the tea," Noah said, appearing in the doorway.

"What sort of problem?"

"There's Bovril," he said, feeling the tears prick his eyes again. This was how it would always be. He felt powerless against fate and destiny – or at least the incompetence of his mother. Things would never align for him like they did for other people. He would always be in the wrong place at the wrong time, wearing the wrong clothes, saying the wrong thing. He would always be the snotty little geek on the edge of the party. Correction: far away from the party. Unwanted. Joked about. And he did sometimes wonder: was that why his dad left? Was it because he was such a poor excuse of a boy? Crap at football? Asthmatic? Crying about being bullied? "Look, I'm sorry," he mumbled, just about holding it together. "Maybe I'm not the right partner for you..."

"Noah..."

"Maybe you should go back in a three with Jon and..."

"Noah!"

He sank down on to the sofa and put his head in his hands. He should never have allowed her to come round. Not without adequate preparation time first.

She came and sat down next to him. Brilliant. *Prolong the agony,* he thought.

"Look, it's been a slightly stressful day, as I'm sure you're aware," he said, his right leg starting to jiggle up and down again. He needed a lie-down. He was in grave danger of having a stroke or something.

"I ignore what people say at school," she said, putting a hand on his knee to stop his leg bouncing. *Why is she touching your leg? What is happening? Oh God! Does she fancy me? I don't have any condoms!* "I know it's just pathetic gossip," she continued, "like what Jess said today, about you wetting yourself on that London Dungeon trip. I mean, I missed that trip because of—"

"Yeah, but I had a bladder infection," he said.

"Oh," she said, removing her hand.

"That's the only reason."

"Oh, right."

"It stopped with some antibiotics and I now have total bladder control, so ... just saying, that doesn't happen any more. No accidents. Not for, like, three years now." He nodded at her. It was vitally important that she understood he wasn't some little kid. He was mature. Sophisticated. Like her.

"Hey, do you fancy coming to the party tomorrow night?" she asked.

"What? Melissa's?" He looked at her suspiciously. Did Sophie not realize that people like Noah had no place at parties like Melissa's? "She'd never want me there."

"Oh, Melissa's all right, she wouldn't mind. I can bring a plus one."

"But ... *what?*" He definitely hadn't heard that right. Why was she being nice to him? He'd done nothing to deserve this. He hadn't even given her a cup of tea. "You could take anyone. Connor ... James ... Josh Lewis from Year Thirteen! Everyone loves him, he's..."

"You're such an idiot," she said, laughing and pushing him so he fell against the sofa arm. "Gimme your phone – I'll type my number in."

He handed it over in a daze and tried to work out what was happening. He wasn't sure if this was pity or actually genuine. He made a mental checklist of the evidence so far:

Being nice ✓

Leg touching ✓

Playful pushing into side of sofa (technical term:
     horseplay) ✓

Invite to party ✓

Offer of mobile number to allow more contact ✓

It was, on the face of it, pretty positive. There was even a slim chance she might *fancy* him. He wasn't sure how he really felt about that... It was something approaching panic, which wasn't great, but he guessed it was just first-time nerves or something. If Sophie did like him, maybe he should like her back? Then he would be a normal boy, doing normal things, and everyone would forget about his mum... Maybe his dad would get to hear that he was dating a girl and he would think, *Oh, that's cool and normal, I'll come back, then*. Perhaps, he thought, he should say something nice back. Something that maybe hinted at the fact he maybe quite liked her. What, though? *You're nice* was lame. *Pretty*. That just sounded creepy. *I really like you* might be pushing it too far; no one likes someone who's too keen. She handed back the phone and his eyes were immediately drawn to the second half of her number... 4412144... Something about those numbers...

You're very kind and sweet... (Urgh! Vom!)

4412144

Me and you, it could be great! (Cheesy.)

44

... 4412144... That number...

Be with me always – take any form – drive me mad! Only do not leave me in this abyss, where I cannot find you! (Words by Emily Brontë, but delivered with heart and meaning by Noah Grimes, so maybe the best choice?)

It was palindromic! 4412144! The second half of her phone number was palindromic!

"I LOVE palindromic numbers!" he squealed.

She looked at him weirdly and managed a half-smile.

Arse! He'd actually *said* that, hadn't he? Oh God, *you even sounded genuinely excited*! She shook her head, turned to him and looked really serious. He'd made himself look like a complete unshaggable geek, he knew he had. Why, when she had been so nice and possibly flirtatious, was this the best he could do? "I love palindromic numbers!" *What was wrong with him?!*

"That's great, Noah, and yeah, palindromic numbers are ... really cool." She nodded, unconvincingly. "Um, look, I don't know if you've heard, but..."

Noah closed his eyes briefly. He knew the sound of bad news when he heard it, and this, *this* was about to be *bad news.*

CHAPTER FIVE

He took a deep breath and composed himself. *Nothing ever went right.* "What is it?"

"I'm leaving," she said.

"What? Now? But what about the…"

"No. Next week. For ever."

He blinked in confusion. "What?"

"I'm having to move house," she explained.

"But … where to?

"Milton Keynes."

"Moving house. I see. Huh," he said, trying to keep his voice neutral-sounding while he let the enormity of the situation sink in. *Bloody brilliant.* Milton Keynes. Somewhere miles and miles away from there. *Of course she was.*

"So, you know my folks got divorced years ago, right?

And I stayed with Dad here because Mum's job meant she was based in Milton Keynes and working away a lot?"

"Yes, right." He had no idea about any of that.

"So now Dad's got a promotion at work that involves *him* spending loads of time abroad, and Mum's not travelling as much from Milton Keynes, so they've decided the best thing is for me to go and live with her..."

"Really?"

"I know, right? Like I can't possibly look after myself! I mean, I'm only sixteen; how will I know how to brush my teeth or shower or even make toast? Never mind that my dad's not even capable of operating Netflix, rebooting the internet or understanding the washing machine programmes, so I do everything anyway. I've told them it's crazy, especially with GCSEs coming up in May and everything, but it all fell on deaf ears."

Noah nodded and tried not to show his devastation. Was this some sort of cruel joke? What sort of All-Powerful Being would dangle all this hope and possibility in front of him and then whip it away again?

"We can keep in touch," she suggested.

Oh yeah, that sounded really good, he thought. "Keep in touch." That sounded full of promise for potential snogging and social redemption. Damn Sophie's dad! Why couldn't he just decline his promotion and stay in Little Fobbing?

"So, what's it like in Milton Keynes?"

"It's OK. There's a multiplex cinema, a theatre," she

said, playing it down like any of these things didn't make it a billion times better than Little Fobbing. "Indoor ski slope, shopping centre..."

"Cool," he nodded, knowing damn well that he would never hear from or see her again, like everyone else who moved away. She would be too busy skiing indoors and having frozen coffee drinks in shopping centres.

"I just thought I should tell you that. You know..."

"OK." He cut her off before she could say, "Don't get your hopes up about the chance of any romance."

She turned towards him, put an arm across his shoulders and gave him a little cuddle. *I should definitely cuddle her back. To show I'm keen and like cuddling. But where do I lift my arm? I can't hug her across her boobs. And round the stomach is weird. So that only leaves the neck. Can you hug someone round the neck? Oh. She's stopped now.*

"Maybe I should get going," she said.

"What about the homework, though?"

"It's easy. We'll be against the proposal. We'll talk about how the new supermarket will decimate local shops, kill the high street and ruin community spirit. It'll increase traffic and pollution whilst eroding the distinctive identity of the town. Faceless corporate giants versus independent, diverse and ethical trading. We'll stand up for the little man. Someone's got to."

Noah nodded and smiled. There was every chance their presentation would be ace. Ace, yet tinged with massive sadness, as the person who had made it ace would be leaving just hours after it was delivered.

"If you can do some case studies on similar proposals in other towns, I'll research some actual employment statistics to show the overall adverse effect on the labour market. We'll busk it from there," she continued. "And I'll come by at seven tomorrow to pick you up for the party, yeah?"

"Is there a dress code?"

"Noah, it's a party. At someone's house."

"Like, casual?"

"Yes. Like, casual. Like any other party you've been to."

"Sure," he said, doubtfully, wondering if the ones with jelly and pass the parcel counted.

"Laters, then," she said, standing up and collecting her belongings.

"Er, yeah, laters," he replied, the word sticking in his throat it felt so out of place.

He showed her to the door, and she breezed out. A really nice girl had been really nice to him. He felt he could justifiably call her a *friend*. Not only that, she hadn't completely knocked the idea of romance on the head. She had merely announced she was leaving for a faraway town and he would probably never see her again.

It could definitely be worse.

And Sophie's very presence in the house ... it had somehow made life seem more joyful. Lighter. He sighed and took a deep breath, filling his lungs with...

AAARGH! What was that ... *stench*?! Jesus! He flailed around, watering eyes eventually settling on a device that was plugged into the wall. What vile thing was this? He bent down and pulled it out of the socket. "AirDivine: Essence of Passion Flower." So! His mother, complaining as she always was about never having any money, had seen fit to purchase some sort of air freshener. God forbid the air should be made clean and wholesome by her *not smoking* or maybe addressing the blocked drains and obvious damp issue. No, better to douse the house in a heavy dose of chemicals that would probably trigger an asthma attack. Heartless old crone. He tossed the device into the bin and returned to the lounge just as his mother came through the front door.

"From Barry at the Red Lion," she said, dropping a carrier bag of raw mince on the table and slinging her fake fur coat on the back of the armchair.

Noah looked despairingly at the mince. His mother liked to be paid cash in hand for her gigs. When that wasn't possible for reasons of accounting and bookkeeping, it wasn't unusual for her to receive payment in kind. Catering-sized portions of meat, vast tubs of ketchup and sometimes even cases of beer all regularly made an appearance. Whatever else he and Mum might want for, they would certainly never go hungry.

"Pity he didn't give you teabags," he muttered.

"What you prattling on about?" she asked, lighting a cigarette and taking a deep drag.

"We're out of teabags."

"Well, what do you care? You don't drink tea," she said, adjusting her hair in the mirror above the gas fire. Her hair looked different, but he couldn't quite place it. Was it blonder? A bit more styled? Hard to tell through the fog of cigarette smoke.

"I had a guest round who wanted a cup of tea, actually."

"Harry's drinking tea these days, is he?"

"It was Sophie," he said, nonchalantly, in the hope she might leave it there.

His mother blew a long plume of smoke out through her mouth and fixed him with one of her piercing stares. "You had a girl round?"

"Mum..."

She immediately scooted round the table and sat down next to him, wiggling her finger in her ear, pretending to dislodge the wax. "I don't think I heard correctly, say that again."

"Mu-um! Stop making a big deal out of it..."

"Oh my God. It's finally happened. The hormones have finally kicked in, haven't they?"

"It's not like that." He hated talking to her about anything like this. She'd once tried to have a chat about puberty with him. He stopped her at the first mention of "testicles". It just wasn't on.

"So, tell me about this Sophie! Is she pretty?"

Noah rolled his eyes. Even though he'd been at school

with Sophie since they were five, his mum didn't know who she was. And even though it was a small town with a small population and even smaller number of teenagers, she *still* didn't know. Because his mother was entirely selfish and wholly wrapped up in her own little world. Other than Harry, she didn't know who anyone his age was. "Mum! All I said was we're out of teabags. That's all. What's for tea?"

"I don't know. I'm popping out, to be honest. Why don't you boil yourself up some mince?"

Noah wrinkled his nose. "I think I'll go and see Gran. Have my tea there."

"Up to you."

"Well, you know, it's nice for Gran to have *some* visitors."

"You know I don't like that care home. Smells funny. *Plus,* she's your dad's mum, so I don't see why she's all my responsibility, like every other damn thing!"

"*Nice,* Mother. *Charming.* You're a shining beacon of selflessness and charity."

"Oh, piss off, Noah. Have you kissed this girl, then?"

"I'm going now."

"I'm taking an interest! Like all the TV programmes tell you to!"

"I don't care," he said, grabbing his coat and heading out the front door. He was in no mood for her drivel. "By the way –" he turned back "– you'll be pleased to know your stupid flyers have been pinned up all over the school."

"Oh, that's good."

"No, it isn't good. I'm a laughing stock." It would take many years for him to forgive her latest idiotic marketing efforts. Thanks to her, his life had plumbed new depths of piss-taking and misery.

"Well, you'll just have to get over it. Do you think Alan Carter's son got all moody when he had his business cards made?"

"He's an accountant!"

"And I'm an actress!"

"You are many things, *Mother*, but one thing you are *not* is an actress!" he hissed, opening the front door.

"Hey! Hey, Noah?!" She threw him a massive bag of Skittles from her bag. "Catch!"

"What are these for?"

"Those 'stupid flyers' have already got me a few gigs, so I'm sharing the spoils."

He took a long, tight-lipped look at her. Did she really think she could get round him this easily? That she could make everything better with a big bag of Skittles?

Yes, of course she could. Epic. He loved Skittles. "Hmmph," he grunted, ripping the bag open and shovelling a handful in his mouth.

"Love you!" she called out as he left.

Bribery. It was just the kind of thing that confirmed for Noah that his mother was the worst.

CHAPTER SIX

He could hear "The Final Countdown" by Europe blaring out of his gran's bedroom even from the far end of the corridor. Noah smiled to himself. She loved her eighties music.

His knocking on the door yielded no response, so he cautiously opened it and poked his head round. "Gran? GRAN!" he shouted.

"George? Thank God you're here!" she said, spinning round from a small bag she was packing on the bed. Her grey hair was coiffed in her normal, elegant style, but she was bizarrely dressed all in black, like some sort of ninja. A ninja who was also wearing floral slippers.

"It's Noah, Gran."

"What?"

"NOAH!" he shouted, above the din.

"I can't hear you..."

He turned the music off. "I'm Noah, Gran."

"Peanut!"

"Yes, Gran, Peanut."

It had been her nickname for him for as long as he could remember. He was maybe four or five and had exploded in a fit of rage in a John Lewis in Nottingham because he'd been denied the opportunity to purchase an iron.

Not a toy iron.

An actual iron.

He'd wanted an actual iron that heated up and made steam and everything. His reasons for wanting it remained a mystery to this day, even to him, but at the time it had resulted in a full-on tantrum in the middle of the small appliances department, during which Noah had been so cross he tore most of his clothes off, flapping around on the floor like a dying cod.

Security were called in the end, as the disturbance was putting off the diners in the store restaurant.

"You're a nutter," Gran had told him on the way home. "You're a nutty little nutcase, aren't you, little Peanut?"

"Peanut?"

"Peanut! 'Cause you're nutty and you're small!" his gran had declared.

And the name had stuck. At first he didn't mind it, but now he was older he had hoped she would stop using it. And, if she must, could she not now choose a more exclusive and desirable type of nut? A cashew or pistachio, maybe?

"Where's George?" Gran demanded.

"Granddad? He's dead, Gran."

"Dead? DEAD? Oh, for bleedin' hell's sake..." she said, slumping down on the bed.

"What are you packing for?"

"I'm trying to escape, Peanut. They are keeping me here against my will. They've killed George, and they want to kill me too. It's a conspiracy, you see. And you know who's responsible? Your no-good father, my terrible son! This is his doing! He's bribing them to keep me here! Bribing them!"

"Gran, no one's seen Dad for, like ... ages," he sighed.

"You mark my words. He has put me in here to get his filthy, lying hands on my money. He's greased a few palms to make it happen. How many times have I told you?"

"Loads," he admitted. But that didn't make it true. It was her paranoia. She didn't want to admit the real reason for her being in this place was that she couldn't look after herself any more. It made him sad. Of course she would prefer to be in her own home. If only he had time, if only he didn't have to be at school, he would have gladly moved in there to look after her. He hated seeing her like this. Miserable, alone, often angry.

"Do you know the code for the main entrance?"

"No," he lied, knowing she'd tried that escape route several times already, luckily to no avail.

"Damn it. Damn it."

Noah sat down in the armchair while his gran, with no immediate escape options left, fished a box of jelly fruits out of her bedside drawer. She opened it, selected one for herself and then offered the box to Noah.

"It's horrible here," she said, conspiratorially. "No, not an orange one. They're my favourite."

"What's wrong with it?" asked Noah, picking a red one instead.

"At night, little boys break in and they hit my knees with toffee hammers."

Noah chewed his jelly fruit and tried to do a face that showed how awful he thought that was. He felt sorry for her. Losing your mind must be utterly horrible. But he felt the loss too, in other ways. He used to be round at hers most weekends, while his mum was doing her shows. Gran would make brilliant dinners, and then they'd watch *Murder, She Wrote* on telly. It was a really good telly, much better than the one they had. And she would cook proper food, with genuine vegetables, and they'd eat it at a proper dining table with all the correct knives and forks. She taught him how to fold a napkin like a swan and a million other social graces he would have had no idea about otherwise.

But it was different now.

Now, it was Noah who felt like the grown-up, and Gran who seemed like a little kid. He wasn't ready for that. He still wanted Gran to tell him what he could and couldn't do and when he had to go to bed and to give him sage advice about school and life in general – pearls of ancient wisdom passed down through generations. If Gran wasn't able to do that any more, then who the hell would? Sure, there was Harry, but he was a kid too. Sometimes a situation just needed an adult. And Gran had been the only adult he could depend on.

There was a knock at the door, and Gran quickly grabbed her dressing gown and wrapped it around herself. "Evening, Millie," said a ruddy-faced matron, pushing the door open with a trolley of food. "Oh, hi, Noah. How are you?"

"All right, thanks."

"Noah's come to visit you, Millie!" she said, brightly.

"Yes, I know, I can see that!" his gran said, rolling her eyes at Noah.

"I've brought your dinner. Do you want some, Noah?"

"Yes, please."

Noah gratefully received his steaming plate of beef stew and mash, which he balanced on his lap. It was funny food, the sort they used to eat in the Olden Days, but certainly a damn sight better than anything he would be given at home.

"Be careful, I think they poison it," Gran said as soon as Matron had left.

"It tastes nice."

"Peanut, we both know that's bollocks, don't we?"

"Yes, Gran." He grinned. He loved it when a bit of predementia Gran shone through. How she used to be. How she *should* be. Classic, vintage Gran.

"Put the music back on. See if you can find a bit of Starship. Track ten, I think."

Noah pressed the buttons on the CD player and flicked through the tracks of his gran's "Greatest Hits of the 80s" album. They both happily ate their food to a soundtrack of soft rock, New Romantics and synth pop, as Gran regaled him with tales of her youth, when she was "queen of the dance floor" and "knew how to throw some shapes". *A pity*, Noah considered, *that I didn't inherit any of those genes.* But he did inherit something, and it was a far, far better gift: up on the wall were framed prints of Angela Lansbury (from *Murder, She Wrote*) and Joan Hickson (the best Miss Marple), looking down quizzically (they were both in character) at their two biggest fans. Yes, that love of detective stories was Gran's gift to him, and much better that than knowing how to . . . *jive*, or whatever the cool kids called it these days.

"I've been invited to a party, Gran!" he said, putting down his plate.

"Peanut, five words. Keep. It. In. Your. Pants."

Noah chuckled. Gran was obsessed with him not having sex under any circumstances. If only she knew how very far away he was from anything of that nature. "No, it's not anything like that. I mean, it's a normal party, not a *sex orgy*."

"Keep it in your pants."

"I'm gonna keep it in my pants!" God only knew he was, like it or not.

"Who invited you?"

"A girl," he said, adding before she could get a word in edgeways, "and I'm totally not going to get it out of my pants, so don't even... But yeah. A girl. Called Sophie. And it's fine, because she's moving house anyway, so nothing would happen, even if I wanted it to."

"Where's she going?"

"Milton Keynes."

Gran wrinkled her nose. "Shithole," she said. "What about Harry?"

"What about Ha—" He stopped himself. What about Harry? How could he have been so thoughtless? He and Harry had rules! They had agreements!

The Rules (as agreed by Noah and Harry in Year Nine on a joyous November afternoon when they both had excuse notes for PE)

(1) Mates before dates. (But we both acknowledge dates are highly unlikely.)

(2) Haribo is an acceptable birthday or Christmas gift.

(3) There is no shame in still watching *Sponge-Bob*, but it doesn't need to be mentioned in

public and will never be used to blackmail or
threaten the other.

(4)   We both will always hate the following:
football, rugby, tofu and, following the
disastrous residential trip in Year Eight,
France.

(5)   We both do solemnly swear that we shall
never leave the other one behind, and if one
of us gets:
(A)   rich
(B)   bow chicka wah wah
(C)   put in prison

the other will do everything possible to
make sure the good/bad fortune can be
shared by (a) splitting the wealth equally,
(b) helping the other to find appropriate
romantic entanglements or (c) mounting a
defence in court and shouting things like
"Objection!" at the judge and channelling
Miss Marple to find exciting evidence that
proves innocence beyond all doubt.

He couldn't believe it. He had fallen foul of sections
(1) and possibly (5b); how was that possible?! The
Rules were sacred. He couldn't break them. Through
everything, through all the crap (and there had been

endless *crap*), one person had always been there for him: Harry.

He eyeballed his gran. "Obviously, Harry is coming too. Of course he is!" Noah bluffed.

Gran gave a little smile. "You better go tell him that, then, hadn't you?"

Damn it to hell, how did she know? The woman was impossible to bullshit! Noah gave her a hug and a kiss on the cheek. "'Kay. Take care, Gran."

"If you see George, tell him I'm waiting!"

"Will do!" he played along, because it was easier.

"And what must you remember?"

"Erm…"

"Keep it in your pants."

"Yeah."

"Say it!"

"I've got to keep it in my pants."

"Good Peanut."

He'd sent Sophie a text that read "OK IF HARRY COMES TO PARTY TOO?" all in capitals because it was VERY IMPORTANT and quite URGENT. She had replied pleasingly promptly with "Of course!" and put a little "x" at the end, to which he'd replied with his own "X". This was practically sex, but he'd kept it in his pants, so it was totally fine. Also, the good thing about sending kisses by text (rather than doing it in real life) was that it was fully hygienic and you didn't have to practise first, so everyone was a winner. Feeling quite the modern, successful *man*, he lay on his bed with his mobile to his ear. "Haz? Guess what?"

"Did you get off with her?"

"What? No!"

"Anything?"

"No. Not really. Look, Harry, this line of questioning is—"

"*Not really?!*"

Noah sighed. Harry clearly wanted to know every little detail, even if things like this, the fine details of a romantic liaison, should really be kept on the down-low. He wasn't a kiss-and-tell sort of boy, after all. "I told her I liked palindromic numbers and she told me she was moving to Milton Keynes."

"Are the two connected?"

"I don't think so. But listen," he said, keen to move on from this, "you and I, we're off to a party!"

"What? How?"

"Sophie invited me. And I told her, *very clearly and in accordance with The Rules*, that I would only come if you came too."

"We like to *come* together."

"We do, yes... Oh, I see, yes, ha ha!" Noah said, forcing an awkward chuckle.

"I do prefer it when we both *come*," Harry continued.

"Right, OK. Yes. That's another ... good *double entendre*."

"Although do you remember my aunt's wedding, and only I *came*?"

OK, for whatever reason, this was clearly a thing. "I *do* remember the wedding. I wasn't well and didn't feel like *coming* that day. But then there was your parent's barbecue, when I *came* first and then you *came* later because you were at swimming?"

Harry guffawed, clearly delighted. "Well, I can't think of any more coming jokes, but that all sounds sweeeeet! You sure, though? I don't wanna be a *melon*."

"It's *lemon*, you twit, and you wouldn't be. It's not that type of thing." Or at least, he wasn't sure if it was that type of thing... Maybe it was. Maybe it *would* be. Either way, if anything did end up happening, Harry would be at the party too and so he would have an equal chance of *bow chicka wah wah*–style activities with a person of his choice. It was only fair. "Why were you so weird this afternoon, anyway?"

"Noah, I was trying to *defuse* the very obvious tension. You're like a tightly coiled spring that just ... explodes everywhere."

For some reason, Harry talking about him *exploding everywhere* made his stomach feel tingly.

"You *explode* everywhere," Harry repeated.

"I heard."

"What are you thinking about *right now*?"

"Shut up," he grimaced, adjusting himself as a boy-type situation suddenly popped up, for reasons that Noah couldn't quite fathom.

Harry laughed. "What's the dress code, then?"

"It's a party, Harry. At a house. A party house ... party. At a house. You've been to a party at a house before, right?"

"Only the ones with jelly and pass the parcel."

"Right, well ... it's hip casual cool, I guess," he said, patiently.

"Hip casual cool?"

Noah could practically hear Harry smirking. "I believe that's the modern term, yes," he sniffed.

"'Kay, well, best get my beauty sleep, then..."

"All right. Laters."

"What did you say?"

"Laters."

Harry blew out a breath. *"You've changed."*

Noah snorted, shook his head and hung up. He lay back and listened to the beautiful silence of the house for a moment. It wasn't *normal* to end a conversation with your best mate and have a boy-type situation come up. He would just have to put it down to out-of-control hormones and ... a conversation that was sort of about Sophie. Yes. He'd had a conversation with his mate – *about a girl* – and that's why he'd ended up like this.

"Noah! I'm home!" his mum called up from the hall, suddenly banging through the front door. With reflexes a fighter pilot would be proud of, he deftly covered himself with his duvet in one swift movement, just in case she were to barge in and see him in this somewhat overexcited state.

"Must be asleep," he heard her whisper.

He decided to say nothing. His bedroom light was off; she might assume he'd gone to bed, and then he wouldn't have to talk to her or—

He froze in terror when he heard it.

The most terrible sound in the world.

From downstairs.

CHAPTER SEVEN

The unmistakable low tones of a male voice. Followed by his mother's coquettish laughter. More low tones. More giggles, then:

"Sssh! Sssh! You might wake him!" (His mother.)

Various low tones. (The Mystery Man.)

Suppressed giggles. (His mother.)

Noah sat on the edge of his bed. Frozen. Wide-eyed. Who was this man she had brought home?

He tiptoed across to his bedroom door and pressed his ear against it in the hope of hearing better, but they were talking too quietly. This piqued his suspicion. She wasn't being all quiet because she was afraid of waking him. She was unremittingly selfish and wouldn't care about his need for reinvigorating rest.

No.

She was being quiet *because she had something to hide.*

He gently pressed the door handle down and slowly pulled the door towards him, millimetre by millimetre, so as to avoid it creaking and alerting the living room occupants to his presence.

But now they were no longer talking.

Now there was a different noise.

And it was something like:

Slurp … sluurrrp … sllllurrrrp…

He was no expert, but he knew what that sound was.

It was the sound of passionate, pre-sex-style kissing.

On every level, this was unacceptable. There were reasons too numerous to mention, but the top of Noah's list was something like:

Reasons why Mum can't have sex with anyone

(1) "Mum" and "sex" are two words that should never be in close proximity to each other because ewwww! And eeugggh!

(2) WHAT ABOUT DAD?! She's acting like he doesn't exist any more! They're not even divorced! What if Dad still loves us, but for some reason can't let us know? Suppose he really had been kidnapped? Or is being held

hostage? How could she betray him like this?

(3) I can't just come home with a random middle-aged bloke and say he's my new dad, so she can't bring home a random middle-aged bloke and say it's her new "fella". ("Fella" definitely being the sort of irritating word she would use.)

Appalling. His mother was downstairs, canoodling and tongue wrestling with a mysterious man! He gagged as his stomach lurched up some of the beef stew from earlier. What if they started shagging right here, right now?

He froze. How could he have been so stupid? Miss Marple would have worked this out by now and gathered everyone in the drawing room. Jessica Fletcher would have tricked the perpetrator into an admission. The clues had been there all along!

Yes . . . it all began to make sense. . . When his mother had come home earlier she had checked her hair in the mirror . . . because *she'd had her roots done*. . . She'd had them done *to impress a man*. . . In the socket in the hall he'd noticed the *plug-in air freshener*. . . "Essence of Passion Flower". . . It had been an odd addition, but he hadn't thought too much of it *until now*! It was some sort of love gas, designed to enhance the mood and encourage the shagging.

Oh God, she was going to bring him upstairs!

She was going to bring him upstairs and they would

engage in intercourse right here with Noah just a paper-thin wall away and *he would hear every single grunt and every single groan of pleasure* and it was HIS OWN MOTHER and it was just all too HORRIBLE...

"AAARRRRRRGGGGHHHHH!" he screamed, with his hands over his ears.

There was a short scuffle from downstairs. "Damn, he's awake," he heard his mother say, followed by some indeterminable words and the front door quickly opening and closing. There was five seconds of silence, and then,

"Noah?"

Shit! Now what? "...Yeah?"

"What the hell's the matter?"

"Er ... I was having a nightmare about my French oral."

"...Fine."

Then silence. Noah turned his head and squinted, like that somehow gave him superhero hearing. But it kinda worked. She was forty, and like most decrepit people, she hadn't turned her mobile's keyboard clicks off. *She was texting.* Texting whomever she'd just been kissing. Probably telling him it was a false alarm, to come back, to have *sexual relations.*

No.

No bloody way!

He quickly wrapped his dressing gown around himself and charged downstairs. He was damn well going to explode.

He was going to explode all over his mother.

(No, not that. That sounded like a Freudian nightmare.)

"WHO IS IT?!" he shouted at her as she looked up, mid-text.

"Who's what?" she said, innocently.

What was the point in denying it? He'd bloody *heard* her! "Whoever you were kissing. *It was disgusting.*"

"No idea what you're talking about."

He wasn't going to let her deny it. "*I know what I heard.*"

She looked him in the eye, sizing the situation up. "Sit down, Noah," she said, making her mind up.

He hated it when she pulled the "I'm a proper adult" card, because whilst it might *technically* be true, a woman who once spent a hundred pounds in a single month phoning premium-rate tarot card lines was no adult in his eyes.

He plopped himself down on the sofa whilst his mother stood by the window and took an extraordinarily long time to light a cigarette. "OK, fine, Noah," she said, finally exhaling smoke into the room, "I *have* met someone. A man. How do you feel about that?"

Noah shrugged, trying to play it cool whilst his heart pumped furious blood around his head. How could she do this? What about him? She had already failed in almost all her maternal duties – he would suffer more now because she would only be focused on some horrific man. And what about his dad? What would he think about all this? In his absence, he should at least have someone representing his views, and Noah was more than happy to take on that responsibility.

"I feel like it's appalling," he said, eyeballing her. "I feel like you're shirking your responsibilities as a married woman. I feel like you've lied and cheated and dodged the truth and behaved in the most despicable manner known to man!"

"Well, I don't expect you to like it," she said. "You've been used to the run of the place. Parading around the house like a peacock."

Noah looked at her, aghast. Where was all this utter rubbish coming from?

"Mu—"

"I'm speaking!" she interrupted. "Now, I'm not saying this is going to go anywhere, I'm not saying this will be for ever, or he'll be moving in, or anything really. I'm just saying it's happened and we'll have to see."

Noah glared at her. So she was already thinking about him moving in, then? She was right about one thing: Noah did have the run of the place, and the thought of sharing that with another person was utterly intolerable. The natural order of things would be upset. He didn't want another toothbrush in the little pot in the bathroom. An extra person wanting to use the loo in the mornings. Awkward and silent "family" outings to the Harvester, pretending everything was cool whilst miserably eating warm cucumber, molested by small children's fingers, from the unlimited salad cart.

"And what about Dad?" he asked.

"What about him?"

"You're still married to him!" he said, desperate for some acknowledgement that Dad was still actually in the picture. How could she act like he didn't matter?

"Noah, we haven't seen him for, what, six years now, is it? He could be dead for all we know. I'm sorry to sound harsh, but it's true."

Noah flicked his eyes down and back again, but tried to keep a poker face. That was the first time he'd heard the word "dead" said in relation to his dad. He'd *thought* it, sure, but for someone else to actually *say* it aloud... A cold shiver shocked up his spine. *Dad couldn't be dead.* He would *know* if he was dead, he was sure of it. It would feel different. Empty. "Well, what if he *isn't* dead?"

His mum shrugged. "We'll never know. I can't base the rest of my life and entire future happiness on the possibility he might be alive and that, if he is, he's changed from being a completely thoughtless bastard into a model husband. Can I?"

"But—"

"I have no desire to talk about your father, Noah."

"But—"

"Leave it! Jesus!" she shouted.

He knew better than to push it. And perhaps, on this one point, his mother was right. If his father really cared about them, he would be here. "Who is it, then?" he said, unable to look at her.

"You don't need to know."

Oh, but he did. And in a small town like this, word got around quickly. He needed to prepare himself for the gossip, the barbed comments, the backlash. "Mum, just tell me. Do I know the guy?"

"Noah, I told you. It's very new. We only met a couple of months ago and it might go nowhere. I don't want to broadcast this all over the town. You know what this place is like."

A couple of months ago? Dear God, the woman was good at keeping nasty little secrets when she wanted to! How had he missed this? "It's not a teacher from school, is it?"

"No comment."

"Or any of the neighbours?"

"No comment."

"Is it someone whom I speak to? Someone from the town?"

"Noah, I'm not going to tell you."

"Why not?!"

"Because this is about me having a little bit of *me time.* I've been a hard-working, career-orientated woman for fifteen years..."

He let that go. *Career orientated?* Ha!

"I've slaved night and day to bring you up," she continued, "and this is about me reconnecting with my femininity. It's about me saying, 'Hey, know what? I'm a *woman.* I have *needs.*'"

74

Noah wrinkled his nose at the word "needs" and felt the beef stew try to come up again. What sort of mum basically tells their kid she wants sex? It was disgusting. Harry's mum would never say she had "needs". She was demure and pure, and would make sacrifices for her child – including not grossing him out.

"Why are you doing that face?" she demanded.

"I'm not doing a face."

"You did that thing with your nose when I said I have 'needs'."

"I didn't do a face."

"You're uptight about sex," she declared.

"*What?*" Oh God, were they really having this conversation?

"Newsflash, Noah, newsflash! People have sex. People *enjoy* sex. It's *normal*. Most boys your age would be trying to get laid themselves, rather than spending every evening locked in their bedroom, stalking people on Twitter and masturbating."

Noah looked at her, open-mouthed. He had never been locked in his bedroom, stalking people on Twitter. The accusation was outrageous.

"Honestly, Noah," she continued. "I'd already lost my virginity by your age."

"Sixteen years, nine months, Mother!" he said, triumphantly. "According to Google that's the average age at which a boy loses his virginity. I've still got nearly ten months! So, who's the abnormal one now?"

"Noah," she said, sitting down next to him, "don't get upset. I want you to find love, to have fun. You're such a … gorgeous hunk, there's no reason why you shouldn't have them banging down our door."

She was quite possibly high. "You know what? If I find someone I really like and we want to have sex, maybe we will. But I don't see what the rush is. *I don't need sex to validate who I am as a person.*"

"Where did you get that line from?"

"From me."

"It's from my *OK! Magazine*, isn't it?"

"No." *It totally was.* "I'm top set for English, I'm more than capable of saying intelligent things."

"Whatever," she said. "Don't make me feel guilty, Noah. In two years' time you'll be eighteen and you'll probably piss off to Nepal on a gap year or something. Do you want me to be all alone? Do you want me to die lonely and bitter?"

He snorted. That was exactly what she deserved.

She looked at him like she might whack him one. "Do you know how hard the last six years have been, Noah?"

He shrugged. Of course he knew. They'd been hideous.

"No, you've no idea," she continued. "I've had to borrow money from loan sharks, I've pawned my jewellery, I've scraped and scratched to keep a roof over our heads.

And that whole time, I haven't seen anyone else. Didn't even think about it because the *only* thing on my mind was how we got by. And now ... someone new has come along and he makes me feel happy and young and carefree again. Like there's a bit of something fun in my life again."

He wanted to say "Don't I make you feel happy? Am I not enough for you?" but didn't. He'd said enough, and maybe he *was* just selfish and stupid and didn't understand anything about normal human relationships. Maybe she was right. He was uptight. So he just sat there. Not saying anything.

"Well, then. Goodnight, Noah."

He sighed and walked out, then turned back at the door. "Just one more thing—"

"And don't even *try* to do a Columbo close on me," his mum said. "I'm saying nothing more about ... my new fella. And you're not going to trick me into it."

He got into bed and stared into the blackness, wiping a rogue tear from his eye.

It wasn't because of *her*. It was his dad. He was on his mind now, and he couldn't stop thinking about him, however hard he tried to shut it away. Strange. Sometimes he longed for him; other times, like now, he hated his guts, because all this, *everything*, was his dad's fault. All roads came back to him and his leaving.

And then, at other times, he was embarrassed about him. Other kids had divorced parents, but they would usually see their dads at weekends and stuff. But not him. It was the stupidest things that hurt the most. Like in French:

"*Je vis avec ma maman, papa et ses frères,*" other kids said.

Noah had to say:

"*Je vis avec ma maman.*"

And half the class sniggered and made snide little comments to each other about his dad "still being on holiday" and "Hey, miss? Shall we do a fundraiser to get Noah's dad released from the kidnappers?" And he'd gone bright red and looked down at the floor, crippled by his intense shame, even though it was no fault of his. That's what his dad had done to him. And he hated him for that.

But even so, more than anything, he wanted him back. And if he couldn't have him back, he just wanted to know he was OK. That he wasn't in trouble. Or living rough on the streets – cold, or hungry, begging for food...

Noah stopped himself. Even though he was alone, and it was dark, and no one could see him, he didn't want to cry. He'd done enough of that over the years. And maybe it was time to accept the truth. He was never going to see his dad again, and he was never going to know what had happened to him. Because once you accepted it, you could lock it away and you could move on. And that's what he would do.

From tomorrow.

But until then, he did the thing he always did, when thoughts of his father kept him awake. He stared into the darkness and said, ever so quietly, just in case the message could somehow get to him,

"I love you, Dad."

CHAPTER EIGHT

Screw it all. He was *going* to be normal. He was going to do *normal* things. Be a *normal* boy. That would show his mum!

It was the night of the party.

And he was going to kiss Sophie.

Maybe. If she wanted to. Because *he* wanted to kiss her. Almost definitely. And not because he was using her to gain popularity. Because she was a girl and he was a boy and … and … that's what happens.

At the very least, he would flirt with her. He would make a start on the first stage of a romantic progression that went:

(1) Holding hands.

(2) A kiss (not with tongues but using the lips of both parties).

(3) Tongue kissing and full snogging.

(4) Wriggling around on top of each other with clothes *on*, whilst saying things like "Ooh!" and "Yeah, baby."

(5) Wriggling around with clothes *off*, with heavy breathing and groaning.

(6) Bow chicka wah wah.

But as he stood in front of the bathroom mirror the following afternoon, he sighed. He wished he was just a little bit taller. And a little bit less skinny. He wished his side parting and glasses made him look a bit more cool, like geek-chic rather than just geek. His jeans were probably too casual for a party where he had to impress. But he didn't like the way his chinos made him look like he didn't have a bottom. And then his T-shirts were either too baggy or too tight – nothing was just exactly the right size and fit.

In the end he decided the best option was to be brave and play the quirky card. He would wear the suit he'd worn for his granddad's funeral, with a shirt and bow tie. Fashion being as it was, he felt sure he could get away with it. Plus, it would make an impact. And an impact might equal another party invite!

"You said casual!" complained Harry when he arrived,

all skinny chinos, hoody and loom bands – even though he wasn't a ten-year-old girl. Although, upon reflection, Harry looked *good*. He looked like someone their age probably should look.

"Well, it wasn't working out."

"Brave choice."

"Thanks," Noah said, as his confidence about the outfit started to seep away.

"No, seriously, it's kinda cute," Harry said, tweaking his bow tie like everyone does when you wear a bow tie.

Noah felt a familiar flutter in his stomach. "God, why do I feel so nervous?"

"Is it 'cause you *lurrrve* her?" Harry grinned.

"Look—"

Harry's eyes nearly popped out. "Oh! There's a 'look'? I was expecting an outright denial, but now there's a 'look'! So...?"

"Oh, I don't know, I was just thinking ... I might flirt with her a bit, that's all."

Harry was all agog. "Flirt with her? Really? Like ... *flirt* with her?"

"So, I'm calling it Operation Flirty-Pants—"

Harry burst out laughing. "Seriously, Noah, just tell her you like her or something. Don't call it 'Operation *Whatever*' like you're a field commander in a war. Just ... keep it real."

"Real?"

"Yeah," Harry muttered, looking down at the floor,

"*real.*" He seemed a bit crestfallen. And Noah knew exactly why.

"Hey, listen. I haven't forgotten The Rules," Noah assured him. "If I manage to do anything with Soph, I'll help you. I'll fix you up with a lovely girl. Some of Sophie's intelligent, sophisticated mates are bound to be there. You'll see! They'll love you."

"Sure," Harry said. "Anyway, you smell nice. Is it Lynx?"

"Well, since we both smell the same, I think you know it is."

Harry stared into his eyes. "It's *very* seductive," he whispered in a sex voice.

"Haz! Stop pissing about! I was generous enough to let you come, don't be an arse, OK?"

"Ooooh!" Harry said, doing a camp little pout.

"OK?"

"Whatever you say." Harry turned and reached into his rucksack. "I brought vodka!"

"Vodka? But how? You're underage!" Noah tried hard not to squeal. Harry had clearly got himself fake ID, been to an off-licence, put on a really deep voice and purchased alcohol. It was all happening. They were being illegal teenagers. His mother would bloody love this.

"Don't fret, sweet-cheeks. Dad let me have it."

Noah gawped at him. He'd never had Harry's dad down as some sort of hugely liberal parent before. Would he be happily doling out cocaine and smack next?

"As long as Mum doesn't find out," Harry continued, "which, you know, she won't. Have you got something to go with it?"

"There's Ribena."

"Er, OK. That's cool."

Harry fixed the drinks and they sank down into the sofa together. "To our first proper party!" Harry grinned, chinking his glass with Noah's. "We've come a long way."

Noah smiled. He was right – they had come a long way. The question was, how much further would they go? Or rather, how much further would Harry go? Harry with his cool attitude and Calvin Klein boxer shorts. Harry with his... OH SCREW IT ALL, HE JUST WANTED TO MAKE SURE HARRY DIDN'T HAVE DESIGNS ON SOPHIE! "Um, so, do you think there's anyone you might like at the party? You got your eye on anyone?"

Harry shrugged, a little smile playing across his lips. "Maybe."

He tried not to scream hysterically as the panic bubbled up inside him. *Take a breath. Play it cool*, Noah told himself. *Play it cool.* "IS IT SOPHIE?" he squealed, completely unable to take his own advice.

"What?!"

"Answer me! It's Sophie, isn't it? You're in love with her!"

"Um—"

"You do! You love her! Oh GOD!"

"Noah, it's fine. I don't."

Noah stared at him for, like … a really long time. A liar would find that uncomfortable. Harry just stared back. Maybe Harry was a good liar? "Prove you're not lying," Noah said.

"How?"

"Take a lie detector test."

Harry rolled his eyes. "OK, fine, but you haven't got a lie detector, have you?"

"Upstairs. It's new," Noah said, without blinking.

"OK, *fine*. Bring it down."

"OK, I *will*."

"OK."

Noah stared at him some more. "OK, so I don't really have a lie detector, but you couldn't have been sure of that and your willingness to take the test gives me hope."

"I'm not lying. Sophie is all yours."

"Well, *merci beaucoup, merci beaucoup*. And yet, you still have your eye on someone, you claim? An unidentified *someone*?"

Harry looked away and shrugged again. "Maybe."

Noah nodded, but his insides were doing flips. Harry was acting like he had an amazing secret plan. Noah had always been playing catch-up where Harry was concerned. Harry got a bike first. Harry's voice broke first. Harry tried alcohol first. It wasn't that Noah was jealous, it was that he wanted them to be the same. To be equals. And he didn't want Harry to have some fabulous grand plan about getting with someone tonight because, knowing Harry, he would probably achieve it. And inevitably Noah wouldn't. And then Harry would have kissed someone first too and ... and that didn't seem fair. It didn't matter if it was Sophie or someone else. It wasn't the identity of the other person that was the problem here ... it was because it was Harry. And Harry was... Well, they were mates.

Harry was *his* mate.

And Noah didn't want to share.

God, he was a screw-up.

They'd had two more glasses of vodka-Ribena by the time Sophie rocked up, in light blue denim jeans that were ripped at the knee, some sort of strappy black top thing, and a checked shirt over it. She looked stunning. Like a person from a TV programme set in New York or something. She scooted upstairs for the loo whilst Noah and Harry fixed her a drink. "Should I have told her she looks attractive?" Noah whispered the moment she was gone.

"Tell her you think she has a '*pleasant manner*' and it makes you horny."

"Hilarious. But I mean, that's what people say, right? 'You look nice.'"

"Yeah. 'You look nice' is fine. 'You look attractive' is too much, borderline creepy."

Noah topped her glass up with Ribena. "You told me I looked *cute*."

"No, I said your *outfit* looked cute. It's different."

"So I should say her *outfit* looks cute?" Noah said, keeping his eye on the door for her return. "Wait. You don't think I look cute?"

"No, you do. You look —" Harry put both his hands on Noah's shoulders "— really nice."

"Oh. Well, thanks," Noah said, slightly taken aback by the fact Harry apparently meant it and wasn't trying to take the piss. He ducked down out of Harry's grasp and returned to finishing Sophie's drink. Add a straw. Slice of … apple. "And you look … if I may say so, you look … *stunning.* Do I mean stunning? It's women who usually look stunning, isn't it? Maybe I mean … adorable? No, that's wrong too. Um… I REALLY like that shirt. It's really, really *fit.* I mean, a *nice* fit! No, I mean, it fits well. On you. It fits you well. It's a nice fit that makes you look nice. Um. Would you like a packet of cheesy Wotsits?"

Harry blinked at him. "I'm good, thanks."

"Why have you got a doll's house?" Sophie said, reappearing in the doorway.

"You've been in my bedroom?!" Noah squealed, mortified. This was the worst thing ever. What else had she seen? The pile of dirty boxers that his mother had failed to put in the wash yet? The heaps of old Lego under his bed which he used to play with, but definitely didn't any more because he was nearly sixteen and, *really? Lego? Ha! No, of course not!* Or worse, his revision wall chart, with its colour-coded subjects and timeline between now and next summer, ensuring all subjects and modules were covered six times over and put on handy postcard-sized reminders, but marking him out as a super-mega-geek to anyone who saw it?

"Only accidentally! I was looking for the loo!" she chuckled, like it was somehow amusing.

Noah narrowed his eyes at her. He felt *violated*. "It's not a doll's house. Well, it *was*. Harry and I made it into a 3D version of Cluedo."

Harry nodded. "It's got all the normal rooms from the regular board game on the ground floor, but the first floor then has five additional bedrooms, two with en suites."

"Oh, right," Sophie said, taking her drink from Noah.

"And we've added extra suspects, including an environmental activist, a disgraced politician, and a social media troll," Noah explained.

"Plus, extra murder weapons," Harry said. "There's an overdose of prescription drugs, a machete, and *wheat*."

"Wheat?" said Sophie.

"Gluten intolerance," Noah explained. "It is actually a thing."

Sophie nodded. Was she impressed? "And you ... decorated it yourself?"

"Uh-huh!" Noah beamed. "We used craft knives and balsa wood for the main construction, then wallpaper and paint samples from Homebase."

Sophie looked at them both. "Great," she grinned. "Should we get going?"

"It's legitimate!" Noah pleaded, worried that she found this amusing and therefore uncool. "Cluedo is a great game. The *best* game. But it's too easy. This version is more involved. Takes more time."

"How long?"

"Five days," Harry said.

Sophie puffed her cheeks out. "OK, boys. Drink up, and let's make a move." She put her glass down and moved through to the hall to put her coat on.

"No, but see, it's realistic!" Noah bleated as she disappeared. "Normal Cluedo takes two hours. Who solves a murder in two hours? It's ridiculous!"

"Yeah. Totally. It's cool," she shouted back through.

He decided the best thing would be to shut up about it, so he did as he was told and downed his drink. Damn it. He was nearly sixteen, for God's sake. What the hell was he doing? He would never get to do things with a girl at this rate.

Harry cocked an eyebrow at him. "What's her problem?" he whispered, conspiratorially. "Why isn't she more excited about this? It's literally the best thing ever!"

"Yes, totally. It's amazing."

"Yes," Harry agreed.

They walked out. Sometimes Noah thought that Harry was the only person in the world who really understood him.

CHAPTER NINE

The front door of Melissa's large detached house was ajar, with people spilling out on to the gravel drive and the music audible from the top of the street. They pushed their way into the hall, Noah doing his best to appear like he was meant to be there.

"Hi, No-ah!" It was Jess Jackson, holding hands with some guy who looked like he was twenty. "Didn't expect to see you here."

"No, me either," Noah agreed.

"Hey, Sophie. This is Kirk, my BF. He's not at school, he goes to actual *college*," she said, clearly impressed she'd bagged herself such a guy. "He's training to be a bricklayer."

"Nice to meet you," said Sophie.

Kirk turned away from the newcomers. "You wanna go upstairs, babe?" he grunted.

Jess giggled, all coy and mock embarrassed. "Kirk's a celebrity."

"Oh right?" Sophie said, giving a weak smile and glancing at him again.

"He was in the national papers loads when he was a kid? The fundraising for his cancer treatment in Germany? He had his photo taken with some of the England football team and everything."

"Ohhhh," Noah said, recalling. "Yes, I donated fifty pence for a cupcake," he smiled, sure that Kirk would be grateful at Noah's generous contribution.

Kirk glanced at Noah. "You're that kid, aren't you?"

"What kid?" Noah said.

"*Yo, ho, ho and a bottle of rum*, my dad's been kidnapped by pirates. *That kid.*"

Noah chewed his bottom lip. "You know, I was *ten*."

Kirk gave a little snort and turned back to Jess. "Babe? Let's check out the upstairs!"

"Mmmmm – whatever you say, babe," she said, as she dragged him off towards the stairs.

Noah watched them go. What was upstairs that was so interesting? OH! Oh, *God*, of course. That's what. Yuck.

"Right, follow me," said Sophie, taking charge and clearing a path into the party proper. "We'll find the kitchen."

A party! Would it be like in the movies? Would there be people with their tops off, all hot and sweaty? Would there be snogging and shagging and would he be involved in any of that? *Would there be nibbles?* Noah hoped so. Even just a pavlova, and cheese and pineapple on cocktail sticks would be fine; it didn't have to be a full-on buffet.

"There are people here with facial hair!" he whispered to Harry as they squeezed past some exceptionally *cool*-looking individuals, one of whom had an actual moustache.

"And?"

"But I thought it would be mainly our year. I don't know any of these people. How does Melissa know them?"

"Because she's popular, Noah. Popular people have a diverse range of friends and they invite those friends to parties."

Noah scanned the room full of those "popular" people... All the usual suspects from school – Jess Jackson, Jordan, Connor Evans, and of course, Eric Smith. Eric got invites to everything because everyone was scared of what he might do if he didn't. He was like a virus: small, unpleasant, and with the ability to fell even the biggest and most popular kids. Blackmail was his talent. Noah didn't know how he did it, but Eric intercepted sexts, hacked social media accounts and procured anything else with a secrecy value attached. He was better than MI5, better than the CIA. Eric's dad (known locally as Mad Dog Razor Jaws Smith) was a vicious bully of a man with underworld connections, and he'd been in prison on and off for years. Nobody was in any doubt that Eric was heading the same way.

"Hi, Harry. Hi, Noah," said Melissa, suddenly in front of them.

"We're here with Sophie," Noah blurted out, terrified they were about to be ejected.

"That's nice."

"Great party," said Harry, nodding enthusiastically.

Melissa did a fake little smile. "The punch is on the table, but if you want to drink it you've got to put your alcohol in too. Up to you."

"Is there a recipe, though?" Noah enquired, keen not to screw the punch up and ruin the night for everyone.

"No. It's just whatever. Don't go in the downstairs loo, someone's puked," Melissa said, walking off as Noah sniffed at the punch bowl.

"You don't want to drink that stuff," Sophie grimaced. "Not until you have to, anyway. That stuff will wreck you. Keep hold of our vodka and the Ribena for now."

Within an hour they were drinking "that stuff". And it was good stuff. Their vodka had disappeared so fast that Noah was convinced someone had been stealing it, although he hadn't quite worked out how, since the bottle had been in his hand the whole time. Meanwhile the Ribena had been caught up in an incident in the kitchen involving a sixth former puking in a microwave, and none of them fancied it

93

any more. Emboldened by alcohol, Harry had to be stopped from getting his boy parts out in front of a group of girls who repeatedly requested knowing "how big it was", and Noah had been faced with the indignity of having to have a wee behind a prickly bush in the garden, as the queue for the upstairs bathroom was long and unmoving. It was turning out to be a night of exciting firsts, and Noah was beginning to see why parties were considered so brilliant. Earlier, in the packed kitchen, *someone* had given Noah's bum a squeeze. He didn't know who, it could have been anyone, but he was secretly quite pleased and flattered. There were some Year Tens dry-humping in the hall, some sixth formers smoking weed in the garden and fabulously dirty rumours about what was going on in the master bedroom. This was where it all took place. All that "growing up" and "first times" and all the wild stuff. And Noah was here. Being a teenager. He glanced over at a Year Nine girl vomiting in the large pot of a yucca plant. Yes. He was living the dream.

Also, his nose had gone numb, and he kept tripping over his feet. But, despite these obvious impediments, he felt GRRRRREEEAAAATTTT! He carefully manoeuvred himself and two plastic cups of punch through the crowd and over to Sophie. "Here you are, m'lady," he said, having decided that calling her "m'lady" was somehow amusing.

"Thanks, Noah."

He decided that now was the time to put Operation

Flirty-Pants into action. He felt confident and *sexy*. Operation Flirty-Pants was go! He went in with his knockout opener, "You look nice, what a lovely blouse."

Sophie looked at him and chuckled. "This is a just a top."

"Oh. Right." *Women's fashions were confusing.* Best not to get into a debate about that. He would press on with his next seductive offering! "Do you want to smell my fingers?"

"What?! No, not really," she said.

"No, but then you can smell my *eau de toilette.* It's nice. I thought you might like it," he said, offering his index finger to her. *Lynx.* She would be impressed. That stuff had magic powers. Smell was an important sense. In perfume adverts people always ended up getting off with each other because they liked the other person's smell.

She batted his fingers away. "I can smell you from here, it's ... really nice."

Noah grinned. Excellent! *She could smell him from there.* Using half a can hadn't been a waste after all! Step three – show an interest in *her* interests! "Do you like music?"

"Um, yeah. I'm really into Mustard Gas at the moment."

Noah nodded, like he knew who they were. "Oh, yeah! Yes! They're great!"

"It's just one person, not a band."

"Yes. I know. I know that. He's great!" *Arse!*

"It's a woman."

Oh, God! "Uh-huh. Yeah, *woman*. What's that well-known song of hers?"

"Which one?"

"You know, it's like, *boom! Sha! La! La!...*" *Why are you randomly making this up and spouting crap? Why don't you go home now? Why are you a moron?*

Sophie looked unimpressed. "She's an indie folk singer, so I doubt her lyrics include 'Boom! Sha! La! La!' Maybe you're thinking of someone else?"

Noah nodded. "I like your blouse."

Silence.

"That had better be your phone sticking out in your pocket and not anything else."

"I haven't brought my phone with me. *Pickpockets.* Can't be too..." He realized what she was referring to. "Oh, don't worry, I haven't got an erection." He pulled out his Mini Maglite. "It's this!"

"Why the hell have you brought a torch with you?"

Noah scoffed. Stupid question! Why not? The Cub Scouts had taught him to be prepared, so he always was. "In case of emergencies," he explained. "Like, a power cut?"

She blinked at him. Blinking was a sign of attraction. He'd read that somewhere in a book about body language. He would be kissing her by the end of the night. He was sure of it.

"I'm just gonna get some fresh air," she said, moving away.

"Copy that, roger and out," Noah replied, giving her a salute.

He turned round to find Harry standing right behind him. How long had he been there? "All right, Haz?"

"How's it going with Sophie?"

"Yeah," Noah grinned, "pretty good, actually... So, we've done flirting and stuff and found out we've loads in common and I've liked her blouse thing and she's told me she likes my smell."

"Cool," Harry said.

"So, have you made a romantic advance towards anyone?"

Harry shook his head. "I'm not really up for all that tonight. But I'm glad you have."

"Wanna be my best man? If I marry her?"

Harry stared at him. "Oh, grow up, Noah!" And he stormed off.

"Harry?!" What the hell was the matter with him?

"Probably drunk," said Melissa, who was standing nearby and had clocked the drama.

Noah nodded. *Probably.*

"Oi! Oi! Sleeping Beauty!"

Noah opened an eye and Connor Evans gradually came into focus, looming over him on the sofa. He had skintight black jeans, a white short-sleeved shirt (wouldn't he be cold?) and hair that was quiffed up ridiculously high and in complete contravention of the laws of gravity. Noah supposed he looked fashionable. Actually, how *was* his hair doing that? What had he put in it – superglue? The music seemed impossibly loud. Everything was strange and spinning, like a dream, a magical vision, a—

"*Oi!*" Connor said again, kicking Noah's feet.

"What ... what... Hello, Connor... How can I help you today?"

"Your mate's upstairs, kicking off in one of the bedrooms."

"Who? Hazza?"

"Yeah, *Hazza*. You need to sort him out. I tried talking some sense into him, but he just kept yelling stuff about you."

Noah blinked at him. What the hell was going on?

"Like, *now!*" Connor said, pulling Noah to his feet.

"I..." Noah steadied himself and took a deep breath. "I'm gonna go sort him out. Man to ... man."

He pushed his way through the sweaty crowd and slid up the stairs, supporting himself against the wall on the way up and dodging an assortment of crying girls with running make-up.

Why was Harry kicking off in a bedroom?

Noah was faced with about eight doors once he was on the upstairs landing, and finding which one led to Harry was like Russian roulette. After two more girls sobbing, some spliff smoking and the beginnings of a lewd sexual act, he flung the fourth door open to find Harry flailing around in a small child's bedroom, sweeping an entire Sylvanian Family off the top of a chest of drawers in a fit of rage. He turned and saw Noah, a wild look in his eyes.

"Harry?"

But Harry just glared at him. Then he bent down, picked up a doll's house and held it aloft.

Not just a doll's house. Noah recognized it immediately from their extensive research for 3D Cluedo. They had dismissed this particular brand of house because it was too expensive, because this, *this* doll's house, was *very* special.

"Harry! No! Not the Barbie Princess Castle!" Noah screamed. "What the hell's the matter with you?!"

"I don't care!"

"You can't destroy a little girl's dream castle!"

He lowered the castle a bit. "How do you know it's a *girl*? Maybe it's a *boy* who likes playing with dolls!"

"A boy who likes wearing dresses?" Noah added, looking at the clothes that Harry had thrown about.

"Maybe! Maybe! Don't make assumptions!"

Noah followed Harry's eyes as they settled upon a wooden sign that read "Emily's Room".

"It could be a boy called Emily," Harry insisted. "But the point is, people shouldn't make assumptions. OK?"

"What—"

"OK?!" he shouted, raising the doll's house up again, his breathing jagged and unsteady.

"OK! OK! Calm down! I don't make assumptions!" Noah said, backing off. He could see the vein in Harry's temple pulsing furiously. Had Harry taken drugs? Was it the drink? Was Harry really the Incredible Hulk or something? He'd never seen Harry like this; it was ... scary, it was ... like he was a savage junkyard dog, or a massive bomb on a hair trigger...

"You *do* make assumptions," Harry snarled. "You make *a whole lot* of assumptions!"

Noah was open-mouthed. Was this somehow all his fault? What the hell had he done wrong? But it was too dangerous to argue. Best just to let it go, talk later. Calm Harry down. "OK, well, if that's the case, I'm sorry!"

"I hate this party!" Harry shouted. "I hate everyone here! We should never have come!"

"Harry, what's happened?"

"It's just shit! It's ALL SHIT!"

Noah nodded, desperate not to antagonize him further. "I think we should go home."

"I think you should SHUT UP!"

He flinched and felt his heart leap. It was like Harry might punch him any second! In the absence of any elephant tranquillizer, Noah attempted his best soothing voice, the one he would use if he ever had to talk a suicide down from a tall building, or negotiate a hostage release. "Put the Barbie castle down," he cooed.

"No!"

"Gently lower it... The Barbie castle is innocent in all this... Just put it down... Put it down..."

"Stay back!" Harry screamed, as Noah inched forward. "Get any closer and I'll smash it!"

Noah stopped and put his hands up, as if to say "fine". And then he tried a trick he had seen used to *great effect* on a TV programme which dealt with insanely crazed bad guys: he pretended his attention was quickly drawn to something to his left, and just as Harry instinctively looked across too, Noah launched himself forward to try and grab the doll's house and restore order.

Only his feet were slow to respond due to fact he was *utterly hammered*, and he tripped over himself and crashed on to the floor. He was expecting carnage to follow, but when he looked up, Harry had put the doll's house back down and was he was now just standing there, quietly sobbing.

Noah scrambled to his feet and tentatively approached him. "Harry? Haz? What's up?"

"Nothing," Harry muttered.

"Come on, what's up?" Noah said, reaching out and putting a hand on Harry's shoulder, giving it a little rub.

"I'm just ... really unhappy."

"But ... but *why*, Harry?"

"Do you really love Sophie? Are you really gonna get together, do you think?"

Noah snorted. Was this really what all this crazy stuff was about? Was Harry jealous that Noah had nearly had a bit of romance with a girl? "Well, I mean, I'd maybe like to, but I doubt it. She's leaving town anyway, so … I guess we're both back at square one on that score."

And Harry just stared at the floor and breathed.

And then he looked up, directly into Noah's eyes.

And something happened.

Something that would blow Noah's little world completely apart.

CHAPTER TEN

"Oh, what the hell," Harry muttered, putting his hand behind Noah's head and pulling him towards him.

He never thought the day would come. Things like this just didn't happen to him. So he'd never given it any thought ... but now ... it was...

It was actually happening.

To him.

Their lips touched, and his heart was immediately all *thump thump thump*. His stomach lurching, heavy, like before an exam, or when someone says "I've got bad news."

Thump.

Lurch.

But sort of nice.

And some sort of terrible.

Definitely weird.

Sick and warm and trembling hands that he didn't know what to do with.

What the hell was going on? What was Harry doing? Harry was kissing him, that's what, but *why*? Why were they kissing? And why was Noah allowing himself to be kissed like this? Was Harry suddenly gay? Harry was never gay before. Not that Noah had noticed, anyway. And *he*, Noah, wasn't gay either. Was he?

They were both drunk.

He couldn't feel his nose.

They were still kissing.

It was tender and soft and ... Harry was good at it. Had he done this before? He was a *master* at kissing. A *pro*.

Noah needed to buy time. He needed to work things out. In the absence of any other options, the best thing to do was to continue kissing. There was literally no other option. If he stopped kissing, Harry might be offended or hurt. That would be bad. If this was his best friend coming out to him, he felt he should at least be supportive. If he broke it off, Harry might think it was because Noah was repulsed by it and was homophobic, which Noah was not. Noah was cool with it. It was cool.

Tongues! Gosh.

Noah knew he had arrived in some form. He was being a teenager. If his mum could see him now, how could she think he was "uptight" about sex? Here he was, doing kissing with tongues, with a *boy*. It was out there. It was daring. He was at the cutting edge of human sexuality ... and stuff.

But this wasn't about his mum, or anyone else.

It was about him and Harry.

And this would change everything.

And it didn't feel right.

But it didn't feel completely wrong.

And yet...

Was it possible that alcohol was responsible for this? They had been drinking a lot... Sophie had encouraged it... She... Sophie... Oh God... Sophie... He'd come here to kiss Sophie, and now he was kissing Harry. This wasn't in the plan! He'd been ambushed by Harry ... and now his first kiss was a big gay kiss and not a girl kiss, like he'd planned ... like he surely wanted?

"Are you..." Noah began, desperate to buy time, "are you ... are you gay ... or...?"

"If wanting to do stuff with other boys means I'm gay, then yes, I'm gay."

"Well, that is what it means. Unless you're bi, or just experimenting. You know, trying things out..."

"No, it's not like that. *I'm gay.*"

Noah nodded and swallowed hard. It all sounded very final. How had he missed this? How had he not realized? He almost didn't want this to be true. If it was true, it had to be *faced*. He didn't want to face it. He wasn't ready. He didn't know how. "So ... is this a recent thing, or..."

"Not really. I've just never fancied girls."

"Right. But maybe ... that doesn't mean you'll never fancy girls. Maybe you just don't fancy the girls at our school. Maybe that's all."

"But I fancy the boys. Some of them."

"Right."

"I fancy you," Harry said.

They both stared at each other. Things were being said that Noah wasn't ready to hear. People shouldn't be allowed to just say stuff out of the blue. They should have to write it down first and send it to you. To give you time to prepare. Spontaneity was no one's friend. Harry could have sent a note, or a text. Explained himself. And Noah could have *thought* it through. Worked it out.

Harry *fancied* him. It was a statement so bold, so extraordinary, Noah couldn't compute its meaning. This was Error 404. This was why Harry had been in here, angry and upset.

Oh, good Lord, Harry was *in love* with *him*.

Silence.

What had they done? The cogs in Noah's brain turned as he tried to make sense of it.

A kiss.

A long kiss.

That's a lot more than "mates".

They were close.

Now they were closer.

Nobody must find out.

Harry laughed first. "Oh, wow."

"Huh. Yeah," Noah muttered, dizzy with it all.

"That was mental."

"Yeah," he said, looking down at the floor, trying to work out how he felt and what would happen next.

"I'm so drunk."

"Yeah! Me too. Yeah." *Was that why this happened?*

Harry gave his leg a little stroke and it gave Noah butterflies. It felt really nice. It felt really weird. This was Harry. One minute they were watching *SpongeBob* together and the next, there were *feelings* and *emotions* and stuff that seemed really grown up. "Come here," he said, pulling Noah towards him again.

And for a beautiful moment, it was him and Harry again.

Just them.

Together.

And there wasn't anyone else. And he didn't want there to be.

But it still felt...

Not entirely right.

Noah pulled back again. "I'm not sure I..."

Harry reached out and took his hand. "I know. It's fine."

"This is a surprise, right?"

"Right," Harry smiled, gently stoking Noah's hand with

his thumb. That movement. So small. Almost imperceptible, but it sent waves of ridiculous pleasure right up his arm and down to his stomach. Made him catch his breath. It was crazy nice.

"Harry, I—"

"Hey, homos!" Jordan Scott was at the door. How long had he been there? Oh, God. "All looking a bit GAY in here!"

Noah snatched his hand away from Harry's. "Oh, hi, Jordan. Hi. We were just—"

"Queering each other up?"

"Shut up, Jordan," Harry said.

"Comparing hands," said Noah. "That's all."

Jordan stared at them both, curling his lip slightly. "Everyone says you two are gay. This just proves it."

"No, it proves nothing!" Noah said. "I had ... a splinter and Harry was—"

"I am *always* walking in on people who shouldn't be together!" Jordan shook his head. "Never expected it to be you two though."

"Jordan, there is literally nothing—" Noah said.

"*People* like *you* —" Jordan gestured to them both "— should be *dead*. Just saying."

And he walked out.

Noah froze, looking at the door.

He didn't even know what he really felt.

He needed time and space.

He was *drunk*! He didn't know what he was doing!

He'd come here to kiss Sophie. He'd come here to be normal. To be like everyone else. To not have drama, but just an easy life, a simple life. A regular, normal life.

Harry *shouldn't* have kissed him. He should have picked a better time if he'd wanted to do stuff like that. How *stupid* can you be?!

He looked at Harry. "Do you think I'm gay?"

Harry looked back, blankly.

"Well, you must, else you wouldn't have done it!" Noah said.

And with that Noah got up and, without looking back, walked out of the room and down the stairs, pushing through the drunken crowds, and headed straight out the front door, down the gravel driveway, round the corner and then ran all the way home.

He caught his breath at the corner of the alleyway that led on to his road. Jordan Scott would make sure everyone knew he'd seen him and Harry holding hands. Now he would be the talk of the school again. Now his life would be hell … *again.*

Now he'd probably gone and lost his best mate.

He kicked the fence in frustration. "YOU STUPID, USELESS, WASTE-OF-SPACE MORON!" he screamed, unsure whether he was talking about Harry or himself. "AAAARGGGHH!"

CHAPTER
ELEVEN

"What the hell time do you call this?" his mother demanded, flinging open the front door as he unsuccessfully attempted to get his key in the lock for the third time.

"I've been at the party!"

"Well, why have you returned? Get back there! It's barely midnight!"

"No..."

"Noah!" she continued, barring his way into the house. "I thought we agreed? You wouldn't be back until at least two a.m."

"I never agreed that!"

"I am *busy*."

"I just wanna go to bed..."

"This is *me time*. Time for *me*."

"Let me in!"

"Piss off!"

"Please, Mum!" he pleaded, on the brink of tears.

"You're as independent as a two-year-old child, do you know that?" his mother hissed in his face, the smell of cheap booze on her breath making him feel even more nauseous. "Ever since the moment of conception you've plagued me. Morning sickness like you've never known. Ten agonizing hours in labour. Had to cut me open in the end, they did! I'm scarred. Scarred for life! Wait there."

She slammed the door in his face while he wiped the spit from his eye. When she opened it again she was brandishing a tea towel.

"What are you doing?" he protested, as she tied it around his head as a blindfold. "It's too tight!"

"Shut up. You know damn well I'm in here with my new man. That's why you've come back early. Trying to catch us at it! Just can't keep your nose out, can you? Well, you've not succeeded. You'll wear this to protect our privacy, I'll escort you right up the stairs and that's where you'll stay."

With that she dragged him across the threshold, flung him in front of her and began pushing him up the stairs.

"Couldn't even stay out at the party until a decent time!" she was muttering, jabbing him in the back as he tripped up the stairs. "I don't know what's wrong with you, I really don't."

"But I wasn't enjoying it!"

"'Wasn't enjoying it!' Can you hear yourself? I should take you to the doctor's – you're not a normal teenager!"

"Everyone's different, Mum, it's fine to be different!"

"No, Noah, it's not," she said, pushing him into his bedroom. "They just say that to make the weird kids feel better. And don't come out!"

And with that she slammed his door. Noah untied the tea towel and listened as his mother dragged a cupboard from her bedroom across the landing and positioned it in front of his door.

"If there's a fire you'll have to jump out the window," she shouted from the other side, once she was satisfied there was no way he could escape.

But the prospect of fire was the least of his reasons for needing to get out. He needed a wee. Quite badly. He hammered on his bedroom door. "Mother? Mum? MUM?! Hello? Help? MUU-UUM! HELP! HELP!" There was literally no response except the sound of her walking downstairs. He jigged about, continuing to bang on the door. "Mum! Listen to me now! This is serious! VERY serious! I'm in the midst of a LAVATORIAL CRISIS! It's very urgent and very important that you let me out. It's ... human rights. You are IN BREACH of my human rights and the UN will arrest you." He waited. Nothing. "Fire! FIRE!" He pretended to cough. "Help me! I'm dying! DYING!"

He frantically glanced around his room in desperation.

He couldn't pee in his bin; it was fashioned from wicker. And a mug that was half full of squash would hardly suffice. OH, GOD! GOD!

"Of course!" he squealed, remembering the window. Pee out of the window! Like they did in the olden days! And desperate times called for desperate measures. Noah could hardly contain his relief as he flung the window open, stood on his chair and was finally able to release an entirely free and unhindered stream of hot piss into the wild.

"Aaaaarrgh!" came a male scream from below.

"What the hell?" came his mother's voice.

Noah froze before toppling back in horror, still spraying piss everywhere. As commotion ensued downstairs ("Aaarrrgh! It's like acid or something … my eyes! My eyes!"), Noah lay on his back and shut his eyes, trying to pretend that absolutely none of that just happened.

"You BEAST! You *ANIMAL*!" his mother screamed, now outside his door. "You twisted little ANIMAL!"

Noah stared up at the ceiling. She was right. He was. He had not only pissed on his mother, he had pissed on her new boyfriend too. On the plus side, maybe that would put him off from moving in?

"It's illegal to piss on people, you know?! Illegal! I could call the police right now. In fact, I will. I'll call the police!"

That would be fine, he thought. They could take him away, far away. Lock him up. Life in prison would be a joy compared to life here. He would have his basic needs met. He would be well fed. He could study in peace. Alternatively, he could just phone social services and ask to be taken away. He was already lying on his bedroom floor, illegally drunk and covered in piss – what more would they want?

Oh, what was the point...?

Tears welled in his eyes as the events of the night all came back to him. He couldn't make sense of anything that had happened or anything he was feeling. Confused? Yes. Horrified? Maybe. Scared? Definitely. He wanted someone to talk to, but who? His mum couldn't care less. His gran had dementia. Dad had vanished. Normally, he would have Harry. Harry, who had seen him through so much in the last few years.

He curled up on his bed and cried, as the room spun round, and an aching dread filled his body. He stared into the darkness. Was this what being a "normal" teenager was meant to be like?

Empty.

Frightened.

Alone.

CHAPTER TWELVE

He writhed around on his bed in just his boxers. He was hot and sick, and his head was throbbing. What was this – cholera? Plague? He felt sure it must be fatal, whatever it was. His Casio digital watch told him it was 11:15 on Sunday morning. He let out a primal moan as a wave of hot nausea flashed across the aching, wasted shell of his body.

A good and attentive mother would have called an ambulance by now. But not his. She was probably too busy having a boyfriend to notice his plight.

"GRRRRAAWWWWWOOOOOOOAWWWW!" he wailed, from deep within his gut, throwing himself over on the bed and suddenly seeing his mum and Harry standing at his door. "OH, GOD!" he screamed, sitting bolt upright.

"Hi, Noah," Harry said.

"Hi, Harry!" Oh, God. He wasn't in any state to face this right now. Everything was fuzzier than it had been last night. What was real? What actually happened? He wasn't sure. He felt sick.

"Harry popped round to visit you," his mother explained. "Why are you making those ridiculous noises? And open a window and spray something, it bloody stinks in here."

He scrambled to his feet, haphazardly pulled on some jogging bottoms and a crusty old T-shirt, opened the window with one hand, and simultaneously sprayed some Lynx around the place.

His mother sighed. "Can I get you a drink, Harry? Tea, or…?"

"Yeah, I'll have a cup of tea, Mrs Grimes, thanks," Harry smiled.

"OK, I'll bring it up. Noah?"

He couldn't face this right now. Couldn't face Harry. Couldn't face the analysis of last night's events. He needed to convince his mother he was too sick to take guests.

"The light is fading!" he moaned, draping himself back on the bed and staring into the middle distance like he was hallucinating. "I am dying… I die…" He coughed and gurgled. "Oh, life! Oh, death! Oh!"

"*Shut up and stop moaning,*" his mum said, backing out of the door and closing it behind her.

Great. Now it was just the two of them and a whole load of awkwardness.

"You've got a hangover," Harry sighed, sitting on the edge of his bed.

Noah looked at him. "A hangover? Me?"

"Yep."

"Oh, Lordy. I hope the school doesn't find out. I'll never make head boy."

Harry smiled and glanced at him. "So, look—"

Noah sprang up off the bed. "I'm gonna stand, if you don't mind? Ooh, that's better. Stretch my legs a bit." Sitting down, *next to Harry*, felt too close, too intimate. It might lead to ... *more kissing.* More kissing would lead to *more confusion* and *more feelings* and that was best avoided right now.

"OK," Harry began, as Noah stood awkwardly in the middle of the room with nothing to do. He should have stayed sitting down. That would have worked better. He was just standing, for no reason, and to sit down now would be odd because he'd just said he didn't want to. *Why was he such an idiot?*

"I just wanted to say I'm sorry if I went too far," Harry said.

"What happened after I left?"

Harry rolled his eyes. "Is that what you're worried about?"

"Well, yeah, a bit. I mean, you know what school is like!" It was bad enough to begin with. The type of boy who doesn't like sport and hands in essays that are four pages longer than they need to be is the type of boy that attracts bullying. And the type of boy that also has a mum who does a Beyoncé tribute act *and* is spotted *holding hands* with other boys is as good as dead. *"What happened?"*

Harry sighed. "Absolutely nothing. I tidied up the bedroom, went downstairs, talked to a few people… Then a sixth former accidentally set fire to the shed, so that was drama. I walked Sophie home, and that was it."

"You walked Sophie home?!"

Harry laughed. "You can't seriously have a problem with that?"

Noah glared at him. If anyone was meant to walk Sophie home last night, and possibly kiss her, it was him. Harry had not only stolen his first kiss and made it a gay one, he'd probably stolen Sophie too and kissed her for good measure because he was clearly a hormone crazed, kiss-everyone teenager now.

"Noah, I'm gay."

OK, so maybe he hadn't kissed Sophie.

"Yes, well, I had sort of gathered that," Noah huffed, playing down the fact his heart had just leapt into his mouth. This wasn't the drink talking now. This was real, cold-light-of-day stuff. This was *truth*. Harry was gay. "How long … have you known?"

"A while. I didn't plan to tell you like this."

Noah nodded. *But he had been planning it.* This was one

hell of a big secret to have hidden. It felt like a betrayal. Why hadn't Harry discussed his feelings when he first started having them? Why wait for an all-or-nothing, dramatic revelation?

"I was scared," Harry continued, "and for a long time, I wasn't sure, and I didn't know what I was feeling. That's why. I wanted to talk to you about it, but I kept putting it off. And then ... the party was happening, and you were talking about Sophie and how much you liked her, and I suddenly thought, that's it. I've missed my chance. I'd had a lot to drink, and I wasn't thinking straight, and I kind of went crazy. So. *Sorry.*"

Noah didn't know what to say. What if he said the wrong thing and it made matters worse? And what about the really big questions? Did *he* feel the same? Was *he* gay? Being gay was not part of the plan. He dreamed of a normal existence – everything his own life hadn't been to date. He would marry a nice girl, maybe Sophie, maybe have a couple of kids one day, and *not* get divorced, or go AWOL. They would have money and a nice house. Neither he nor his wife would do a Beyoncé tribute act.

"You gotta say something," Harry said. "What do you want to do?"

He swallowed and sat down weakly on the bed. "I ... I kinda want things to go back to normal. Or something approaching normal."

"Me too."

Noah breathed a sigh of relief. "'Kay. Good."

"But I can't."

"What do you mean?" Noah said, a sting of fear stabbing his stomach.

"I mean, yes, it would be great if things could just go back to how they were, but, being totally honest, I want more than that. I really ... I really like you, Noah. More than just mates. I mean, I could kiss you now..."

"We can't!" Noah bleated. "My mum! She'll be totally here any minute with the drinks, and she won't knock!"

"Chill – I'm not gonna do anything – I was just saying *I would like to*. If you wanted to. That's all."

Noah put his head in his hands because it was all too confusing. "Oh, *God*," he muttered.

"I don't know," Harry said. "There's something about you that I just want to..."

"Shag?" Noah suggested, looking up.

"I was gonna say 'protect'."

"Oh," Noah said, looking down again. "Well, why? Because I'm a bit short, or something? A bit weedy? I'm not some little mouse. I don't need *protecting*."

"Sure." Harry smiled. "I just meant, the way you see the world. Your, I dunno, your innocence. It's nice."

Noah smarted. "My *innocence*? I've seen stuff on the internet! I've seen some pretty *mature* sites, if you know what I mean?"

"Yeah, well I think we've all looked at porn."

"Well, that is actually *illegal*, Harry. That is against the law. I was talking about news and current affairs sites, aimed at adults. They give a very raw and uncompromising view of the world."

"You've never looked at porn?"

Noah looked Harry straight in the eyes and swallowed.

"Refreshments!" his mum announced, barging into the room with a tray.

He looked up – a teacup and saucer for Harry, actual sugar cubes with some serving tongs (where the hell were *they* from?!), a plate *with a doily on it* and a biscuit selection. There were party rings, Jammie Dodgers, chocolate fingers and pink wafers. Noah narrowed his eyes. *Clearly his conniving mother had a secret stash of top-quality biscuits hidden within the house.* He would find them. As God was his witness, he would find them. He would Jessica Fletcher it up, follow the clues, and find them.

"Thanks, Mrs Grimes," Harry smiled.

His mum went, and they sat in silence for what seemed like ages, the tea going cold on the tray, the biscuits untouched – which was when you knew serious shit was going down.

"Look," Harry said, "I'm sorry to have caused chaos, and I know it's confusing—"

"Confusing?!" Noah said, springing up from the bed. Why did Harry assume he was confused? When Harry was ruthlessly decimating that Sylvanian Family, he had been

121

barking on about "making assumptions". But now who was making assumptions? "*You* assumed I wanted to kiss you, even though you knew I liked Sophie, and *you're* now the one assuming I'm engulfed in some sort of sexual confusion over the whole thing!"

"And are you?"

"What if I didn't want my first kiss to be with another boy? What if I didn't want to kiss you?"

"Then maybe you shouldn't have kissed me for so long."

"It was the punch!"

"Sure. Fine. I was a drunken snog. Brilliant."

Noah scowled at him. "You've had time to think about all this. You've had months or years or whatever. You sprang it on me and it was all KABOOM! This is happening if you like it or not."

"And did you like it? Or *not*?"

He tried to control his breathing. Why was Harry trying to force an answer out of him? How was that fair? "I don't know. All right? Happy? *I don't know.*"

Harry nodded, while Noah tried to work out if what he'd just said was actually some sort of admission that he *might* be gay. Well, whatever it sounded like, it didn't matter. The truth was, *he wasn't sure* if he liked the kiss, and he *wasn't sure* about anything. If Harry had left him alone last night, he might have kissed Sophie. And then he might have liked that. And then this little chat would all be pointless.

"Well, I guess just think about it and … see," Harry said.

"Right. I'm sorry I shouted."

"No worries. I deserved it."

"Take a Jammie Dodger. You can have it on your way home."

"Oh. Right, yeah, I should probably get going, then."

"OK. Cool."

Harry took a biscuit and went to the door.

"What about school?" Noah asked. "We'll get so much hassle."

"It'll be fine," Harry said. "Remember Zach Donovan from three years ago?"

Noah nodded. "But the thing with Zach Donovan is that he was a six-foot-two football player with model good looks and everyone loved him. In case you haven't noticed, most people don't seem to feel that way about us. Plus, he went to uni shortly after he came out and hasn't come back since. You can hardly compare the situation."

"What I'm saying is, people these days are more open-minded than you think. Anyway, who cares? We were seen holding hands – big deal! People have better things to think about, right?"

Noah looked at him, doubtfully. "You'd better be right."

CHAPTER THIRTEEN

"Let us pray."

"Our Father, who art the gay boy? Noah be his name..."

Oh yes, "people have better things to think about."

"He makes Harry come. He gives him one. On earth as it is in heaven..."

Noah looked over at Harry, a few rows down. He had his eyes closed and head bowed.

It was almost all OK yesterday, or at least as OK as it could be when your best mate has snogged you and declared his undying gay love and you were like, *That's great, but I don't know if I feel the same and now my whole life has been turned upside down. Cheers for that.* But standing in Monday morning assembly, the eyes of the school on him, the red-hot gossip of the day, with some halfwits (*who was it standing behind him?*) making fun of him – it was quite clear the simple act of holding hands with another boy had unleashed a new form of total hell.

"And lead him straight into temptation. Right into a gay bar. For Noah is a gay boy. Who likes to suck cock. For ever and ever. He's gay."

"OK, sit yourselves down!" said Mr Baxter, head of year.

The Year Elevens all shuffled back into their seats. Noah despondently plopped back down, straight on to a banana that the hilarious occupants of the row behind had placed on his seat during the prayer.

"Awww – right up his arse!" said one of the lads. (It wasn't.)

"He loves it!" said another. (He didn't.)

"Oh, Harry! Do it to me!" sighed a girl. (Not a phrase he would ever use. He wasn't a porn star with no class.)

"Right, folks!" said Mr Baxter. "The Christmas Fayre is coming up…"

Noah wasn't sure what to do about the banana. If he pulled it out from underneath him it was bound to elicit further jibes from the knobs in the row behind. Yet to leave it there, when he had so obviously sat on it, seemed odd. There was also the fact the banana had been very ripe and had burst open on impact, the mush and juice now seeping into his trousers.

"He's still sat on it!" giggled the girl behind. "He's getting off on it!"

He glanced across at Harry again, who was staring straight ahead and clearly had no idea that any of this was happening. Right. That was enough. Screw them. Noah shifted slightly and reached underneath himself to extract the banana.

"He's gonna pull it out his arse!"

"Dirty bastard!"

"Noah, do you have ants in your pants?" said Mr Baxter, cocking an eyebrow.

Laughter. All eyes turned to Noah. "No..." he muttered.

"OK. Well stop shifting about and sit nicely, then. If you can't sit still on a chair, you'll sit on the floor."

Noah sat still and bowed his head in shame while the kids behind pissed themselves over their brilliantly mature joke. The mush had even soaked through his boxers. He could feel it against his skin now. He was going to spend the day smelling of banana – probably the worst fruit of all to smell of.

With Mr Baxter continuing to deliver exciting news about how this year's Christmas Fayre was to be a German-style outdoor market affair, Noah very slowly moved his right hand under his bottom, so he appeared to be sitting on it. Ignoring the gasps of disbelief from behind ("He's got his whole hand up there!"), he subtly attempted to scrape together the bits of banana that had pressed themselves to the seat of his trousers. As it turned out, the adhesive qualities of bananas were quite considerable. He needed more leverage. There simply wasn't enough height between his bottom and the seat to get enough purchase on the banana skin. He was so deeply involved in the manoeuvre that he hadn't noticed Mr Baxter was no longer talking, but was instead looking directly at him, horrified, as he apparently fiddled with his bottom. When Noah finally looked up he realized the whole room was back looking at him again. He froze, his hand still wedged underneath him, mid-grope.

"You may well go bright red," said Mr Baxter, giving Noah a look of utter disappointment. "Stand up, please."

Noah looked back at him with startled eyes. He really didn't want to stand up. Couldn't he just apologize and promise to sit still?

"Noah Grimes!" Mr Baxter shouted. "If you still want to be on the prefect list for next year, STAND UP!"

Noah sprang up, the adhesive properties of the fruit immediately failing, and clumps of banana falling from his bottom like elephant dung.

"What the *hell* is that?" asked Mr Baxter.

"I accidentally sat on a banana, sir," Noah explained, desperately trying to salvage the situation by adopting a strategy of complete honesty.

Noah was expecting laughter, but the room was totally silent. Horribly silent. Oh God. Noah knew exactly why. Everyone already knew about the gay holding hands

127

thing, so they would be thinking this was just a natural progression. He must remedy the situation. He must explain. Else things would only get worse...

"It's not a sex thing, sir," Noah ventured.

Mr Baxter looked at him, aghast and silent, which Noah interpreted as an expectation of further explanation.

"I wasn't putting it up my bottom."

Somewhere, someone quietly said, "Oh my God."

"Right, Year Eleven – assembly over!" Mr Baxter shouted, suddenly jolting himself into action. "Everyone to classes now, please! Noah Grimes, remain here. And absolute quiet on the way out, please. Go!"

Noah stood motionless as the lines of students filed out of the hall in hushed silence. He glared at Harry as he moved off with the line. Yeah, it was definitely all "fine". It was going really bloody well.

"OK, Noah," Mr Baxter said, walking over to him as the last stragglers left.

Noah swallowed in panic. "Will I still be on the prefect list? Because I can explain, I—"

Mr Baxter put a hand on Noah's shoulder. "Are you being bullied? Be honest. Tell me."

"Um, well...?" What was the best thing to do in this situation? Should he be a "snitch", a "squealer", a "grass"? Answer: yes, of course. Those *fools* deserved their comeuppance! "Yes, Mr Baxter, sadly I am. I'm unsure of the exact identity of the students behind me, other than they were from Form 5B, so I suppose the best thing might be to put the entire form group in detention, I don't know."

"Listen, kids play pranks sometimes, they get high-spirited, there's 'banter' and so on. But I want you to know you can come to me, OK? You can talk to me about it any time. I want to crack down on this sort of nonsense."

Noah looked at Mr Baxter. He was somewhere between thirty and sixty, Noah had no idea. He'd been at the school for ever, though, and had shaved his balding head, which gave him the slight look of a right-wing extremist. That was probably one reason why he was head of Year Eleven – he was terrifying when he needed to be. But now ... he was being nice. Very nice. OK, he wasn't really *doing* anything to help, but was making a show of caring. *Why?*

"How's ... stuff at home? Everything OK?"

Noah's eyes widened. Why was he so interested in this? What was he getting at? "Everything is fine, thank you very much," Noah said, quickly.

Mr Baxter stood looking at him and smiled. "Hey, you like theatre? Plays?"

Noah gave a tentative nod.

"Great! I'm helping the English department organize the Year Eleven theatre trip. I was thinking ... *The Mousetrap*?"

Noah's eyes lit up. "*The Mousetrap*? That's an Agatha Christie, I *love* Agatha Christie!"

"Yeah, I know," Mr Baxter chuckled.

"Excellent. That is an excellent choice," Noah beamed.

"Well, let's make it happen, then. And pop in and see Mrs Peters at reception. She can, er, arrange for some lost-property trousers *sans* banana mush for you."

He patted Noah on the back and strolled off, humming. Noah watched him go and smiled. Maybe things would be OK after all, and a trip to London to see *The Mousetrap* would be WAIT A MINUTE HOW DID MR BAXTER KNOW HOW MUCH HE LIKED AGATHA CHRISTIE?!

Noah looked around in panic, replaying the exchange. He'd said that he loved Agatha Christie. "Yeah, I know," Mr Baxter had replied. *"I know."* HOW DID HE KNOW? And why, WHY was he being so nice and ... *fatherly*?

Noah was totally channelling Miss Marple, Jessica Fletcher and Poirot, all at once.

Was Mr Baxter his mother's new man?

CHAPTER FOURTEEN

Noah walked round to reception in a daze. This was all he bloody needed. If it turned out his no-good mother was dating the head of Year Eleven from school, he couldn't be held responsible for his actions.

Now he came to think of it, he remembered Mr Baxter had recently caused a stir by driving into the car park in his new two-seater convertible sports car. He was showing all the signs of a midlife crisis and was therefore exactly the unstable sort of man his mother would be naturally drawn to.

It. All. Made. Sense.

And then he shut his eyes because, horrifically, that would mean he had recently pissed all over his head of year. *Brilliant.*

This insane relationship could not be allowed to continue. *He must drive them apart. He must plant seeds of doubt in both their minds, and then water those seeds with the poison of paranoia.*

He wasn't a bad person. This was for the good of all parties.

They would thank him. One day.

Mrs Peters was the surly woman who guarded reception (and photocopier access) like it was Fort Knox and, like most people who worked in schools, she utterly despised kids.

"Mrs Peters? I've been told I have to wear the lost-property trousers," Noah said.

"You're a Year Eleven, aren't you?" she asked, narrowing her eyes.

"Yes."

"I don't think we've got any trousers for Year Elevens. Year Elevens don't normally wet themselves."

"Yes, but I haven't wet myself."

"Why do you need the lost property trousers, then?"

"I accidentally sat on a banana."

Mrs Peters scowled at Noah and went to hunt in the cupboard at the back of reception. She returned and flung a scabby old pair at Noah, who was dismayed to discover the label read "11–12 years".

"I think they'll be too small," Noah told her.

She wasn't listening. She was staring out through

the glass doors of the main entrance. Noah turned to look, and watched as Josh Lewis from Year Thirteen walked by outside, in his rugby kit.

Josh Lewis – captain of every sports team. Josh Lewis – loved by the school so much they kept him back a year. Josh Lewis – heart-throb, prefect, role model. Girls loved him. Boys wanted to be him. Teachers adored him. He had gone through every step of puberty at precisely the right age. He had real stubble on his face and proper muscle definition that came from playing a lot of sport. He was so butch he could pull off wearing a square, glistening diamond stud in his ear, although Noah had noticed he hadn't had it in recently – not that he had been obsessively checking or anything, because he definitely hadn't.

Josh waved at Mrs Peters, who gave a cheerful wave back, accompanied by a girlish giggle. Then her eyes refocused on Noah, her lip curling as she took in the complete contrast between Josh and him. Noah lifted the trousers up into her field of vision.

"Sorry, Mrs Peters, but I'm worried these might be too small."

"It's that or nothing. You're pretty skinny, so they'll probably fit," she suggested, biting into a Weight Watchers digestive.

"Right," Noah sighed. "Well, thank you for your time."

Remarkably, the trousers did fit around the waist, although the legs were too short by a good two inches and the crotch was incredibly tight, displaying in vivid high definition his most private of regions. "Skinny fit" trousers might well be *en vogue*, but Noah wasn't convinced they were meant to cut off circulation to your entire lower body.

"Wow!" said Jess, looking at his crotch as he made his way to his seat in geography. "It's got a bit X-rated in here!"

"Nice penis, Noah!" someone shouted.

"Jeez, that should be *illegal*, man!"

Beyond caring now, Noah pulled his chair out from under the desk and flopped down on it, the trousers wildly constricting as he sat, slicing his testicles in twain whilst simultaneously ripping into his flesh from the top of his thigh and across the bottom. He gaped in agony as he felt his bollocks ricochet into his stomach and back again, trying to find someplace to be.

"All right, Noah?" said Sophie, who arrived to sit next to him with a small pile of supporting papers for their presentation. "I'm looking forward to this; we've got a strong case." She stopped and looked at him. "Are you OK?"

Noah nodded, a wave of nausea passing through him. "Yeah," he squeaked.

"You're very white. Are you ill?"

Noah shook his head. This was agony. What if he'd actually chopped something off?

"I hope you're not getting too much hassle. Harry told me everything that happened at the party."

"Everything?" he croaked.

"Yes. And I know those idiots were taking the piss in assembly, but I think it's great you've maintained a dignified silence. Like you've risen above it. Are you sure you're OK?"

"I think I've done something," Noah gasped.

"What kind of thing?"

"I think I've sliced off one of my balls!" he whimpered, the tears welling up in his eyes.

"Oh... God... Really?"

Noah nodded, his bottom lip wobbling. "At the very least it's twisted and if that happens you've only got five minutes before it dies and they have to surgically remove it," he said, as every horror story he'd ever read from unreliable medical websites came flooding into his head.

"Oh God... I'll..."

"No! Don't tell Miss Palmer!" Noah pleaded, not wanting an iota of further attention to be lavished upon him.

"But, Noah!"

"No!"

"Noah! This could be serious!"

"Please!"

"It's nothing to be embarrassed about!"

"It is! It..."

"Right! Settle down!" Miss Palmer shouted as Sophie put her hand up. "What is it, Sophie?"

"Sorry, Miss Palmer, it's just I think Noah might have twisted one of his testicles and he may require medical attention."

Miss Palmer crossed her arms. "Is this some sort of ruse to get out of the presentation?"

"No, miss!" Noah said. "All the papers are here..." He haphazardly opened a folder as they all spilled out over the floor. "All the papers! All the work! Aarggghh!"

"Miss, he *needs* to see someone about his testicles," Sophie insisted.

"Well, how's he done this to his testicles?" Miss Palmer asked.

"Can everyone please stop saying that word?" Noah squeaked.

He closed his eyes. If it wasn't for the incredible pain this would be horrendous, but as he hobbled out in an agonized blur, leaning weakly on Sophie and Miss Palmer, he didn't care. He didn't care that everyone else was loving this. He didn't care about the howls of laughter. He didn't care that someone said,

"Friggin' hell, is he wearing *SpongeBob* boxers?"

He just didn't care. When you've reached the very bottom, there's nowhere else to go. There are no further depths to which you can fall, so there's no more bad stuff that can possibly happen. And this was the bottom. It was definitely the bottom. His mum was dating a teacher, he'd kissed his best friend, the girl he liked now thought he was gay and his testicles were ruined. It couldn't possibly get any worse than this.

Could it?

CHAPTER FIFTEEN

"Well!" declared Mrs Sawyer, snapping her latex gloves off as he stood bollock naked in the middle of sick bay. "I think we can all breathe a sigh of relief. Your testicles will live to fight another day."

Noah pulled his boxers back up while Mrs Sawyer made a note in the accident book. The first person to ever fondle his balls had been a sixty-year-old woman with a receding hairline and whiskers sprouting from her chin. It was not as he had hoped or imagined.

"Has the pain subsided?" she enquired.

"Yeah," he grunted, avoiding eye contact with the woman who now knew him more intimately than anyone else on the planet.

She flipped the book closed and gave him a kindly

smile. "OK, so you stay here whilst I source some new trousers for you. Have a little rest in the bed there and we'll get you back to new in no time!"

"OK. Thank you."

She bustled out of sick bay and Noah hopped into the little bed and snuggled himself under the mean blanket. Mrs Sawyer was a notorious pushover. With any luck, he could spin this out all day, by which time some other poor kid would have encountered some hideous misfortune, and everyone would have forgotten about him.

No sooner was he settled than the door swung open again.

"All right, Noah? Heard you were in here," Harry said, bearing a black eye and a bloody lip.

"Jesus! What happened to you?"

"Fell over on the gravel by the tennis courts."

Noah stared at him. "Riiiight."

"So, silly me." Harry shrugged. "That'll teach me to run, won't it?"

Noah nodded. "Sure. Very silly."

Noah leaned back against the wall. He knew damn well there was more to the story. It's what made it so scary. Wouldn't be the first time a gay kid got beaten up. Wouldn't be the last.

"I'd quite like a hug right now," Harry told him.

Noah swallowed. He supposed that would be OK. After all, a hug was just a hug. It doesn't mean anything much.

He went over to him and they buried their faces into each other's shoulders. It didn't seem too bad when it was just them. It was everyone else that made it difficult. It felt fine. It felt normal.

"Oh God, that's enough," Harry said, backing off. "I'm getting a ... *you know.*"

And all at once it seemed wrong again.

How could this all feel so right and then so messed up, at the same time?

"Look, Harry, I don't know, but what with the stuff this morning and now you ... having fallen over on the gravel, I mean – I just wondered if we should maybe not be seen together for a bit? Like, not hang out at break? Maybe not walk home together?"

Harry shook his head. "Screw that. You're not serious?"

"I just thought, until it all goes quiet again. I mean, all that happened is that *one person* saw us holding hands. Imagine if Jordan had come in ten seconds earlier when we were... Well, imagine that!"

"But he didn't. No one saw, no one knows, no one's gonna do anything about it."

"But if they see us hanging out, talking, it'll fan the flames!" Noah said. "People will be looking out for any little thing now, any hint that we might be..." He did a vague thrusting motion with his hips. "You know, whatever. There'll be more trouble."

"I don't care if there is. So what?"

"I just want everything to go back to how it was. I can take the stuff about Mum and Dad. There's nothing I can do about that any more. But *this*..."

"What? Am I an inconvenience to you now? Is that it?"

"No! Harry, definitely not!" Noah sighed. Why couldn't he see his point of view? Normally he and Harry agreed on everything. Now, they agreed on nothing, it seemed. "I just don't want to give them any more ammo."

"Stop wimping out on me. No way. No way is that happening."

"But—"

"NO WAY! Jesus!" Harry paced to the wall, ran his hands through his hair and looked back at him. There was a flash, just a flash, of the angry stranger that Noah had encountered at the party. It scared him.

"Sorry, it was just a thought. Stupid."

Except it wasn't stupid. Harry might be fine with it all and not care, but Noah wasn't. He didn't want everyone talking, calling him gay and making his life miserable. He hadn't even come out! He hadn't done anything except let himself be kissed by his best friend. And nobody even knew about that, except possibly Sophie! All anyone knew for sure was that they were caught holding hands. Holding hands! God only knew what it would be like if they knew about the rest.

The door pushed open and Sophie edged in. "Hey? How's the patient?" she asked.

"Fine. My balls are fine," Noah said, keen that she should know there was no damage and he was still perfectly capable of having children and being an excellent father, just in case she was thinking he might be suitable for that type of thing.

She looked at Harry. "God, are you all right?"

"Yeah, s'fine."

"This school is such a dump and the people in it are all utter Neanderthals," she declared. "Present company excluded."

"Lucky you're leaving, then, isn't it?" Noah said.

"You know, I've been thinking, you two are the only lads in the school I actually *like*. How mad it that? There's, like, five hundred boys and only two who are decent! You've got the right idea, you two aren't even *trying* to fit in."

Noah felt his heart plunge. *She liked him.* OK, she was totally wrong about the trying-to-fit-in thing, but if she was staying, and if she wasn't at least half wondering if he was gay, he might be in with a chance. He wished she could stay. If she stayed, something might happen. She'd as good as said it was a possibility.

"Look, you know you can come and visit any time, yeah? Both of you."

"Noah's not sure he wants to be seen with me," Harry said, "so I doubt we'll visit you together."

"Haz! Shut up! God!" That conversation had been private. Why was he telling Sophie, making him look bad?

And it clearly looked bad, especially taken out of context like that.

She pursed her lips and looked at him. *Yep!* That was the look! The look that said "You're a total jerk, how could you?" and "Now there's only one boy in the school I like, and it's not you!"

"That's not exactly what I said!"

"Yeah. You did," Harry chipped in.

"Look, Sophie, I just thought it might make things less awful if the others didn't—"

"Shut up," Sophie said. "That's a terrible idea and really mean, Noah. You and Harry should stick together. You're mates. You love each other."

What did she mean by that? What did she think, after what Harry had told her? "I do love Harry," he said carefully. "We're chums, but not *bum* chums. We're friends, but not *willy* friends. We're—"

"Noah, this is totally unnecessary," Harry said.

"I'm just clarifying—"

"You don't need to. I'm really embarrassed, just leave it."

"Right, anyway, I've got to get back to class. And *you* —" Sophie pointed at Noah "— don't be a dick."

He nodded. "Totally. No. I won't be."

She went, and Noah turned back to Harry. "Why did you do that?"

"I dunno. I was just pissed off."

"Well, fine, but don't involve other people. Especially ones that have just revealed we're the only boys in the whole school they like."

"Sorry, should I have left at that point? Did you want to lose your virginity to her on the sick bay bed?"

Noah threw his hands up. "Well, who knows? Maybe. Maybe I did! Maybe, if you had gone and not made me out to be a total *bastard*, I would have seduced her and we would have made sweet, sweet love. Or not. I just don't know."

Harry laughed and gave Noah a playful push. "You're an idiot."

"Bingo! One pair of trousers, ages thirteen to fourteen years!" Mrs Sawyer announced, pushing the door open with her massive breasts and bustling triumphantly back into the sick bay, as the boys casually shifted apart.

"But I'm fifteen to sixteen!" protested Noah.

"Beggars can't be choosers. What's happened to you, Harry Lawson?"

"He fell over on the gravel by the tennis courts," Noah explained, giving Harry a sarcastic smile.

"Does it need stitches?" Harry asked.

"It'll need some wet paper towels, that's what. I don't know! Falling over on the gravel! Tch! Who's a silly boy, then?"

"I am," Harry grinned, playing up to it, "I'm a silly boy."

"I've got a fun-sized Mars Bar for brave boys. Do you want a fun-sized Mars Bar?"

"Yes, please, Mrs Sawyer," Harry replied with puppy-dog eyes.

Noah smarted as Mrs Sawyer shuffled back out of the room. Why hadn't he been offered a fun-sized Mars Bar? His predicament had been far worse than Harry's. Harry just had a few cuts and scrapes; Noah had full-on twisted testicles that had as good as been sliced up by cheese wire. He wanted his Mars Bar, damn it!

"So, meet you by the wall tonight? Like usual?" Harry said.

Noah nodded. "Sure." *And I'll carry a placard reading "WE'RE OFF TO BUM" because that's what everyone will be thinking anyway.*

"We good?"

"Of course we are." Although it felt *different*. It felt like stuff had changed. It felt like *everything* had changed.

"Catch!" Mrs Sawyer said, poking her head back round the door and throwing Harry the fun-sized Mars Bar. "Noah, do you feel well enough to get those trousers on and get back to lessons?"

"Not really, I think I'm suffering from a sugar low due to the shock," he said, enviously eyeing Harry's Mars Bar.

"OK, then. You stay here just as long as you need to," she said. "I'll see if I can find you a Polo mint."

Noah grimaced. *It was a Mars Bar he really wanted.* He looked back at Harry, who was grinning at him. "Everything's gonna be all right, you'll see," Harry said.

"Sure."

"Here." Harry threw him the Mars Bar. "Don't eat it all at once."

CHAPTER SIXTEEN

"Noah?!"

He looked up and smiled, delighted to see Sophie dart round the corner of the sports hall and hurry towards where he was sitting on one of the benches.

"Your text said 'Meet me behind sports hall – URGENT'," Sophie said, flopping down next to him. "What's happened?"

"Nothing. I just thought we didn't say goodbye properly earlier."

Sophie rolled her eyes. "OK, first, if you put 'urgent' in a message, that normally implies some sort of emergency, by which I mean death or injury. Second, what exactly does saying goodbye 'properly' entail?"

"Well, just—"

"Because people only normally hang out behind the sports hall to smoke or snog."

"Well, I haven't got any cigarettes," Noah said.

Sophie's eyes widened.

"Oh, and, er … I haven't got any … lips?"

She shook her head. "Right, that's just … obviously stupid because I'm looking right at your lips. Look—"

"So, this is goodbye!"

"Noah, we don't have to do a big goodbye thing because—"

"I just wanted to say a few words—"

"There's Skype, there's social media, there's even these things called trains—"

"I just wanted to say—"

Sophie sighed and sat back. "Fine. Go on, then."

"I know we've only really been talking to each other for a few days, but in that time you've definitely become one of my best friends. But now you're going to Milton Keynes…" He looked at her. Here was the crux of the matter. Here was the reason for the sense of urgency. Matters may have been somewhat derailed, but he couldn't let this chance slip through his fingers. "And the thing is, Sophie, do you think there will be *boys* in Milton Keynes?"

She blinked at him. "Well, I would say there's a high chance. You lot seem to be pretty much everywhere."

"We do. We do." Noah nodded. "But I wonder what the boys there will be like?"

"Oh! Oh, I see what you mean. Well, there might be some you like. When you come visit we can—"

"No!" Noah squealed. "I'm not asking for my own pleasure. No. I just meant ... er... Look, it doesn't matter. Just remember that boys from big cities can sometimes be ... you know, they can be *very* dangerous. They're often hardened by tough lives, pollution and low-level crime. Some may be pickpockets. Others will be drug mules. I'm just saying, trust no one and best not to get involved if there's any doubt, and there's plenty of doubt, so my advice is don't get involved. Anyway, with your exams and everything coming up, you really don't want to think about starting a relationship. Not with some new boy you don't even really know. That's what I think."

Sophie burst out laughing. "Oh, Noah!"

"This isn't a joke though."

"I know. And that makes it all the more amusing." She ruffled his hair. "You're so clueless, it's cute."

"But, Soph—"

"No, it's *great* advice, Noah. Much appreciated," she said.

Noah nodded, unsure if she was being sarcastic. And what the hell did she mean by "clueless"? He was completely *au fait* with how the modern world worked. Why, just the other night he watched a TV documentary about an outbreak of kinky sex parties in the Cotswolds, that had led to a marked rise in STIs amongst the over-fifties. He was nothing if not informed. "Anyway, I thought you might like this." He pulled the warm and soggy Mars Bar from his pocket. "Sorry it's a bit soft, it's been in my pocket since this morning. It's a Mars Bar."

"Yes," she said. "Happily, I can read the label. It's very kind of you. Thank you."

"Yes," Noah said.

"Can I give *you* some advice?" she said.

"OK…"

"Rather than sitting here giving me top tips on dating, which, you know, really are appreciated, how about going to meet Harry? Because that's the thing you should be sorting out right now."

Noah flinched. "Yes, well, I *am* going to see Harry. I'm just seeing you first. But next I'm just going to pop to the boys' toilets, then go see Harry." *Why have you told her you're going to the boys' toilets? She already knows about the bladder infection fiasco. Now she'll think you really have got a weak bladder. That's what she'll think.* "Of course, I could go to the toilet at home, I've just decided to go here. No real reason. I could take it or leave it, to be honest."

"Good to know," Sophie said, standing up. "I'll text you when I'm in Milton Keynes. I'm not starting my new school until next week, so I'll have plenty of time on my hands to check up on you and Harry! If you see my dad wondering around, dazed, confused, starving and in dirty clothes, can you help him work out how to use domestic appliances?"

"Of course," Noah said. "Good luck in your new town. I hope you don't get sucked into an urban vortex of heroin and violent street crime."

"Thanks, Noah."

Noah stood at the urinals peeing, checking his watch because he was late to meet Harry and he wanted to get over and see Gran while visiting time was still on. On the plus side, at least most of the other students should have left by now, meaning the chances of any more trouble today would be slim. It was only as he zipped up and turned that he realized he wasn't alone.

One of the cubicles was occupied, and the person inside was very quietly sobbing. Noah tiptoed to the furthest edge of the room and ducked down to see through the gap at the bottom of the door. He could only see the occupant's rucksack, but it was the same rucksack that Harry had. And the person inside was wearing the same shoes that Harry wore.

Chances were, it was probably Harry inside. Noah hesitated and stared in the direction of the cubicle, listening to the quiet, muffled gulps and sobs. He felt terrible. He should help him.

But...

What should he say? What should he do? This was uncharted territory.

Noah felt awful. And Harry clearly felt awful. This whole *gay thing* was making them both feel awful.

He wished it had never happened.

"Haz?" he whispered, outside the locked door. "Haz? It's me. Your friend Noah Grimes. You OK?"

There was a silence, then, "Yeah … yeah, I'm fine, Noah. Look, you're right, maybe it's best if you walk home alone today."

Clearly, it wasn't fine. Noah tapped on the cubicle door. "Can I come in?"

Harry sighed from inside. "Seriously, just go away."

"Are you engaged in legitimate lavatorial business?"

Harry slammed the lock across and flung the door open. "No, I'm not 'engaged in legitimate lavatorial business'! What's wrong with you? Can't you just leave me alone?"

Noah stared at him. Harry had red eyes and tear tracks down his cheeks. He looked *wrecked*. "What's happened?" Noah said, desperately wanting to reach out and touch him.

Harry took a few unsteady breaths. "Nothing's happened… I guess … it's all just got to me a bit. I'll be fine. I'll be fine tomorrow. Just being stupid." He nodded, looking like he was trying to convince himself. "You OK?"

Noah shrugged. "Suppose."

Harry nodded again and wiped his eyes with his palms. "Get off home. Let's just lie low and let things cool off for a bit."

What the hell had happened? Something had, that was

for sure. Something to make Harry change his mind. "How bad is it?" Noah asked.

Harry took a deep breath, then looked directly at him. "I don't know what you're talking about." He shut the door in Noah's face.

"Haz!"

And slid the bolt.

Noah sighed. This was all too much. This was all one stupid, crazy mess. He needed to talk to someone about this. He needed *Gran*. He shook his head and walked off, slipping silently out into the corridor.

"All right, Noah?" said a voice from behind him.

Startled, Noah whipped round and saw Eric Smith staring at him, greasy hair stuck to his sweaty-looking face. "All right?" Noah replied, immediately sensing that Eric was up to something illicit and shady.

Eric stared at him for what seemed like for ever, with an entirely expressionless face. "You're here late," he said eventually.

"So are you."

And Eric nodded and smiled. "See ya, then."

"Yeah. Bye," Noah said, unable to walk away fast enough. God, that boy creeped him out.

"George! At last!" his gran said, turning the volume down on "Livin' on a Prayer" by Bon Jovi as Noah poked his nose into her room.

"It's Noah, Gran."

"Where's George? What have you done with him?"

"We cremated him two years ago, Gran."

"You've BURNT him? BURNT him alive?! He wasn't Joan of friggin' Arc, you nonce!"

Noah didn't have the energy to argue, so he muttered a quiet "sorry" and sat on the edge of the bed, loosening his tie because it was so insanely hot in there. Gran closed the door and shut the curtains. In the half-light provided by the miserable energy-saving light bulb, she pulled a rolled-up sheet of paper from her underwear drawer, sat next to Noah and unfurled it.

"What's this, Gran?" he asked.

"Look carefully."

It appeared to be a ground plan of the Willows, complete with dimensions, elevations and a series of dotted red lines.

"Oh! It's—"

"Don't say!" she interrupted. "They bug the rooms! They're listening!" she whispered. "I KNOW YOU'RE LISTENING!" she suddenly shouted into the room.

"What are you doing with this, Gran?"

"Dickie stole it from the admin office. Our codebreakers have had no luck trying to crack the combination for the main door. And that's even with Vera, who worked at Bletchley Park in the bloody war! This was a woman who helped crack the Enigma machine, for pity's sake. I said to

her, I said, 'It's four sodding numbers, how hard can it be?!'
She can't even do the *Sun* sudoku now, poor cow. Anyhow,
we're having to look at other options. The main door is a
no-go, but the emergency *trouser presses* are not! As you can
see from this plan, those *trouser presses* are located here, here
and here," she said, pointing to sections of the map where
fire escape doors were.

"Gran, what are you planning? Some sort of jailbreak?"
he asked.

"Sssh! No! We don't say that word. What we are doing,"
she whispered, "is *taking some laundry to the launderette.*"

"OK. And when are you going to the launderette?"

"The best time is in the early hours of the morning.
That's when they have only a skeleton staff on. Vera has
agreed to pull her emergency cord at zero three hundred
hours, and in the ensuing mayhem me and Dickie will take
our laundry to the launderette using the closest *trouser press*
at the end of this corridor."

She seemed pleased with what she obviously considered
to be a foolproof plan, but Noah had his doubts. The
emergency fire escapes may not be locked, but they would
almost certainly be alarmed. And what were she and Dickie
planning on doing once outside? Would they be scaling
the fence like ninjas, with her replacement hip and his
pacemaker?

But Gran clearly felt she had it all sorted out. "From
there," she continued, "a waiting ice-cream van will take us

down to Dover, where we shall board a ferry and set sail … for *Barbados*!"

"You're going to Barbados on a ferry? Really?"

Gran tutted. "Oh ye of little faith!" She rolled the map back up and handed it to Noah. "Put it in the top drawer," she instructed him, "good and hidden."

He did as he was told, then sat back down and gave her a gentle smile. The details of her plan, taken in isolation, were funny. The reason for them most certainly was not. He didn't want to have to humour Gran about her crazy escape plot. He didn't want her to come up with the ideas in the first place. He wanted her like she was before – when she was together and conversations made sense. When she remembered stuff. *When she was his gran and she looked out for him.* But maybe, just maybe, she still could. "Everyone's saying stuff about me and Harry," he said.

"Why's that?" she sniffed.

"'Cause they saw us… He was holding my hand. No, not *holding* it exactly, more just *touching* it."

Gran raised an eyebrow. "Go on—"

"I mean, it was totally innocent. Totally. A misunderstanding, really."

"I wouldn't call a handsome young man like Harry holding your hand a 'misunderstanding'. I'd call it a bloody *result*!"

Noah chuckled. *Classic* Gran. "OK, it wasn't a misunderstanding. But it was a surprise."

155

"Oooh!" Her eyes lit up. "Tell me *everything*!"

He dropped his eyes to the floor. "There's not much to tell, really. We were at a party and we held hands ... and he kissed me, but that bit's totally secret 'cause no one knows about it and it doesn't mean I'm gay."

"Uh-huh." Gran grinned.

"But you know that, right? It doesn't mean I'm gay."

"Gay, straight, it's all the same. Kiss who you want, I say. You can't help whom you love. I had a dalliance once with a girl called Meredith Southgate."

"What? Really?" said Noah, not really wanting to know, but at the same time, *really* wanting to know.

"Don't you be wrinkling your nose like that!" she scolded him. "You should be a bit more open-minded. I used to be your age, you know. And one day you'll be mine, and then you can reassure *your* grandchildren that all the nonsense they've got up to is nothing new and you've already been there, done that, got the tea cosy."

"T-shirt."

"Just chill out about it, Peanut. You're probably making it a hundred times worse for yourself by worrying. If you don't care, no one else will either – react and you play straight into their hands."

Maybe she was right. Old people usually were. People could probably see it was stressing him out, so they were just winding him up even more.

"You know what I did when they found out about me

and Meredith?" she said. "I *embraced* it. I didn't deny it. Although I didn't confirm it either. I was aloof about the whole thing. Maintained an air of dignified silence and mystery. And you know what happened?"

"What?"

"I had young men flocking to me! People love someone who is a bit exotic. They are *drawn* to them. Especially if they handle their exotic-ness well."

"How do you handle it well, though?"

"You must be bold, Noah. You must be bold and brave. Be dignified in your silence and watch them fall into your lap."

Even placed in the context of her dementia, it did seem like it might work. If he didn't give them bait, they would stop biting.

When he was with Gran, everything seemed to make sense. Massive problems didn't seem so massive once Gran had dealt with them. He got up and kissed her on the cheek. "Thanks, Gran."

"Young Harry's a nice lad."

"Yeah. He is. He is nice," Noah said, sadly. The nicest person he knew. He didn't want *not* to be best friends.

"Maybe you'll think about it," his gran said. "Nice people are hard to find. You should hang on to them."

"We're still mates. It's just..." *Complicated now?*

"You know what I would do? What I *did*? Don't try to label it. Don't even think about what it is. Just enjoy the moment. And remember that no moment is for ever. And other moments come along. And sometimes they're even better. Sometimes they're worse. But don't fret about it. People always like to talk, but ask yourself: in the grand scheme of things, in the total insignificance of our tiny lives in this massive universe, *who gives a shit?*"

Noah smiled. He felt a bit better. Surely he could cope with a bit of ribbing, and they would get bored once they weren't getting a reaction from him, and it would all die down.

"In other news," Noah said, "Mum has clearly given up all hope of Dad coming back, thinks he's dead and is actively dating."

Noah watched as Gran tried to piece together what he'd just said. "Who's dead?" she said, finally.

"No, he's not dead. At least, I don't think he is. But that's what Mum thinks. Probably." He screwed his face up, acutely aware he was not making this any clearer. He tried again. "My dad. Your *son—*"

"Yes..."

"Is missing. Hasn't been here for years."

"Well, where is he? Little toerag; when I get my hands on him—"

Noah breathed in for five, held for three, out for five. "I know, you'll kill him," Noah said. "In the meantime, as far as Mum is concerned, he's already dead, because even though she's still married, she is dating a *new man.*"

"I never liked your mother. I told Brian not to marry her. 'She's trouble,' I said to him. 'She's fickle!' He wouldn't listen. Never listens. And now she's killed him!"

"No, Gran, that's not exactly what I—"

"Who is it? Who's this new man?"

Noah shrugged. "She won't tell me."

Gran sat up, clearly intrigued. "She's trying to keep him secret, eh? He's probably in on the whole thing – keeping me locked up here so I don't cause any trouble too! Got suspects?"

"Affirmative. One at present."

"Evidence?"

"Nothing that would stand up in court. *Yet.*"

"Keep a low profile. People slip up eventually. A word here, a look there. You'll spot the clue you need. How do you feel about it, anyway?"

"Pretty grossed out," Noah said. "I mean, she's forty; surely celibacy would be the best thing now?"

Gran stifled a grin. "You don't think people over forty should have sex?"

"Well…"

"Because I can tell you, since Dickie got his new pacemaker, and a job lot of Viagra, things have certainly been more interesting around here."

Noah froze and stared at her with horrified eyes.

Gran gave a heavy sigh and shook her head. "You really need to lighten up, mister."

He felt his cheeks glowing. "What? No, that's great... I mean, it's really cool. I love the idea of old people having sex. No, wait, that came out wrong. I mean..." He floundered to a halt. It wasn't just the *image* that was now burnt into his brain. It was the fact that literally everyone else was doing it. Except him. And he was the teenager. It should be *him* having all the sex. It said so in books and TV programmes. It was all wrong. He was being left behind by the rest of the entire world.

"I'm pulling your leg."

"Oh."

"It was a joke."

"Oh. Ha ha. Yeah. Good one, Gran."

Gran nodded. "Get off home. And if you see George, tell him I'll find him just as soon as we've made the escape. There's a tea shop on the promenade in Broadstairs. Tell him I'll meet him there."

Noah sighed and stood up. "Righto."

"Who are you again?"

"Noah, Gran! I'm Noah."

His mum was out of the house. He was alone. And *hungry.* He was on his knees, rifling through the detritus that was stacked up at the bottom of his mum's wardrobe. All manner of garbage was here – from Christmas decorations to boxes of old photographs and even some old exercise books from when his mum was at school.

There were her algebra assignments, which he had pleasure in noticing were covered in red crosses and had been graded "D" – which was probably the teacher just trying to be encouraging, because as far as he could see she hadn't got a single sum correct.

Somewhere in here she must have hidden the special biscuits she brought out yesterday for Harry's visit. And he would find those biscuits. They were his destiny, his *birthright*. The wardrobe was the only place left; he'd already searched the whole house, even sifting through his mother's knicker drawer with a pair of barbecue tongs, carefully lifting each thong like it was radioactive waste. But there had been no delicious biccies anywhere.

Exploring deeper into this pound-shop version of Narnia now, he came across a metal biscuit tin. *Ha!* Now he could have all the Jammie Dodgers he wanted. He prised the lid off and raised an eyebrow.

What the hell was this? A wad of ten-pound notes, maybe a hundred quid's worth? They were skint! They never had enough money for anything nice and only just about got by paying the nasty red bills in the nick of time. A hundred quid was a lot of money. To him, anyway.

The tin also contained a small bundle of envelopes. Addressed to his mother. *Letters.* Presumably these were from his mother's distant past, written by horse-riding suitors, perhaps, asking for her hand in marriage once the war was over ... and other stuff that used to happen in the nineties. To his surprise, however, the first letter was dated just a year ago.

Under the light of his torch he read down, his throat tightening on every word, his breath quickening and his heart pounding.

"No one has heard from him for six years," his mother had said. "He's assumed dead, Noah. We just have to move on."

The letter was from his dad.

CHAPTER SEVENTEEN

Calle Santa Maria 21 – 3a
*   28012 – Madrid*
*   Spain*

Lisa!

How's tricks? You good? I'm great! Life here continues to be a picnic… sun, sea, sand … but nothing else beginning with "s" – I'm behaving myself, sort of! Ha ha!

How's Noah? Say hi from me and give him some fatherly advice – stick a rubber on it! Wish someone had told me that all those years ago! Ha ha!

I'm still at the same address if you want to contact me, but I've changed my name! Who wants to be boring old Brian Grimes when I can be Jon Mortimer. Sounds pretty good, eh? Great name for a top businessman! Ha!

Filthy lucre enclosed.

Peace out,

J. xx

He had to read it five times before it sank in.

His dad wasn't dead.

He was alive.

Alive, living in Spain and *sending money to support them.*

He grabbed another letter from the tin and opened it with trembling hands:

Hola from España!

How you doing, Lisa? Things are good here. Had to get rid of a business partner this week – he wanted the spoils but didn't have enough skin in the game, you get me? No sweat though, bagged myself five new investors since then. Means we can start the build next month and then BOOM! That's a cool million in pure profit. Just gotta keep the bank sweet for a few weeks – wanna come over and do a little show to distract them?! Ha ha!

I'm between addresses at the moment, so I'll
write when the new one is sorted out.

 Bit of dosh enclosed. Sorry it's not the normal
amount. Am selling the car so I'll make it up next
time. I'm doing my best, Lisa. I'm trying, babe. Give
me a chance, yeah?

 Peace & love,

 J. x

Riffling through the rest of the box he found more
letters, all along similar lines, all sending "filthy lucre",
"moolah" or "spondulicks". Why his dad couldn't just say
"money" he had no idea, but it didn't matter. Here was an
entire history, undiscovered and shut away – a man he
barely knew, but wanted to, desperately.

The sadness in his stomach flared up into red-hot
rage. His mum had no right to have kept all this from
him. What about his persistent questions over the years,
asking about his dad? Didn't Noah have a right to know? A
right to decide if he wanted to see him or not? His mother
had not just evaded his questions, she had downright
lied to him! She had painted a picture of a man who had
selfishly abandoned his family and left them high and
dry, struggling to survive, neither of them knowing how
to replace a fuse or put up a shelf. But the truth was very
different. The exact reasons for his father's departure and
the full details of his life in Spain were left unexplained by

the letters, but he was clearly full of remorse and was doing his best to make things good. Every letter was an apology. What could he have done that was so bad he couldn't be cut a little bit of slack?

Noah counted a total of fifty letters, sent over the course of four years, and every single one made mention of enclosing some money. And the five birthday cards and six Christmas cards that were addressed to Noah each made reference to "a little loot to get yourself something". So where had all that money gone to over the years?

Noah looked around his mum's bedroom, his eyes lighting upon the Ruby Devine outfits, the TV on the wall, the satin sheets on her bed. These were expensive things – where had the money really come from to buy them?

He punched his fist into her pillows, blow after blow, imagining his mum's face. He wanted to charge downstairs, scream at his mother and rip her lying throat out. But he couldn't. In typically selfish fashion, she was out.

And what about his dad? His poor old dad who had written to him for years and who had never received a reply from him? His dad must only assume that Noah didn't want anything to do with him either – that's how it looked! *Oh God...* It all burst out of him, tears of frustration and fury and at the same time relief that his dad was actually alive and clearly cared.

He gasped down air, feeling like he was drowning.

And then ... finally ... calm.

And a new resolve came over Noah.

He wasn't going to be a victim of circumstance any longer.

He was going to be a man of action!

Back in his room, Noah powered up his computer and googled "Jon Mortimer Spain." It was indeed an impressive-sounding name. And a scan of the search results was even more impressive. It looked like his dad owned some sort of massive apartment block. There was a website – "Mortimer Holdings", offering luxury flats for sale, with pictures of his tanned father, smiling, shaking hands with various men and women in suits. God, his dad was *handsome*. He had fashionable hair and bright white teeth and sharp outfits. And there was a picture of him in casual clothes, drinking a cocktail on a yacht! In a bloody Ralph Lauren sweater! Holy shit, he must be *minted*!

In the absence of an email address, Noah had to do it the old-fashioned way: he opened his desk drawer, pulled out a crisp sheet of writing paper and his best fountain pen and set to work with trembling hands.

Dear Dad,

You might be wondering why I haven't written before. Well, that's because Mum is a total bitch and had been hiding all your letters to make me think you

*hated me / were dead and has clearly been using all
the money you sent to buy cigarettes and bras and
stuff. I can see now why you left her! It's lucky for
you that you were able to get away, whilst I must stay
here and suffer horribly.*

*I've really missed you, Dad. I honestly
didn't know what happened or where you'd gone.
Sometimes I thought you were the worst father in
the world because you clearly didn't care about me
or what I was up to. But now I feel bad about that
because I can see you did care. And now it looks like
I was the one who didn't care about you, because I
never replied.*

*Things have been pretty bad, to be honest with
you.*

*Why exactly did you leave? What did Mum do?
You don't have to tell me if it's private, but I would
like to know. Was it her stupid Beyoncé act? She's
still doing that, by the way.*

*I like girls but recently some people have been
saying that I am gay, but that isn't true because it was
complicated and I. . .*

A text came through on his phone.

"HI NOAH IT'S ERIC FROM SCHOOL. GOT
SOMETHING I THINK U WILL WANT. REALLY

WANT. MEET ME IN PARK IN 20 MINS. BRING
MONEY. UNLESS YOU WANT YOUR LIFE TO
GET WORSE, GAY BOY."

CHAPTER EIGHTEEN

It felt like the words were burnt into Noah's eyeballs. "UNLESS YOU WANT YOUR LIFE TO GET WORSE, GAY BOY." His mouth was dry. What had Eric got? Noah racked his brains for anything he might have sent or said that Eric could have got hold of, because he clearly *had* got something. Eric didn't waste his time. What choice did Noah have but to go? Lie awake all night worrying about what it was? No, thanks.

Noah took one of his dad's letters and all the birthday and Christmas cards and hid them in his room. As for the money, he had taken the lot. After all, it was rightly his. And if his mother found it gone, she could hardly accuse him of taking it because she would have to admit her own appalling treachery. Most of it he'd left at home. He could perhaps use it to start an investment portfolio – something responsible anyway. Twenty he had stashed about his person – five of it in his trouser pocket, five down his sock and a further tenner down his boxers. *Yeah.* He knew how to fool potential muggers. In addition, he grabbed his trusty pocket torch, a first-aid kit and a whistle, because at this time of night you never knew what could happen.

Ahead, silhouetted in the orange glow of a street light, was Eric. Noah steeled himself and strode up to him with as much confident swagger as he could muster.

"You hurt your leg?" Eric snorted.

"No."

"Why you doing that funny walk, then?"

Damn it. He'd seen other people strut down the street like they owned it; why couldn't he? "Good evening, Eric."

"Know what this is?" Eric said, smiling smugly and holding his hand open.

"A memory stick."

"*Wrong.* It's the answer to your prayers, that's what."

"You're speaking to an atheist. I don't pray," Noah replied, like a *boss*, which was a miracle because he was totally bricking it.

"All right, then. It's the solution to all your problems."

"How?" Noah could feel his heart pounding in his mouth. What the hell was on that stick?

"Because on this little device is three beautiful gigabytes of video footage from the party on Saturday.

Everything that happened in that little girl's bedroom is on this little stick."

He felt his stomach lurch in horror. "Everything?"

"Oh. Now you're interested."

"I was always interested, Eric. If I wasn't interested I wouldn't be here." He felt like his knees might give way. "What's on it, exactly?"

"About half the year getting off with people they shouldn't. You and Harry..."

Noah swallowed hard. "Yeah?"

"Oh, yeah. I reviewed that footage *most* carefully," Eric said with a dangerous smile playing across his lips. "I knew that's what you would be most interested in. It wasn't just holding hands at all, was it? You two had a nice long kiss."

"No!"

"Very romantic!"

"You're ... lying!" Noah spat.

Eric shrugged. "Cameras don't lie, Noah. And *I'm sure* the whole school will agree, when they see it."

Shit. Video. Him and Harry. *The kiss.* His classmates' interest might have died down in a couple of days, but now ... *with this* ... all it would take was an upload to YouTube, or for someone to make a GIF, whack it on some sites... Him and Harry, everyone seeing ... everyone knowing ... it would no longer just be hearsay, a bit of gossip that people had seen scant evidence of. It would be real. Hard fact. Immortal. Noah would forever be known for that gay kiss. Nothing else would matter.

"Two questions," Noah said, trying to buy a bit of time. "First, how did you get the footage?"

"HD video camera hidden on top of the wardrobe. I put it there when I arrived. Like always."

Noah looked at him, dumbstruck for a few seconds. Eric was such a disgusting excuse for a human being. "OK... Well, fine... And why me? Why offer this to me? Sounds like loads of kids would wanna buy this off you."

"Got a lot in common, me and you."

Noah stared at him. *In your dreams*, he thought.

"So ... how much you got?" Eric asked, squaring up to him so they were nearly nose to nose.

"How do you know I want it?"

"Let's not mess about. We both know you do."

"I need to think about it."

"No can do," said Eric, sucking in a breath. "Special offer, you see. Available today only. Take it or leave it."

"Give me until tomorrow, at least?"

Eric shook his head. "I've got other buyers lined up. Thought I'd do you a favour by offering to you first. No skin off my nose either way, 'cause if you don't want it there are plenty of others who will. This will be in someone's hands by midnight tonight. It could be in yours, Noah. It could be in yours."

Noah swallowed. He couldn't risk the footage going viral. "How much do you want?"

"Make me an offer."

He had no idea what the going rate for extortion was. "Four quid?"

Eric laughed. "All right. Sorry I troubled you, Noah. This is big boy stuff, yeah? See ya," he said, turning and starting to walk away down the path.

"Wait! Eric, wait!" said Noah, scurrying after him. "That was just my opening offer! Obviously I've got more... How about a tenner?"

"Go home, tuck yourself up and go to sleep."

"Eleven? ... Twelve?"

"Oooh! We're talking big numbers now!" Eric mocked.

"Twenty? Twenty pounds? I've literally only got that on me! Please, Eric! Twenty quid!"

"Not enough."

"How much, then? How much is enough?"

Eric turned and eyeballed him. "I want a hundred."

Noah gasped in disbelief. That would mean handing over all the money he had. "No way!"

"Then that's tough for you." Eric shrugged. "Like I said, there's plenty of people who will pay. Believe me. I know the going rate."

"How about fifty?" Noah pleaded.

"The price is a hundred."

"Sixty, then? I'd need a bit more time to get it, but..."

"A hundred."

"*Please!*"

"Why should I do you any favours?"

Noah glared at him and wished he was the sort of boy who could stride over to a heinous enemy and smash their stupid face in, until they were possibly dead. "Why? Why would you do this? What have I ever done to you?"

"It's just business. Stop taking it so personal."

And then he recalled... Eric had been hovering outside the toilets after school earlier. And inside those same toilets had been Harry, crying his eyes out. It didn't take much of logical leap to see the two things were connected.

"Harry didn't want to buy it, then?" said Noah.

"Well done, Einstein," Eric replied, his eyes flicking sheepishly from Noah back to the ground.

"Tried to blackmail him too, did ya?"

"I offered it to him. That's—"

"I'll do it," Noah said, cutting him off. He knew there would be no chance Harry would be able to buy the video – how could he? Harry got pocket money from his folks, but it would never be enough to pay off Eric. And normally Noah would be in the same boat ... if it hadn't been for his mum's little stash. Fate was smiling on him a little bit, maybe. For about half an hour, he'd been rich. Now he would be poor again. But it didn't matter because he would put Harry's mind at rest that the video would never see the light of day. They would get through this, *together*.

"I'll take the twenty you got now as a deposit. The remaining eighty I need by tomorrow, else I sell it to someone else. Look, you also get the footage of the other kids too, remember – pretty priceless stuff. You'll be sorted at least until the end of Year Eleven; no one will touch you if they know you've got shit like this on them, promise!"

"All right. *Yes*," Noah said. He wasn't a natural blackmailer, and he probably would never use the video, but there was no harm in having a little insurance policy against his bullies.

"Good boy. Now, the twenty, please." Eric smiled, holding out his grubby little hand.

Noah looked at him with as much contempt as he could muster and extracted the money from his sock and (much to Eric's bewilderment) boxers. He held his hand out for the memory stick.

"No." Eric smiled. "The deposit means I won't sell it to anyone else. You get the goods when you pay the balance."

"What?!"

"I'm not an idiot, Noah. You pay the rest tomorrow, like we agreed, and it's all yours."

Noah scowled at him, but what choice did he have? He could hardly wrestle Eric to the ground and get the memory stick; Eric would win. A gnat would win.

"Well, that's that, then. I don't need to be standing here chatting when I got other business to attend to. See you tomorrow, with the cash." Eric turned and walked away, leaving Noah standing alone in the shadows. That boy was such a grubby little waste of atoms.

CHAPTER NINETEEN

Noah pounded down the pavement on his way back from the park, beating himself up about all the devastating and powerful things he *could* have said to Eric, but which he'd only thought of right now. "Do your worst," he could have sneered in his face. "You don't scare me, you dastardly knave," he might have snarled.

It was bin day tomorrow, and he almost didn't see her as he rounded the corner on to Gordon Road. She was sitting, hunched over, between two wheelie bins, knees drawn up to her head, crying her eyes out.

Noah stopped, frozen between wanting to pretend he hadn't seen her and wondering if he should do something. He made a subtle coughing noise to attract her attention but failed to get any sort of acknowledgement. He waited a few

177

seconds, and – suddenly fearing that she might actually be injured – he got out his pocket torch and shone it straight in her face.

"Gerr-off!" Jess Jackson shouted, shielding her eyes and squinting up at the torch owner. "Noah?"

"Oh. Hi."

"Shouldn't you be in bed with your *teddy bear* or something?" she said, sniffing back the tears.

"No. I'll have you know I haven't got a teddy these days, so..."

"Just leave me alone."

Noah considered the situation. He absolutely hated her guts, and he owed her no favours. But ... a young lady, alone on the streets... This was the time of night when murderers were at large. How would he explain it to the authorities if Jess Jackson were to fall victim to a terrible crime? How would it look if he had left a vulnerable teenage girl on the streets at the mercy of all manner of bandits? He would be spotted on CCTV footage or something, and the headline would read: "Noah Grimes leaves defenceless girl to be MURDERED because he had a PETTY GRIEVANCE with her!" Oh God. He probably wouldn't get into uni if that happened, due to him lacking any sort of moral fibre.

"Stop shining that stupid light at me!" Jess screamed.

"Sorry."

"Just piss off!"

"Are you all right?" he ventured.

"You're still here. Why are you still here? Go back to your ... books."

Noah smarted. His *books*? What did she mean by that? That he was some geeky loner? Well! He was damn well going to show her there was a whole lot more to Noah Grimes these days. A whole lot more!

"You can't stay here, Jess," he said, in as manly a voice as he could manage.

"I can stay where I like!"

"It's bin day tomorrow. What if you fall asleep and the bin men don't see you and scoop you up into the masher lorry?"

"You saying I look like trash?"

"No!" he said, resisting the urge to tell her it was "rubbish", not "trash". They weren't in America.

"That's what you think of me!" Jess screamed, with unnecessary volume. "I'm just trash! Pointless, waste-of-space, thick, stupid trash!"

A bedroom window opened on the other side of the street. Not wanting to alarm anyone, and fearful that the police might be called, Noah turned and gave a small, friendly wave up to the bedroom occupant. "It's OK. We're not a dangerous teenage drugs gang or anything," he assured them.

"Noah – get lost!" Jess shouted.

"Is that young man bothering you?" called a female voice from the window.

"Yes!" Jess shouted back.

"No!" cried Noah.

"This is a respectable street!" the voice shouted down.

It wasn't immediately clear to Noah what he was supposed to do with that information, but in any case Jess provided response enough by replying, "Shove it up yer fanny!" quickly followed by a "Leg it!" as she hauled herself to her feet and started sprinting, unsteadily, down the street.

"I'm calling the police!" the female voice yelled. "This is a neighbourhood watch area! Barry?! Code red!"

In a panic, and with no other option, Noah turned and ran in hot pursuit of Jess as a burglar alarm started wailing from the house opposite. It didn't take him long to catch up with her as she was, it transpired, pretty drunk and was lurching from lamp post to garden fence, careering down the street like an out-of-control fairground dodgem.

"This way!" he said, pulling her left, down an adjoining road. The pair twisted and turned through the streets of Little Fobbing, only coming to a stop when Noah could run no more.

"Wait…" he gasped, sucking on his asthma pump, pressing the little canister down to spray the Ventolin deep into his tight little lungs. He held his breath for a moment, then jumped as he felt Jess Jackson's hand on the small of his back.

"All right?" she asked.

Noah nodded, still holding his breath. She took her hand away and started laughing.

He exhaled. "What's funny?"

"Who'd have thought it? Me and Noah Grimes, on the run from the law!"

"See? I'm not just into books and stuff!"

"Maybe," she said doubtfully. "What you doing out, anyway?"

"Had to see someone about something," he said, all mysterious and Mafia-like.

"Oh, yeah? Had to see your little boyfriend, you mean?"

Noah was about to launch into a response but remembered his gran's advice and stopped himself, giving only the slightest hint of a smile. He watched Jess's face as she awaited his reply, smiling curiously herself when she didn't get one. She was intrigued.

"Dirty boy," she muttered.

But again, he remained silent. And there was no follow-up from Jess, no additional teasing. Nothing. It was quite possible that Gran was right. Old people really did know what they were talking about.

"Well, you basically walked me home ... *ran* me home, I suppose, so thanks for that," she said, indicating her rather plush detached house with a BMW parked on the brick driveway. Noah reckoned there were more bricks on that driveway than in his entire house. "Guess I'll see you at school and we'll both pretend none of this happened," she continued. "Don't want people to think we're hanging out, Noah, no offence."

"Feeling's mutual," he said.

In the not-too-far-away distance, a police siren started wailing.

"Shit!" said Jess. "The old bitch grassed us up to the cops!"

"Oh no!" Noah said, again resisting the urge to inform her they were not "cops" but in fact "the Constabulary" or "police force". *They were not in America.*

"Quick," she said, pushing him towards her front door, "get your ass inside!"

"But I have to go home now!" Noah protested. He couldn't set foot inside her house! This girl killed hamsters, provoked swans and stole horses! She would probably tie him up in the cellar and torture him...

"Noah! If she really did call the cops, she will have given your description and they'll be out looking for you... God knows if they pick you up you'll blab your mouth off in no time, and I'm already on a warning. If there's any more shit I'll be in court; you'll have to come in and lie low for a bit."

"But why? What have you done?" Noah wailed, wondering if he would be guilty of whatever it was by association.

"Shut up, get in!" she said, pushing him in through the door and slamming it behind her.

They both stood breathless in the hall as the police siren wailed in the distance. Noah took in his surroundings. He had to admit, it was an impressive residence. There was art on the walls – *proper* art, not just some framed print from Ikea. And the furniture in the hall was made of some sort of solid, dark, highly polished wood. And in fact, the hall was *big enough* to actually have space for furniture in it, more to the point. Cream carpet. Very fluffy and soft. This was nice. But it was also a trap, surely? A hallway designed to lull him into a false sense of security before she hit him over the head and dragged his unconscious body downstairs.

"I can't hear the siren any more, should I go?" Noah suggested, desperate to get out of there.

Jess shook her head. "They'll be out on patrol for at least an hour. They've got naff-all else to do round here."

"An hour?!"

"Chill out," Jess said, with an edge of annoyance in her voice. "Pity my folks aren't here – they'd love it if they thought I'd come home with a boy like you."

"A boy like me?"

"Good at school. Neeky." She looked at him for longer than she needed to, and a smile gently played across her lips, like she was momentarily thinking of something else, and then *click!* Back in the room. "Do you want a drink?"

"Um ... Robinsons Barley Water? Or Kia-Ora?" he suggested, reckoning she would probably have the sort of mum who could afford quality branded squash.

"I mean a drink-drink, idiot!" she laughed.

"Oh! Oh, a drink-drink. Oh ... like, *alcohol*?"

"Yeah. But what?"

"Well ... what are you having?"

"Pear cider."

"OK, pear cider it is, then," he said, figuring it was safest to drink whatever she drank, in case she drugged it or something. Perhaps he would secretly switch their bottles, or quietly pour the contents of his into a pot plant – anything to thwart the wicked scheme she was doubtless plotting,

"Go through to the lounge," she said, cocking her head towards an open door that appeared to lead into a vast space. "Make yourself at home."

And with that Jess Jackson smiled a cheeky little smile and ushered him inside.

CHAPTER TWENTY

Jess was an absolute rascal, bringing bottle two before he had even finished bottle one. And even if the conversation had been desperately awkward to begin with, about halfway through that second bottle he had begun to delight her with witty repartee and sparkling observational comedy. He felt charismatic and confident and utterly brilliant.

Mmmm. *Cider.*

This was nuts. Normally Jess Jackson wouldn't give him the time of day. Normally she would only make jokes at his expense. She would not, *normally*, be sitting next to him on a sofa, sharing her pear cider with him, whilst laughing at *his* jokes.

Mmmm. *Cider, cider, cider.*

Something else was weird too. Jess had somehow morphed from being a terrifying horror-clown from hell into a rather charming and beautiful young woman, who was capable of funny jokes and almost-intelligent opinions. And in the warm glow from the floor lamps (which Noah was pretty sure he recognized from the Conran Shop website), her hair looked natural blonde, so maybe it just looked fake under the harsh glare of school strip lights? Her lips were a dark, voluptuous red, and he became hypnotized by them, watching them move as they spoke words. Words of agreement and mutual respect, because somehow, she was acting like they were friends.

It felt so good to be on the inside for once. One of them. No teasing now. No life being made hell. Harry wouldn't approve, but sometimes you've got to think of yourself... Why should Noah be made to feel miserable all the time? He and Jess would never be *best* mates – *God, no* – but couldn't they at least get along? He sat back into the sofa with his legs obscenely far apart, which he assumed would give him the look of a confident and capable man. He wanted Jess to see that he really wasn't just a geeky little virgin. *He was one of the lads.* One of the *straight* lads.

"Why were you out by yourself crying, anyway?" he asked.

"Kirk dumped me."

"How come?"

"We had a row at Melissa's party. He wanted me to ... he wanted to do stuff."

"Oh. And did you ... do that stuff?"

Jess sighed in a depressed sort of way. "Of course not. Never done nothing with anyone. Kirk was like, 'What's the problem?' and I was like, 'We're at a house party!' I dunno, guess I just wanted the first time to be right and ... *special*, or something. Anyway, seems he's sick of waiting, because he didn't speak to me for the rest of the weekend, and this afternoon, he dumped me."

Well, that's unexpected news, he thought.

"Everyone's wrong about me, Noah," she continued. "Like they're wrong about you, I guess."

"They are! They're wrong about me!" Oh my gosh, they were so alike! A bit. Well, not really, but at least there was some common ground.

"But, I mean," she continued, "you're a virgin too, right?"

"What?" he asked, nervously trying to buy time – as if a few seconds would make any difference anyway and someone would shag him in the time it took to answer.

"I mean – unless you and Harry really are..."

"No! No, not at all. We've done nothing. 'Cause all that is crap," he assured her, grasping his chance to set the record *straight* and stop the gossip. "It was the alcohol. Harry and me are best mates, but that's all. He's nice, and we weren't properly holding hands, he was ... helping me get a splinter out, but it was misinterpreted... So, yeah."

"So ... why were you out so late tonight? If you weren't seeing Harry?"

"Well ... you see, that's the thing..." he began. What was he going to tell her? He was certainly *not* going to tell her that he had been out buying video footage from evil Eric, which he could potentially use to blackmail half the year. "I just needed to get some air, you know? *Man*, I needed some air!" he said, adding the "man" part for extra cool points, because that was definitely a word that cool people said a lot. "Mum ... doing my head in, *man*."

Jess nodded and smiled like she knew what he meant. She didn't know the half of it, though. He clenched his jaw as he thought about his mum's heinous duplicity. How could she possibly justify what she had done? Even if Eric hadn't texted him, Noah probably would have needed to go out to clear his head anyway. Either that or there was a high chance he would have slipped some cyanide into her tea ... or thrown a live hairdryer into her bath.

He felt Jess's hand on his leg, stopping it from bouncing up and down. "Oh, sorry," he muttered. "I was just thinking about ... stuff."

She smiled again. "Chill out, yeah? Parents just don't get it."

"Yeah," he agreed. But his parent not only didn't "get it", she was hurtful, selfish and had totally screwed him over.

"So, if the Harry thing was just a *thing*, do you like girls, then?" Jess asked, downing what was left of her drink.

"Love 'em," he said quickly, feeling really quite rebellious for dropping the "th".

"That's good."

"Is it?"

"Yeah," she said softly, snuggling up to him on the sofa, apparently pleased about that.

He knocked back the remainder of the cider in a terrible panic. Jess Jackson was now snuggled into him. Her hand dropped on to Noah's lap. He looked at her in surprise, but her eyes were closed and she had seemingly drifted off to sleep, snuggled into his shoulder. He bit his lip. This was most awkward. If he was going to be in close proximity to a girl, it should really be Sophie. Not Jess. He and Jess weren't even proper friends. He was almost the only boy in the school that Sophie liked. He felt like an unfaithful husband.

"Mmmm, Noah ... how about we both stop being virgins, huh?" Jess slurred gently into his ear as she stirred again.

He must have misheard. "Say what?"

"You *know*," she purred, "we could *stop being virgins*."

"How?" *How?! How do you think, you UTTER KNOB!*

"Oh, Noah!" she giggled as she struggled on to her knees and ran her hands haphazardly through his hair. "Geeky boys are so cute. But, really, you want it just as bad as the other boys."

"No... I really don't..." he assured her, his pulse quickening. What was she on about? There was absolutely NO WAY he would ever consider sex with a girl.

Like her!

A girl like her. Yes, he would probably like to have sex with a girl, but a really *nice* one. Like Sophie, maybe. Not Jess.

"Mmm, *you're cute!*" she smiled.

He had to stop this. And, like any upstanding teenager in this situation, he must draw her attention to the legal ramifications. "Look, I'm still only fifteen and stuff, so..."

"Big boy now. *So I've heard!*"

Damn! Of course she didn't care about the law! She planted a drunken, slobbering kiss on his lips, which he immediately wiped away with the back of his hand before doing the buttons on his shirt back up as fast as she was unbuttoning them.

"We can't do it with our clothes on, silly!" she giggled.

"No, well, that's fine..."

"I'm hot for you, Noah!" she purred, like a bad porn actress.

"Oh, God!" he screamed, panicked by how fast things were happening and trying to fling her off him. It was no use. She was stuck like a deranged, sex-mad limpet. "Look, if you're *hot*, maybe you should *cool down*?" he said. "I could run you a cold bath? Or maybe hose you down in the garden? Have you got a hose?"

"*You've* got a hose!" she grinned, making a grab for his trousers.

"Oh! Urrgggh! No, God, no you don't ... no. It's not for you!" he wailed, batting her away as she tugged at his belt in an utterly cack-handed manner. "No, please... Pull your shorts back up! Jess! Your shorts have come down, I can see... No... Jess! JESS! Jess – this is serious now, that is something I *do not* want to see, because it's actually illegal? That is illegal what you are showing me now! Illegal. There are laws, and you are breaking those laws! You're on a warning, remember?! One more thing and you'll be in court...? Well, this is that thing!" He hoped the clear threat of a substantial prison sentence would deter her; did she really want to end up in a borstal for bad girls?

Apparently she didn't mind. They continued to battle it out on the sofa, him trying to keep his clothes on and her doing everything possible to get them off. And then, it being evident that ALL of Noah's clothes were going to remain firmly attached to his body, a new and dangerous look came into her eyes as she shuffled up towards him, pressing and grinding herself into his crotch.

"Mmmm, you're *hard*, baby," she cooed, pressing herself up against what was actually the Mini Maglite in the pocket of his trousers. What was he going to do? She was clearly hell-bent on engaging in some form of horrific sexual activity with him. It was terrible. Terrible because it was her and terrible because he felt like it was about the worst thing that could happen to him, but then WHAT SORT OF BOY DID THAT MAKE HIM? A GAY ONE?!

Oh, GOD! He should be enjoying this! He should be all horny for it! His head was chaos, and, just like with Harry, there was no time to properly think because everything was happening so quickly.

She kissed him on the lips again, broke away and sashayed over to a small clay pot on the mantelpiece, from which she extracted a condom.

A *condom*.

Who the hell kept condoms in a pot on their mantelpiece?!

There was no time to ponder the question. She tore the packet open with her teeth, in direct contravention of every sex ed class they had ever had.

"Now! *Make love to me!*" she exclaimed, hurling herself at him with renewed vigour. Terrified, and by reflex, he pushed her away, and she staggered backwards, tripped headlong on to the sofa, slammed her head on the wooden armrest and passed out unconscious.

Mouth open, arms still outstretched in front of him – it was like Noah was frozen in time and space. He didn't even dare breathe. He waited in the pin-drop silence for any slight stirring from Jess. A murmur, a twitch, a breath? But there was nothing. Oh, *God*. She wasn't moving. At all. He cautiously edged nearer. Was this a trick? Would she spring up like a horny jack-in-the-box and try to shag him?

"Jess?" he whispered. "Jess? You OK there?"

Nothing.

"Jess ... it's been fun, but I do need to go home now..."

Nothing.

"It's been nice having a chat, and all that stuff just now was just the drink-drink, right? We can put it all behind us. A misunderstanding. Like what happened with me and Harry. Like grown-ups. Jess? Can you hear me?"

He poked her, and her arm dropped down and hung limply off the end of the sofa. He stared at her, shaking, his mouth dry.

She did not appear to be breathing.

There was every possibility that Jess Jackson was dead.

CHAPTER
TWENTY-ONE

"What the merry hell are you doing now, Noah Grimes?"

He looked up from the flames to where his mother was standing, in her baby-doll nightie with fur trim and fluffy pink mules. She looked like mutton dressed as poodle.

"Just burning some stuff," he snapped, resisting every impulse to hurl her into the flames too.

"It's two in the morning! The neighbours!"

"Best time to burn stuff. Doesn't disturb anyone!" he said, like everything was totally fine with this situation and there was nothing odd happening.

Of course he hadn't just left Jess. After placing her in the recovery position, checking her pulse and establishing she *was* in fact breathing, he'd made an anonymous call to 999 from the phone box at the end of her road. Posing as a "concerned passer-by" he told the operator he had seen Jess Jackson "doing a gymnastic display" through the window of her lounge, and she had "apparently slipped whilst performing a split leap into a Yurchenko loop and they should send paramedics ASAP". Adding detail, he knew, was what makes lies believable.

Hiding in a bush, he watched in terror as the ambulance arrived at the same time as her parents, sure they were about to bring her out in a body bag. But they didn't. They didn't even take her away on a stretcher; her parents just shook the hands of the paramedics and waved them goodbye instead. *Not the actions of grieving parents.*

Then again, this was Jess.

Oh, she probably wasn't dead or seriously injured. But she clearly couldn't be trusted. She had lied to him and tried to seduce him. What else was she capable of? What if she claimed *he pushed her with intent to kill*? What if she planned to press charges against him? What if the police wanted to investigate? He could not be linked to the scene of the crime!

Mum made her way across the patio and towards the shabby excuse for a lawn, where Noah stood, wearing just his boxers under his dressing gown, using a large stick to prod the bonfire. "These are your clothes!" she declared. "Why are you burning your clothes?!"

"I was sick of them."

"Sick of them?! They were perfectly decent clothes! Frigging mentalist!"

195

"They didn't fit!"

"Don't give me that! You're a short-arse, just like your father!"

"Mum!"

"Nobody burns their clothes apart from murderers and sex offenders," she said, suddenly changing tack from outrage to suspicion. "What have you done?"

"Nothing," he muttered, wondering how she'd got so quickly and dangerously close to the truth. Was she actually psychic or something...?

"Nothing, huh?" His mother nodded, sagely. "Well, that 'nothing' took you out of the house until gone midnight, so that's a whole lot of 'nothing' to be occupying yourself with."

Noah glared at his mother. He had seen criminals burn their clothes on TV detective series, and he knew this was a good start for getting rid of his DNA. His mother, on the other hand, was a loose cannon. A *selfish, lying loose cannon.*

Well, how dare she treat him like this? How dare she make his life hell when she had been keeping this MASSIVE, HUGE, UGLY SECRET from him?! Who the hell did she think she was? Oh, he knew who she was, all right! A TOTAL BITCH MOTHER FROM HELL!

Well, it was time to play the ace card, time to drop the A-bomb.

"I know about Dad," he said.

Noah's mum stared back at him for a few moments, the bomb quietly whistling through the air, plummeting towards its destination and exploding in a mushroom cloud of utter devastation.

"I suggest you come inside for a chat," she said, turning and walking calmly back indoors.

Noah furiously rewrapped himself in his dressing gown, prodded the bonfire one last time and followed her in. Damn it to hell, she was going to pay for her duplicity and she was going to do his bidding! He stomped through to the lounge, where she was sitting with uncharacteristic serenity on the sofa, dabbing a tissue at the corner of her eye – without an actual tear in sight.

"So, you've found out, have you?" she said, glancing up at him with faux tragic eyes, "Well, I'm sorry, Noah. *I'm sorry.*"

"That's it? That's all you've got to say? I thought he was dead, Mum!" She was going to have to do a lot better than that. He wanted answers. He wanted *reasons*. He wanted to know why the hell he'd had such a godawful life for the last six years. The heartache. The misery. The terrible sadness, deep in his gut. *Why?*

"I never said that. *Assumed* dead, that's all."

"But he wasn't assumed dead! You *knew* he was alive!"

"OK, I'd had a few letters from someone purporting to be your father, but how was I to know it was really him writing? Could have been an impostor!"

"An impostor who sends hundreds of pounds? That sort of impostor?"

"Do you think I did it lightly?" she said, turning to him. "I know you think I'm selfish, but actually, I did it to protect you. He's a no-good man, and if he were part of your life, he'd upset you. Worse, he'd *destroy* you. He uses people, then spits them out. And ... I'm your mum. And believe it or not, I don't want bad stuff to happen to you."

Noah snorted. "Bad stuff happens to me all the time! You're not doing a very good job!"

"Well, I do my best, but you never listen to my motherly advice. Smart-arse."

"I should have had the choice, though!"

"You're a kid. I was gonna tell you on your birthday anyway. Sixteen – old enough to make up your own mind."

Noah shook his head in disbelief. "Oh, yeah! Happy birthday! And ... surprise! Your dad isn't dead after all!"

"Oh, go and meet him for all I care. Don't say I didn't warn you."

"Mum! He sent us money! You said we were skint!"

"We *are* skint, darling."

"So where's all the money gone?"

His mother paused and looked around wildly. "You know ... the holidays we took in Scarborough."

"A static caravan in February doesn't *break the bank*. Where's the money gone?" he growled.

His mother shifted uncomfortably. He knew he had got her. He was determined to make her admit it. Admit that she had selfishly taken the bulk of it and lavished it on herself and her opulent ways. He narrowed his eyes. "Where's the money, *Mother*?"

"It's gone. Spent."

"I know that. But what on? *I've* not seen any of it!"

"You've seen a bit of it! Costs a lot to bring up a kid … the rent … bills, clothes, food … school uniforms and trips… You've no idea how it all goes."

"But you've been earning money too! Not much, I'll grant you, but some! And there's the welfare state that you so merrily sponge off. So where's it all gone?!" He stood there, glaring at her, breathing heavily.

"Christ, Noah, why do you have to be so…"

"Just say it, you old crone! Tell me!" he demanded.

His mother sighed. "The thing is, Noah," she finally said, "if it was just you and me, we would have seen more of the money."

"What?"

"But it wasn't just for you and me."

His fists unclenched and he looked at her, more confused than ever. "Then … who else?"

"It was for your dad's other kid. The one you don't know about."

CHAPTER TWENTY-TWO

Noah stared at his mother as her flippantly delivered words hung in the air. "Now, I know this might be something of a shock—" she began.

"Who's the kid? Who is it?" he said.

"Well, now, that I can't say."

"I have a right to know!" he shrieked.

"No, Noah, you don't. We all made a pact, see. At the time. This town hasn't changed in sixteen years – same back then as it is now. We all knew if this got out it would be the biggest scandal to hit Little Fobbing, ever. So we all agreed: we would never speak of it again. No one must know."

"The town hasn't changed in sixteen years?"

"'Sright."

"So this happened sixteen years ago, then?"

"Well…"

"SO THE KID'S IN MY YEAR AT SCHOOL?!" Noah screamed, utterly beside himself. What if it was Harry?! What if it was Sophie?! What if it was Jess?!

"Oh God, I've already said too much!" his mother said, clearly flustered.

"OH SHIT, OH SHIT, OH SHIT!" People would find out! They would gossip and point…

"Noah, you're getting hysterical… Do you need your asthma pump? Just breathe … breathe!"

"I don't wanna breathe! I just wanna DIE! First you hide my father from me, then you date Mystery Man, even though you know Dad's still alive! And by the way, *I'm pretty damn sure I know who Mystery Man is* and you should know he's a notorious cad who's always picking up unsuitable love interests in his stupid sports car, so I would cancel the relationship if I were you!" He nodded in an attempt to make the lie more convincing and took in the expression of surprise on her face. "I mean, all that considered, why should I trust another thing you say? What's next? Have I got a twin? Is my cousin really my dad? Am I, in fact, the result of you being impregnated by some form of alien life, visiting Earth?" The latter would be no surprise whatsoever – and would actually explain quite a bit.

She got up from the sofa, notably failing to deny any of

201

the outlandish things Noah had just mentioned. "Have some milk..."

"NO!"

"Just..."

"AAARRRRGGGHHH!" This whole mess could only end in tragedy and total embarrassment.

"Noah—"

He needed facts. He needed to know. He needed to prepare and then decide on a course of action to save his sorry arse. "WHO IS IT?"

"No."

"WHO THE HELL IS IT?!"

"Noah, it's not that simple. Please. And it doesn't matter anyway."

"Actually, you *cantankerous hag*, it does matter. It matters an awful BLOODY lot! You're talking about a sibling I never knew existed! Family! Someone I could have shared the *disappointment of our parents* with for all these years! I mean, the kid's in my year!" His mind reeled. "And what if I happen to share a moment of *passion* with another kid in my year? Hmm? What if I accidentally share such a moment with my secret sibling? Would you have me commit incest now?"

"A moment of *passion*?!" His mother grinned. "*Passion*, Noah? Is that what the kids are calling it these days – *passion*?"

"WHAT IF I HAVE SEX WITH SOMEONE IN MY YEAR?!" he barked at her.

"Well, Noah, that statement makes a lot of assumptions. First, that you are *capable* of sexual relations…"

"My voice has BROKEN!" he squealed.

"Second, that you would *want* to have sex with them – because they could be a boy or a girl, remember. Although I've always suspected you might be bi after you asked for tickets to *Wicked* for your twelfth birthday…"

"That doesn't make ANY sense, and anyway, I'm STRAIGHT!"

"And thirdly, that the other person would want to have sex with you anyway, and I'm not being funny, but you hardly seem flooded with offers…"

"WRONG, actually, pretty much had *two* offers in the last three days, but go on…"

"And then it wouldn't actually be full incest because they're only your half-brother or sister, so it's unlikely you'd go to prison as it's no different than marrying your cousin, really, and if you did have kids with them there's only a fifty per cent chance of a genetic disorder, so all's well!" she chirped.

"Oh, great. Brilliant!" he said, flinging his arms up at the crazy logic. "You've obviously put a lot of thought into this. Just brilliant."

"Milk?" she said, edging towards the kitchen door.

"Do *they* know who they are?" he asked.

"I don't know. Like I said, we all agreed. Sweep it under the rug."

"Dirty little secret that it is."

She sighed and came back to sit on the sofa. "I told you your dad was no good. That's exactly why I kept his existence away from you. Knew he'd only cause grief, and look! Mum's right again! Hadn't even been married two months when I found out he'd gone and shagged that other woman. It had to be kept quiet because..." She looked guiltily at Noah. "Well, for various reasons it would have been unfortunate if people knew the truth."

"What the hell does that mean?!" Noah squealed.

"Doesn't matter," his mum said. "But eventually the pressure was too much for your father. He couldn't take the heat and then finally he just disappeared and left us all to it, occasionally sending a bit of cash in the post. That's your dad, Noah. That's your brilliant dad."

"I hate you both more than anything in the world right now."

His words hung in the air for a moment. "Well, I don't blame you. I hate me," she muttered.

And then she started crying.

Noah was speechless. He'd never seen his mum cry before. She was hard as nails; he didn't even think she was capable of genuine feeling. So what was this? And what was he supposed to do? Parents were not meant to cry. *Kids* cried. *Parents* made them feel better. That's how it worked. Not this! What was this?! "Er, Mum? Er ... look, there, there," he said, gently tapping her arm. "Please ... don't cry..."

"I've tried so hard, Noah," she sobbed. "I've always done my best to keep our heads above water. Found the money for this and that – the French trip, or a new uniform. I know you've not had as much as other kids, but I gave you what I could. I *wanted* you to have nice stuff – would get you anything you wanted, if I had the money... It could have been so different... But it's all his fault. *Please*, Noah."

Noah sighed. "So he sent you money, and you sent some of that to the secret kid's mum?"

"Yes."

"Well, why? Why didn't Dad just send it direct to her?"

His mum looked down. "There are reasons. That's all I'm going to say."

"Tell me."

"It won't help. Don't dig it up. *Trust me.*"

Noah shook his head. Trusting her was the last thing he'd ever do again. "Does Gran know about this?"

"Oh, Noah, who knows? She's got dementia. I've no idea what she knows, or thinks she knows, any more."

"But she *did* know?"

His mum shrugged. "Well, *I've* never told her. Can't speak for your dad."

He got up and walked to the door. "I'll find out, Mum. I'll find the clues, and I'll work out the links and piece the whole thing together. You'll see."

"It's a can of worms you don't wanna open. OK?

You don't." There was something in the way she said it, something *awful.* Something dark and terrible and full of fear.

But that would never have stopped Jessica Fletcher.

And it wouldn't stop him.

CHAPTER TWENTY-THREE

He sat on a little bench by the lockers with his rough book and a pen. It didn't matter that his mother wouldn't tell him who his half-sibling was. He was cleverer than her, *far cleverer*, and with some sharp detective work (and possibly a series of photos and clues stuck to his bedroom wall, linked with pieces of string to indicate various connections), he felt sure it was only a matter of time before he identified the culprit.

Not that they were in fact a "culprit". They were probably just as much a victim as him in all this. A poor kid, left to deal with the endless mistakes of the adults who were meant to be bringing them up.

It had been established that the individual was in his year at school. That narrowed it down to just over a hundred people. Whilst it being any of them would be awkward and embarrassing, there were certain people that he definitely did not want it to be, and it was here he needed to spend his initial energies. He scribbled frantically, hoping a logical deduction might come out of his wild thoughts:

1)   SOPHIE. Sophie was the best girl he'd ever met. Maybe it could be love? Maybe not. But if she turned out to be his half-sister, these possible feelings would be DISTRESSING and WEIRD. Unfortunately, the fact that Sophie was mixed race didn't rule her out as a sibling, as it was her mum who was black, not her dad.

2)   HARRY. His best friend. Noah had always felt close to Harry; they had a connection. But why was that? Was it because they were, in reality, half-brothers?! Was it because they actually shared some of the same DNA? This would also be WEIRD because Harry had already admitted to having feelings for Noah — feelings that would be considered INCESTUOUS feelings if things turned out for the worst. BUT it was hard to imagine that Harry's mum, who was a member of the Women's Institute and

owned a pashmina, would be the type to
cheat on her husband.

3)   JESS JACKSON. Nothing had happened
between them, but she had shown him
private areas of herself that he didn't want
to see, and attempted to initiate an act of
sexual intercourse. If she turned out to be
his half-sister, these feelings and actions
would be CRIMINAL. He knew Jess had
parents (plural), but he didn't know enough
detail to be sure she wasn't originally the
product of depravity some sixteen years
earlier. He must prioritize research on her!

"What's this?" Eric said, whipping the book out of his
hands.

Noah sprang up, grappling for the book. "No! Eric!
I—"

Too late. Eric was already reading through it, and
batting Noah away every time he tried to get it back. "Eric!
Please!"

"Number one, Sophie – love, love, love. Want to do
sex. Incest, question mark. Sister, question mark. Number
two, Harry – mate. Gay stuff, exclamation mark. Weird,
question mark. Incest, question mark. And number three,
Jess Jackson. Attempted sex. Little shorts." Eric looked up.
"Wow. You've got issues, haven't you?"

Noah swallowed hard, his heartbeat throbbing in his ears. "Give me it back," he said.

"Always good to know how folk get their kicks," Eric said. "Reveals their innermost desires, and therefore their *weaknesses*." He gave Noah a smug smile. "Where is it, then?"

Oh no! The money! In all the drama of the previous night, Noah had completely forgotten about it. "Eric, I..."

"You'd better have it!"

"I've got it, Eric. I have got it. I just haven't got it *with me*," Noah explained.

"We had a deal!" Eric blurted out, a look of genuine panic in his eyes.

"And I will honour that deal, Eric. I will! I'll get you the money."

"How? When?"

"Tomorrow?" Noah suggested.

"Not good enough. Too late!" Eric loosened his tie as beads of sweat formed on his forehead.

"Well, when do you expect me to—?!"

"After school. I come home with you. You give it me then. All of it."

Brilliant. One thing he didn't need right now was people seeing him walking around town with Eric Smith, like they were mates.

"Whatever." Noah shrugged.

"Yeah. Good. Don't let me down." Eric waved the

rough book under Noah's nose. "I keep this as insurance. You let me down, this gets photocopied and distributed round school. I'm sure everyone will love your little wank diary," Eric grinned, walking off.

Noah flopped back down on the bench and, totally in line with his usual luck, Jess Jackson came into view and was making a beeline for him. She would surely be furious after their tussle last night. Had she told the police about him? Was she about to present him with a bill for compensation?

"Thanks for calling an ambulance," she said, sitting down next to him.

"Oh, you're welcome."

"I was being sarcastic," she said. "I was totally fine. My parents were livid, but don't worry, I didn't tell them anything. Naughty boy."

"But I didn't mean to push you, though!"

"That's not what I mean."

Noah gulped and snuck a look at her. "What ... what do you mean? *Naughty boy?*"

She smirked at him. "We had a good night, right?"

"Right," he agreed.

"That's all." She shrugged. "You're funny. I like you."

He squinted at her, trying to work it out. Was she saying she wanted to be mates? That they could hang out a bit? That he could be one of the cool gang?

She must be after something. But what could he

possibly offer her? "Have you done the French homework?" he asked.

"No."

"I suppose you could look at mine, maybe. I would need to think about it, but I suppose you could have a quick look during short break." He winked at her, hoping she would be impressed about how daring he was being.

"Thanks, babes," she said. "That's great."

"Sure. No worries . . . *babes.*"

"What were you doing talking to Eric Smith when I came down the corridor?"

"Oh . . . nothing much. Just . . . you know." Noah trailed off, really not wanting to get into it. The memory stick wasn't his yet. The real facts were still out there. Dangerous.

Jess nodded. "Watch yourself. That guy's a douchebag."

Noah grimaced and desperately wanted to retort that Eric might be a "tosser", he might be a "heathen", he might even be "an uncultured swine", but since *they were not in America* he would *not* be a *douchebag.* But he swallowed down his irritation because he and Jess were talking now. Like normal people. "Uh, yeah!" Noah said, forcing a chuckle. "And he's not just a douchebag!"

"No?"

"No! Hell no! He's a. . . a. . ." *Arse! What was he?* "He's a . . . *Douchebagasaurus Rex!*"

Jess looked at him, stony-faced. "What's that? Some sort of. . ."

"Dinosaur," Noah interrupted. "A real *douche* of a ... dinosaur. Like, probably the one that told all the others, 'Oh, don't worry, that huge speeding meteorite won't harm us, we're dinosaurs, we're unstoppable, just stay out and enjoy yourselves.'"

"Huh." Jess nodded. "You're ... funny. I don't get it, but you're funny."

"Well, it's because the way scientists think dinosaurs became extinct was—"

Jess held her hand up. "That's cool, Noah."

"I'm interested in palaeontology," he said, before realizing that perhaps it wasn't as cool to her as it was to him. "But I like other stuff too. Like ... music!" Music was a safe bet. Everyone liked music. Music was cool.

"Yeah?" Jess smiled. "And what's your *jam*, Noah?"

He swallowed hard. He knew she couldn't possibly be asking what sort of preserves he favoured. He smiled at her. "I like so many jams," he said. "I like *all* the jams."

"You're so cute," she said, pecking him on the cheek and getting up. "Laters!" And she flounced off up the corridor.

Oh my God. It had finally happened. He'd become normal. Soon he would be fashionable, use teen slang, post inspirational images on an Instagram account...

He turned to go and nearly bumped into Melissa and a few of her friends who were trying to catch up with Jess. "All right, Noah?" she said. "Heard you had fun last night."

"Er, yeah. Fun, yes," Noah said, waiting for the inevitable vicious punchline to land.

Melissa smiled. "Cool. Oh, by the way, I googled your mum last night and watched some of her Beyoncé show on YouTube? You know, it's not bad. I quite liked it."

Noah stared at her. "Riiiight—"

"Serious," Melissa said. "And way cooler than my mum – she's an *office manager*, for God's sake. Like, what even is that?"

"Office managers calculate payroll, organize meetings and supervise the work of secretarial, clerical and administrative staff," Noah said. It was a good job *someone* had been paying attention at that careers fair.

Melissa gawped at him. "Well, *whatever*, sounds dull to me! Your mum is way more creative."

"Uh-huh?" Noah said. This was making him feel nervous. This sort of normal interaction with the cool kids just wasn't, well, *normal*.

"Catch you later," Melissa smiled, giving him a little fist bump on his shoulder and walking off.

Noah stood in a daze.

For reasons he didn't remotely understand, it felt like he had turned some sort of corner.

CHAPTER TWENTY-FOUR

"Is this some sort of pathetic attempt to try and prove you're not gay?" Harry dropped his lunch tray on the table, kicked out the chair and slammed down opposite. "Messing around with Jess?"

Noah froze, mid-mouthful. *"What?"*

"Because that's what everyone's saying. That's what *she's* saying. That you two..."

"We two, *what?*"

"Had sex," Harry muttered.

Noah felt the pasta in his mouth turn to sand as he did his best to swallow it down. "That's what she's saying?"

"That's what *everyone's* saying! You were round at hers, you had several bottles of cider and then one thing led to another. Is it true?"

"It's—"

"So it's not true?"

"It's—"

Melissa being so friendly, the idea his mum was now cool, not being bullied for being gay (so far today) – it all began to make sense. Everyone thought he'd had sex with Jess! And by association, he was now suddenly acceptable. And while that was utterly pathetic, school had felt *nice* today. It had been pleasant. And if this was the reason, he could presumably look forward to more of the same. Obviously the sex thing wasn't true, and he wasn't sure how this misunderstanding could have occurred. Jess would hardly be lying to big herself up – it wasn't as if having sex with him would improve her own social standing. Maybe she mentioned something about him coming over and people just took it the wrong way? Or maybe she couldn't remember – what with being knocked out and all.

"Why are you hesitating? Yes or no?" Harry said, staring at him.

"None of that matters," Noah said. "I did something for you last night that I think you'll be very pleased about."

"Having sex with Jess?"

"No, something else."

"OK, so you're just ignoring the whole sex-with-Jess thing?"

"I agreed to purchase a little something from Eric Smith."

There was a second or two of silence whilst Harry took it in. "What the hell?" He frowned, massively unimpressed. "It better not be what I think it is. Not the memory stick?"

"Well, thank your lucky stars, because it is! Cost me a hundred quid, but I'm gonna get it. Get it for *you!*" Noah grinned.

"You bought that crap off Eric? Is that what you did?"

"Yes..." *Why was Harry not down on his knees, licking Noah's shoes?*

"You wanker!" Harry hissed at him.

Noah was stunned. What the hell was Harry's problem now? He'd just spent his own money making sure their *antics* weren't plastered all over the internet! "Hey! I did this for you!"

"Did it for *you*, more like. Ashamed of kissing me, was that it?"

And there it was. Back to the kiss again. Back to being gay. That's what everything boiled down to now. That's where every path in their friendship led. Things would never be the same, because everything was now connected to this. If he didn't want to get chips after school, it would be because he was *ashamed of kissing him*. If he didn't answer his phone, it would be because he was *ashamed of kissing him*. If he didn't want to join Harry and his parents on one of their godforsaken garden centre trips, it would be because he was *ashamed of kissing him*!

"I don't care! Get it?" Harry continued. "I don't care if

Eric shows the world that stupid video, I'm not hiding any more and I don't care who knows! And I'm not gonna be blackmailed by him 'cause I've got nothing to be ashamed of!"

"Harry, I just didn't want everyone to see the video! I didn't mean... It would be embarrassing! And you saw how everyone reacted when they just thought we'd held hands. What'll they do if they see we kissed? Twice?" He lowered his voice and leaned in to Harry. *"With tongues!"*

"I don't care! You know why I was crying in the toilets yesterday? Because Eric tried to sell me that video and I said no. And I knew that when the video got out, just like Eric threatened it would, things would get worse for us, you're right about that. They would. And I knew that would probably make things even more difficult between you and me. Maybe even... Maybe everything would be lost, I don't know. That's why I was crying – because of how I knew you would react. But at the same time, I wasn't going to be made to feel ashamed of who I was. Who I am."

"Yes, but..."

"Everyone's talking behind my back! *My parents* even know about it, somehow. We had to have this whole talk. Mum's doing this thing where she's *acting* fine, but it's obviously an act. Like she's acting the act, making it obvious she's acting, you know? And I kept hearing her crying in bed last night, and I mean, *really*?!"

"Crying 'cause you're gay?"

"Something about never having grandkids."

"Yeah, but you could, because you could give some sperm to a surrogate mother or a lesbian couple or something," Noah helpfully proffered. "Although I guess your mum wouldn't be massively keen on that either."

Harry gave the slightest flicker of a smile, and Noah was overcome with a terrible sadness. He was sitting opposite the only person he knew whom he didn't have to pretend around. He didn't have to be someone he wasn't; him and Harry just *were*. And without Harry having to say it, Noah knew that this stuff with Harry's parents would be hurting him. Unlike Noah, Harry actually quite liked his folks. He was paranoid about disappointing them even by just getting half marks on a maths test, so what was happening now must be off the scale.

"Look, Harry, I'm sure we can sort this out, I'm sure—"

"Yeah? Really? See, I don't get you any more, Noah. You maybe sleep with Jess, maybe don't, but it's definitely *nothing* to do with what happened between us. Then you buy the video off Eric, but *not* because you've got a problem with gay stuff. I mean, it was a *kiss*, Noah. A kiss! So what? Who cares?"

"Look, Harry, I can explain everything… I mean, when you put it like that, sure, I agree, it sounds awful. And –" he lowered his voice again "– you know, I'm cool with the gay stuff, like, I mean, with you being gay … even if

I'm not ... gay, not that I've... I mean, I don't entirely know what I'm trying to say really, but *please* don't be mad at me. Maybe I made a mistake, then... Got it wrong about the video. But, please... We're ... best friends. Aren't we?"

Harry shrugged. "I thought we were."

"Well, yeah!"

"You won't be buying the video, then, will you?"

Noah stared at him, cornered. It was a no-win situation. Buy the video, upset Harry. Don't buy it, have the world see what they did. "You don't think we should have it? Rather than... I mean, you want it all over the internet, then?"

"Have you heard anything I've said?"

"Yes, but—"

"I've had enough."

Harry stood up abruptly and stormed out of the dining hall as all eyes turned in their direction.

"Ooooh! Lovers' tiff!" said a Year Eight kid at a nearby table, to appreciative laughter.

Noah put his head down and pretended to be preoccupied finishing his pasta. He aggressively speared the last of it on to his fork. *This. Whole. Situation. Really. Sucked!*

"What's the pasta ever done to you?" chuckled a fully broken male voice.

Noah looked up and froze in terror. There, looking down at him and for some reason placing his tray on the same table as Noah's … and now actually sitting down opposite Noah, was Year Thirteen's Josh Lewis. THE Josh Lewis! Noah turned to look behind him – surely Josh was talking to someone else?

"What's up with your mate?" Josh asked, starting on his lunch of chicken breast and salad.

"Oh … he … er, he's … you know, so, yeah." *What are you doing here, Josh, surely you've made a mistake!*

"Uh-huh." Josh nodded, chewing on his chicken.

Noah sat staring at Josh, unaware his mouth was slightly open, mesmerized by this beautiful boy eating his no-carbs lunch. He watched Josh take each mouthful of tender grilled chicken and crisp salad, chewing slowly, exuding that confident, charming and in-control air he had about him. Josh had never spoken to him before. Never even noticed him before. So why now? Did he think Noah was someone else? Or had Josh gone blind, perhaps? A freak sporting accident, robbing him of his sight, disorientating him in the canteen…

"So … you and Jess, then?" Josh grinned.

This was unbelievable. A rumour that he might have got with a popular girl and suddenly Noah Grimes was worthy of being spoken to by Josh Lewis. It was brilliant, but terrifying. Brilliant because he finally wasn't a social pariah. Terrifying because the things that had made him so weren't actually true. What if Jess Jackson's memory suddenly came back, in crystal-clear detail? Or what if Noah

221

himself couldn't keep the pretence up and said something that immediately proved it was all a facade?

It would be like the kidnapping story he made up about his dad.

"Hmm, ahhh – hum..." Noah muttered, smiling and trying not to actually say anything that implicated him one way or another, just as Gran would advise.

"Cool," Josh said, taking a swig of mineral water from his sports-capped bottle.

"I like your bottle," Noah said, desperately grabbing on to any conversation topic he could find.

"Yeah? You like sports? You into anything?"

Noah flailed around for something to say. Josh Lewis was talking to him. He had to talk back. This was his chance. This could be acceptance. This could change everything. "Badminton?" he finally offered.

"Bro, badminton is for pussies."

Noah gave a nervous laugh. "Oh, yes. Yes, er, *bro*, I... It was a joke. 'Course not! Badminton!" he scoffed. "As if! Ha!"

"You should join the rugby team. We could use a scrum half."

"Oh, right, I'm not sure...?" Noah said, quickly hiding his trembling hands under the table.

"Or a winger? You fast on your feet?"

"Not ... sure..." Noah repeated.

"Cool." Josh shrugged. "So. Jess."

Noah nodded. "Jess."

"She's a *fine* girl. Lots of lads be jealous you're hitting that."

"Oh. Right."

"But I gotta hand it you, bro. S'always the quiet ones!" Josh chuckled and pulled a protein shake out of his bag. "Listen, yeah, I know we've never talked before, but you seem cool. And I like your style. Lot of boys brag about it endlessly. I like that you're being relaxed."

"Right!" Noah said, staring at Josh, unblinking.

"And most lads I know are full of it. But you seem different. So ... mates?"

"What?" Noah whimpered, in utter disbelief.

"Wanna be mates? We can compare notes, *on the ladies*?" he said, winking at him.

"Sure! Yeah! Deffo!" Oh my God, this was bloody BRILLIANT!

"Now," he continued, "what marks would you give her?"

"What? Marks? Marks for who?"

"Jess, you bellend!" he chuckled. "Gotta give your girl marks out of ten."

"In what categories?" This was a whole new world, and he didn't much like it.

"How good the sex was!"

"Oh! Oh ... er ... what are the grade boundaries?"

"Zero is crap, ten is out of this world. What would you give Jess?"

"Um… I… Five?" he said doubtfully, thinking it seemed like a safe sort of number. In the middle. Average.

"Five, huh?"

"Could be a six?"

"Well, which?"

"Five, then. Let's say five."

"You're hard to please. I like that. You've got standards."

"Sure have!"

"And so have I. Me and you are gonna get along just fine! Do you fancy a Coke?"

"Oh! Yes!"

Josh handed him a two-pound coin. "Grab me one too, will ya? Make sure they're cold!"

Noah took the shiny coin and bounded off to the vending machine. He was going to have an ice-cold Coke with Josh Lewis. A boy who wasn't going to try and kiss him. A boy that was happy to engage in a bit of light banter, nothing heavy. No accusations. No problems. He might not be his best friend, but he was sure as hell a better one than Harry was being right now.

He approached the Coke machine and inserted the coin in the slot, just as he felt a warm hand come down on his shoulder.

"Afternoon, Mr Grimes!"

Noah turned to come face-to-face with a smiling Mr Baxter. "Getting something from the vending machine?" Mr Baxter said. "Chocolate, or a nice beverage?"

Noah squinted at him. Why was he engaging in pointless chatter?

"Just a Coca-Cola," Noah said. "For me and *Josh Lewis.*"

"How's things?" Mr Baxter continued.

Noah rubbed his nose. *This was his chance to plant seeds of doubt.* "Well, Mum's got an horrific fungal foot infection. She's prone to them, it's fully gross, so it's lucky she's still secretly in love with my dad, because he's the only person who loves her regardless, you know? And she does really, really love him. Even though she sometimes lies and says she doesn't. Of course, she's always on the lookout for a *naive rich middle-aged man* who she can ultimately fleece, but hey, that's my mum!" Noah pulled at his collar and gave Mr Baxter a wide smile.

Mr Baxter blinked back at him, blew out a breath and patted him gently on the back again. "Excellent. Crack on, kiddo."

And he walked off. *Kiddo?* A word you would only use if you were being some sort of try-hard stepdad.

Noah's blood ran cold. How much more trouble did the universe want to send his way?

CHAPTER
TWENTY-FIVE

"FIVE OUT OF TEN?!" she screamed.

Noah had been making his way across the playground towards the gates, but he spun round as a furious Jess Jackson stormed up to him, looking about ready to gouge his eyes out with her impossibly long nails. "FIVE out of TEN?!" she repeated. "FIVE?!"

"Hello, Jess."

"Disrespectful! That's what it is! You've disrespected me!"

"No..."

"Why are boys all the same? Can't wait to brag about it to your mates, can you?"

"I haven't!"

"And I wouldn't mind, but at least give me a decent score! *Five!*"

"Five's good!"

"FIVE!"

"It's a good, respectable score... It's average..."

"AVERAGE?!"

"I've nothing to compare it to!" he pleaded, furious that Josh Lewis had clearly blabbed his mouth off at the nearest opportunity.

"Well, thanks, Noah. Thanks a lot. It's *really nice* that you're going around, telling everyone about how we had sex!"

"I haven't been! Everyone's been saying that anyway!"

"You know, that makes me feel really special! I thought you were different, Noah! I thought you had respect for women! I thought you were intelligent and caring..."

"I am *all* of those things, and so much more," he assured her. "But the point is—"

"I'll tell you what the point is!" she said. "I've seen how things have changed for you. People being nice. No one's bullying you about being a gay boy now, are they? Suddenly, you're Mr Popular!"

"Well – I mean, there is possibly some truth in that."

Jess nodded. "Isn't there just? So, do you want all that to end?"

Noah's eyes nearly popped out. "No! Jess! I gave you the French homework! And there's more where that came from. Think, Jess! I could up your grades tenfold!"

"In return for what, exactly?"

"Just ... keep quiet about the fine details. *Please.*"

She looked at him like the sad little loser he felt. "So, you're asking me to say we had sex?"

"No, just don't necessarily deny it. Keep it ... mysterious." *Just like Gran had advised.*

She stared at him for about ten fully awful seconds. "Whatever. *Dick.*"

Noah suddenly saw Eric in the edge of his field of vision, waiting for his money, Noah's rough book in his hand as his insurance policy. He wanted to get Eric over and done with, but he knew he needed answers. Noah cleared his throat. "Jess, I know you're angry, and this probably isn't the time..."

Jess stared at him with cold eyes.

Noah cleared his throat again. "Um ... but here's the thing... And what I'm wondering is, do you ever think that your dad might not really be your dad? At all? Do you ever think that?"

"Are you fully serious right now?" she asked.

Noah took a step back, eyes darting between Jess and an impatient Eric. "Yes, I know it's—"

"Why would you even ask me something like that? Are you actually *trying* to piss me off?"

He stared at her, his pulse racing. "I ... am ... doing ... a survey. A survey! Yes. It's a thing for ... maths? I'm going to make it into a graph, ultimately. Maybe a pie chart, I don't know. This is one of the questions."

She stepped right up to him. "I don't think my parents are my parents at all. I think I'm adopted. We have nothing in common, and I hate them. So shove that in your pie chart!"

She flounced off, leaving him in the middle of the yard. Damn it. Asking her had not only failed to solve the mystery, it had made her more angry towards him. Miss Marple never got called a dick when she was making enquiries. Where was he going wrong?

He took a deep breath, checked the coast was clear and Harry was nowhere to be seen, and walked over to the gate, towards Eric.

Noah was sick of being a victim of other people's actions. Whether it was his mum, his dad or Harry, why should he suffer just because someone else decided to do a Beyoncé tribute act, abandon their family, or kiss him? Noah had a right to buy that video if he wanted to, and he wanted it out of harm's way.

He barely glanced at Eric as he passed by. Just enough for Eric to know he should follow. Noah certainly wasn't going to stroll down the street alongside him, like Eric wasn't a total blackmailing little shit.

"We're attending to some business upstairs for a bit," Noah said to his mum as they passed her in the hall on their way up the stairs.

"What sort of business?"

"It's private, Mother. You have secrets. I have secrets."

"Hello, Mrs Grimes!" Eric chirped sweetly.

"Hi, Eric," his mother muttered.

Noah showed Eric into his room and pulled the bottom drawer of his bedside cabinet out, revealing his secret stash in the cavity beneath.

"Neat hiding place," said Eric, eyeing the assorted contents.

"Thanks."

"*Sex and Growing up: A Guide for Kids*," Eric said, reading aloud the title of a book hidden in the space.

"Er, don't know how that got there, must have slipped down years ago..." Noah muttered, shrugging it off and grabbing the money.

"Sure." Eric smirked.

"Here you go – twenty, forty, sixty, seventy, eighty," he said, counting the notes out into Eric's sweaty hand.

"I like a man who sticks to his word," Eric said, folding the notes and putting them into his pocket.

"Sure," Noah said, sliding the little drawer back on its runners. "So..." he continued, standing up and finding himself awkwardly close to Eric.

"Nice doing business with you." Eric grinned, seemingly finding some perverse pleasure in the closeness.

"And you," he lied.

"So, here's the memory stick," Eric said, handing it over.

Noah took it and placed it deep in his trouser pocket, wedged beneath his handkerchief. No one must know he had it. Especially not Harry. Later, he would have to find a suitable place to keep it.

"And your rough book too," Eric said, handing it to Noah. "Anything else I can do for you?"

"No. What like?"

"Like … anything."

Noah swallowed. What did he mean? "No."

"OK," Eric grinned, "but if you change your mind…"

"I'll see you at school, Eric. I've gotta get on with homework," Noah said.

But Eric didn't move. "So what's the deal with you and Harry?"

"There is no deal, and it's not really any of your business," Noah said. "Not that you've helped whatsoever."

"He's angry you bought the memory stick? Maybe you shouldn't have. I didn't *force* you to buy it."

Noah laughed. "Oh, right. You're serious. Yeah, *you did.*"

"In a way, it's a shame. The way you two kiss…"

Noah glared at him. "Eric—"

"What? You obviously like each other. You shouldn't care what other people think. That's a free bit of advice for you."

"Well, thanks for the tip."

Eric stepped closer again. Really close, his breath hot on Noah's neck. "Moving forward, us two could help each other out in other ways," he said.

Noah swallowed. "What – what do you mean?"

"I dunno," Eric smiled. "Just saying."

The walls seemed to wobble. "Er, no thanks. But I appreciate the offer."

Eric gave a little smile and nodded. "OK, well, think about it."

Eric turned, headed out and straight down the stairs, letting himself out of the front door.

Noah took a deep breath. *That had been a truly horrible and weird experience.* But at least it was over now. Noah had what he wanted. He didn't need to speak to Eric ever again.

CHAPTER TWENTY-SIX

He put a new cartridge into his fountain pen and took up where he'd left off.

> *Dad – nearly twenty-four hours have passed*
> *since my last sentence, and in that time I can tell you*
> *that I am now definitely not gay because I almost had*
> *sex with a girl whom I don't even like and saw her*
> *real live boobs. But never mind all that, Mum's told me*
> *I have some sort of half-brother or sister! I can't believe*
> *no one ever thought to tell me! You and Mum owe me*
> *an explanation. People already think I'm weird thanks*
> *to you two – this will only make it worse. How could*
> *you do this?! Please write back within three working*
> *days and explain everything. Kind regards, Noah.*

He didn't put a kiss at the end. His dad didn't deserve one. He folded the letter up, rammed it in an envelope, addressed it and shoved five first-class stamps on it. That should cover delivery to Spain. He would put it in the postbox on the way to school tomorrow.

His phone pinged:

Hi Noah! Have arrived in Milton Keynes. You OK?
Soph x

Damn it. With all his own drama he had been a selfish and bad potential boyfriend and hadn't even bothered to ask her if she'd got there OK. He quickly hammered out a message back.

So sorry, was just about to text you but you beat me to it! LOL! Ha ha! Glad you got to Milton Keynes OK and didn't die in one of those multi-car pile-ups or anything, lol. Hope your new house is nice. I'm fine. Sophie? Do you ever wonder if your dad isn't really your dad? (Doing a survey, that's all.)

She texted back: ?
He replied: Yeah, it's for maths. Just wondered. Do you?
She texted back: Frequently.
Noah grimaced. It was quite possible that everyone

thought they weren't related to the people claiming to be their parents. Come to think of it, how could Noah himself be the result of his mother's hideous egg being fertilized by his father's useless sperm? Would such a union really produce a boy as intelligent and sophisticated as him? Unlikely.

She texted again: How's everything with Harry?

He wondered if she'd already heard things. What if Harry had already texted Sophie to say that he was really upset about Noah's behaviour? He didn't want Sophie thinking that he was an unfeeling cad, incapable of emotional sensitivity and stuff. He hit the caps lock. This text would all be in capitals, because it was VERY important.

JUST TO CONFIRM, I'M BEING NICE TO HARRY BUT IT'S SOMETIMES DIFFICULT BECAUSE HE IS VERY EMOTIONALLY UNSTABLE EVEN THOUGH I AM TRYING REALLY HARD TO DO NICE THINGS THAT WILL HELP HIM, EVEN IF HE THINKS THEY WON'T.

Yes. That was fine. It was true, after all. Noah'd just misjudged the memory stick situation. Catastrophically, as it turned out. *Ping!* She'd texted back: *Really?!?*

Noah narrowed his eyes at the screen. She had replied with one word and an assortment of punctuation that implied she didn't believe him *one little bit*. Aaargh! She had no idea how tricky Harry was being. Harry was the one being unreasonable! Harry was the one...

He sighed. Oh God, Harry was furious with him. Noah had royally screwed up.

He couldn't leave things like this. He had to do something. Make amends. At least one aspect of his life had to be drama-free, surely? He made a list of things he needed to say. This time, he would be prepared. Preparation made everything better.

Stuff I need to say to Harry

I'm so sorry.
It's all my fault.
I was a fool/plonker/coxcomb. (Decide on best
    word at the time.)
We can't end our friendship like this.
We can't end our friendship at all!
Give me another chance; I'll prove myself!
You owe me three pounds from when I paid
    for your cheese puff and a Coke at lunch
    last week. (Only say this if it's going well,
    otherwise mention at a later date.)

He practised three times so it came out right, then grabbed a small toy guitar from his bedroom – he'd only ever managed to plonk out a piss-poor rendition of "Memory" from *Cats* on it – and headed out to Harry's house.

"Haaaaa-rrrryyyyy!" Noah sang tunelessly, as he strummed away on the lawn below Harry's window. Thinking about it, it would have been easier to ring the doorbell, but maybe less dramatic. *He needed to prove himself.* Like those scenes in romcoms where someone stops the person they fancy from boarding a plane to New York by making a loud, inappropriately personal speech in front of everyone. "Haaaaa-rrrryyyyy! Woo! Yeah, Haaarrrr-rryyy! Open ya windooow! So I can come see you!"

He opened his window. "What the hell is this?"

"Surprise! I've come to say it's all your fault."

"What?!"

"I mean, *me*! My fault! Sorry. Yes. I'm singing you a song."

"Why?"

Noah shrugged. That was a good question. "Seemed like a nice thing to do?"

Harry frowned and shut the window. *"My* fault, *my* fault," Noah muttered. Damn it, he had over-rehearsed it now, hadn't he? He had built it up into something important and big, and now nerves were taking over. He wished he had some water to sip. His mouth was bone dry.

Harry came out the back door and looked at him.

Noah needed to get it all out before Harry had chance to say anything. If Harry started first, he might say something unexpected, and then all Noah's preparation would—

"Is this all a joke to you?" Harry said. *Damn it, too late! Arses!*

He wouldn't be deterred. "Look, you're sorry it was all my fault, plonker, but don't end our friendship this way. I'm a coxcomb, and you need a chance to prove myself to you." He nodded. That was certainly some words in a sequence that more or less summed matters up. "And you owe me three quid."

Harry ran his hand through his hair and sighed. He came closer, and Noah held his breath, unsure if Harry was about to kiss him or hit him. "Did you tell Eric what to do with his pathetic little video?"

Noah gulped. In his pocket, right there, was the memory stick. If he came clean, he knew that would be it. Harry and him would be over. And that would be the worst thing that could happen. "Yeah, I told him what to do," Noah said, his heart racing.

"You told him you didn't want it?"

He felt like his knees were going to give way. "Uh-huh."

Harry nodded and stared at him for a long time. Noah shuffled from leg to leg, Harry's eyes burning into him. "I mean," Noah muttered, "that stupid video – not worth losing my best mate over, is it?" All he could feel was the memory stick, sitting in his pocket like a huge lump, really *obviously* there. He didn't dare look down. He didn't want to draw attention to his pockets. What if it was sticking out? It *felt* like it was sticking out. It felt like he was carrying a massive neon sign with a huge arrow, reading "MEMORY STICK RIGHT HERE!"

Worse, he realized he didn't want the damn thing at all. Harry was right. *It didn't matter.* What really mattered was them, their friendship, the years they'd spent together. What mattered was *Harry.* The best person you could ever hope to be with. Harry. *His* Harry.

In spite of himself, tears starting welling in Noah's eyes. And, to his horror, Harry was crying too.

"I know you're lying," Harry said.

"What?"

"I saw you walk home with Eric. I watched you, Noah. I hid and I watched you. I know what you did."

They both stared at each other, eyes wet. There was no recovery from this. There was nothing Noah could do to save himself. To save them.

Harry smiled sadly, tears still streaming down his face. "See ya, Noah."

And he turned and went inside.

Noah stood, motionless in the dark.

Him and Harry were no more.

CHAPTER TWENTY-SEVEN

"Cheer up, bro!" Josh Lewis said, striding over to Noah as he sat on a bench at the furthest corner of the yard, unable to eat his lunch.

"Oh, hello, Josh," he said, barely able to smile. He was engulfed in despair about Harry. "I'm just..."

"Dealing with some *guy* stuff?"

Noah nodded. "I've had a massive row with Harry. We're not mates any more."

Josh sat next to him and put a matey arm across Noah's shoulders. "Bro, here's the deal. *People change.* Want to know what I think?"

"OK," Noah said, feeling the comforting warmth of Josh's manly embrace.

"You've both reached a crossroads. Harry's realized he's gay and got feelings for you."

Noah's heart sank. Josh, too, it seemed, was aware of the hand-holding episode.

"Now," Josh continued, "based on how you bagged Jess, I'm guessing that you don't feel the same? Like, you *like* Harry, but you're not necessarily gay for him? Am I right?"

"OK." Noah nodded.

"So, you both want different things now. And that's what happens. You were best mates, but now your paths have taken you in different directions. And yes, that's sad, but it's also a natural part of life. Everything moves and changes and turns. And you'll meet new friends, like Jess. *Like me.* It's life, man. It's the whole crazy way of the universe. Life and death. Don't be sad. Be glad for what you had, but be excited for new adventures. New people."

Noah managed a small smile. Josh was *very* good with words. Very philosophical. Noah liked that. And how refreshing to have someone want to be mates with him, but not want to snog him. A conversation that wasn't about being gay. Josh got him. Right? Josh was *ace.* Right?

"Josh, I am slightly cross," Noah said, "about you telling everyone Jess Jackson's sex score."

"Bro, I'm sorry, all right?"

"That's OK. I accept your apology." Noah would just have to let this one go. He didn't want to make Josh feel too bad.

"Look, I mentioned it to Alfie Bell. Alfie's normally cool, but suddenly he's gone all dickhead on me. Blabbed it to everyone, little virgin that he is. Meant to be going to a festival with him at the weekend, but I've bailed on him now. I'm sorry, mate."

Noah smiled at him. Josh was so utterly lovely. "No, really, that – is – fine."

"Was she pissed?"

"Pissed? As in . . . drunk?"

"As in pissed *off*?"

"Oh! Oh . . . yes. Yes, she was! She felt she deserved a higher score."

"In the future, we'll keep the banter between ourselves, yeah?"

"Oh, yes! *Yeah!* Banter! Just between us!" Noah nodded, pleased. He felt so cool, using words in a conversation like "banter" in a non-ironic way. He had arrived. He really was *one of them.* "So. . . Did you . . . do any sex last night?"

Josh raised an eyebrow at him. "Bro, that is really not cool. You don't ask that sort of thing. What bros do in private stays in private. If a bro wants to share, he shares. But you do not ask."

"But you asked about Jess! Yesterday!" Noah said.

"Bro, I asked only because everyone knew. *You* had shared, bro."

"I am *so* sorry," Noah said, kicking himself that he'd been so forward, so stupid.

"Cool."

"Oh no," Noah muttered, seeing Jess and Melissa walking over to them. "Don't mention the sex score thing," he said to Josh. "She's proper angry at being a five."

"No sweat, bro," he replied. "Yo! Come in, Number Five!" he shouted over to the girls.

"Josh! Aaargh!" Noah squealed, throwing his hands over his face.

Josh slapped him across the back, fracturing his spine. "Just banter, bro! Doesn't count if it's banter!"

The girls sauntered up. "Hi, Noah, it's Miss Average for Sex here. How are you?" said Jess.

"Fine, thank you," he grimaced, going red.

"Still bragging about our little evening together?" she said, giving him a dangerous smile.

He didn't want her to reveal the truth. How humiliating would that be? "It *was* a lovely evening, Jess... *Amazing*, in fact..."

"Was the sex out of this world, Noah?" Melissa asked.

"Oh, *yes!* Yes, it totally was." He leaned back, spreading his legs apart. "Yeah. *Man.*"

Jess seemed satisfied. "Good. As long as it was." She handed him a little black-and-white printout.

He blinked at her. "What's this?"

"It's an ultrasound scan," Jess said. "I'm *pregnant*, Noah. Pregnant with your baby."

CHAPTER
TWENTY—EIGHT

Hilarious. Very damn funny. "Ha ha," Noah said. "That's very amusing, Jess." He stared at her, trying to read her face. Oh, yes, she was good. But not that good.

She looked at him quizzically. "This ain't no joke, Noah."

"Double negative. That means it *is*," he retorted with a satisfied smile, to a blank stare from Jess.

"Shit, man, shoulda used a condom!" Josh laughed, slapping Noah on the back again, dislodging his lungs in the process.

"I, totally... Condoms were absolutely a thing," Noah assured him.

Jess snorted. "You sure about that, Noah?"

"Yes! Quite sure!" he barked. This was ridiculous. She

was clearly doing this just to make him feel embarrassed and awkward, to see how far she could push it, in punishment for the sex score fiasco. "Right, OK, biology lesson, Jess. You don't end up with a baby you can see on an ultrasound scan after sexual intercourse two days ago. Right? Not possible." He handed it back to her. "This probably isn't even a real anyway. You got it off the internet or something."

"Fine," Jess said. "Let's see what you say when my dad turns up at your house tonight. And he is *mad*, Noah, let me tell you. Never seen him so angry. He blames you entirely. Says it's always the boy's fault." She smiled maliciously, turned and walked off.

Melissa gave Noah the finger. "Typical lad," she hissed.

He wasn't buying this for one second. She was just trying to scare him as a punishment. Unlucky for her that he wasn't that gullible.

Noah blew his cheeks out and turned to Josh. "Mental."

"Shit, man, though—"

"It's obviously not true, Josh."

"But, I mean, you *did* have sex... So, I mean, that doesn't look good... And maybe, look, sometimes the best thing a bro can do is man up and take responsibility. You get me? You hold your hands up and you say, 'You got me, but I'll do the right thing.' Yeah?"

"But I – I can't do that!"

"*Bro*, hear my words! Kids can be cool. Life takes us to unexpected places sometimes. Embrace the change!"

Noah opened his mouth and was about to tell Josh everything, what *really* happened that night – then he saw Harry across the playground, walking and chatting quite happily with Connor Evans, like they were best buddies. Huh. Didn't take him long to find a new friend, did it? Noah saw how it was. There was Harry acting all hurt last night, and now ... just hours later, *totally fine, everything cool,* like it hadn't happened. Laughing and joking with Connor, whilst Noah was the one still feeling like the whole world was on his shoulders.

Well, *fine.* Noah wasn't about to lose Josh as a mate, in that case. He was going to make Josh his *best mate of all time.* Josh was going to see that he was a funny, hilarious, confident lad who was ace at banter and awesome at ... sex ... and stuff. *Hell, yeah!* "Well, I have to tell ya, Josh, THE SEX WAS BLOODY EPIC!" he shouted, hoping Harry would hear from across the yard.

Josh seemed a bit startled by the outburst. "Yeah?"

"Oh, yeah. I was really good at it. But I totally used a condom. I'm not a dick."

Josh looked thoughtful for a moment. "Any chance the condom could have broken accidentally? What sort did you use?"

Noah looked at him like a deer in the headlights. "What do you mean, what sort?"

"You know, there's so many different types."

Noah nodded. *Was there?* Surely a condom was a

246

condom? *Types? Shit!* He racked his brains for any memories of changing-room banter between hideous lads, boasting and talking crap. He had a vague recollection of a brand name... "Yeah, yeah, I like to use the Dulux range..."

"Dulux?"

"Uh-huh. Yeah, they've got one called the ... Mega-Hung Donkey Stud."

He froze as Josh stared at him in silence.

"Aarrrggh! Banter!" Josh finally laughed, whacking him on the back again. "You're so funny! Mega-Hung Donkey Stud! Dulux! Ha!"

Noah picked himself off the ground and brushed himself down. He wasn't sure what he'd said that was funny. And Harry was nowhere to be seen, and clearly hadn't clocked any of this brilliant exchange between really good mates, damn it. "Yeah, *banter*," he said.

God, this was exhausting.

"Look, bro, I need to go and ... catch Harry," said Noah.

"Know what else you need to do?"

"What?"

"Think about your respon-sibil-ities!"

Noah nodded. "Uh, sure."

"Harry! Hi!" Noah gasped, jogging up to where he and Connor Evans were standing by the wall. *Their* wall.

Harry sighed. "What do you want, Noah?"

"I just—" He turned to Connor. "I'm sorry, would you mind? I need to talk to Harry, you know, in a private way?"

"Uh, OK? Whatever." Connor shrugged, turning to Harry. "See you later, dude."

Noah watched him walk off. "Dude?"

"What's the problem with that?"

"*Dude?*"

Harry sighed. "We're friends, so what?"

"Friends?!" Noah spluttered. "So you're actual friends now? Wow. Gosh. OK."

Harry crossed his arms. "How's *your* amazing new friend, Josh Lewis?"

"Cool, he's cool."

"You know, it amazes me that you are finding so much in common with him."

"I don't know what you mean. We're very alike. We connect on all sorts of things. We have high-minded, intellectual *banter.*"

"He's having to repeat a year to get his A levels."

"Er, *no.* I think you'll find the school *begged* him to stay on a year for the good of the sports team."

"For someone who's top set for everything, you really are quite stupid sometimes," Harry said.

"Right, well, you're quite … irritating sometimes," Noah countered.

"Great, well, nice chat, thanks," Harry said, starting to walk off.

"No, Haz! Come on!"

Harry spun back round. "No, Noah! I won't 'come on'! No! You've made it clear how you feel about me. *Fine*. Have a nice life, then."

"You don't understand!" Noah blurted out. "I'm going through hell! My mum told me I have a secret sibling – in this school! In our year! It could even be you, I've no idea. And she's having an affair. Probably with Mr Baxter, who I've accidentally also weed on. And Jess Jackson is pregnant and saying it's mine even though we didn't. . ." He lowered his voice. "We totally didn't do anything. At all. So, I mean, you're here laughing and joking with your 'buddy' Connor Evans, and, you know, I could really use some advice right now. Like we used to. Like we always did. I'd tell you stuff, or you'd tell me stuff, and we'd help each other work it out. Harry?"

Harry stared at him.

"Please, Harry?"

And he carried on staring. Emotionless. Cold.

"Harry?"

"Know what? Why don't you go and talk to your new friends who are so pleased you're straight? That's what I'd do. I'd go and talk to them right now, actually. If anyone sees you chatting to me, God knows what they might think. Right? And I'd hate to be the cause of any more problems for you, Noah. Sounds like you've got quite enough."

"So, that's it?"

"Yeah. That's it. Oh, but I can take one worry off your mind. This idea that I might be your sibling? No chance. I don't think we share a single strand of DNA, Noah. I don't think we've got a single thing in common any more."

CHAPTER TWENTY-NINE

"Noah, can you come down here, please?"

He trudged down to the front door, where his mum was standing, cross-armed, in front of a stocky man with a very pink face, who was wearing a suit with wide pinstripes. Noah swallowed hard. He knew that when there were men at the door wearing suits, it was never good news. And sure enough, just behind his right shoulder was Jess Jackson.

Oh absolute crap.

"Hi!" Noah bleated. Was Jess actually going through with this, then? How did she possibly think she was going to get away with it? It was crazy!

"Jess says that you slept with her," his mother said.

"No. That's not true," Noah replied.

"See?" his mother said to Mr Jackson. "Anything else you want to say to waste my time?"

"You're saying nothing happened between you and Jessie?" Mr Jackson said, glaring at Noah.

"I regret to inform you that Jess Jackson, your daughter, is a liar. She is lying about all this."

"I see. What exactly is the nature of your relationship to my daughter then?"

"Well, strictly speaking, we did hang out ... a bit."

"*Hang out?* Tell me, what does that mean? Does it mean you kept your clothes on?"

"Well, *some* clothes were removed," Noah conceded. "Your daughter removed a lot of her clothes. I did not remove hers, or any of mine."

Her dad crossed his arms. "So it's not true that you've been bragging about having sex with my daughter at school?"

Noah swallowed.

"That is, until you found out she was *with child*," her dad continued, briefly glancing over his shoulder to check no one else was listening. "Apparently you gave her a 'sex score'?"

"You did *what*, Noah?" his mum said, with a look of devastating disapproval.

He wanted to crawl under a rock and die. "Well, I... See, that was just *banter*. You know, between *bros*?"

"Did I bring you up to be that disrespectful towards women?" said his mum.

"Well, I…" Noah flailed. "It was a *joke*!"

"It's not funny," Mum said. "And why say it, when it's not true?"

Noah mouthed words, but no words came out. There was no answer to give. Not denying the rumour was an act of staggering stupidity.

"So, you tell me, who looks like the liar now?" Mr Jackson said.

"Well … me," Noah admitted.

"Indeed!" Mr Jackson said. "You're that ridiculous pirate kidnap boy, aren't you? Good at making up lies, aren't you?"

Noah breathed heavily. "Look, even if I did, which I didn't, I would have obviously used a … protective sheath. I'm not an idiot; in fact Jess even…" Noah trailed off, realizing what he was saying.

"Jess even *what*?" Mr Jackson said.

Noah swallowed. "When she was wanting to have sex with me, she removed a … protective sheath from the pot on your mantelpiece."

Mr Jackson didn't even flinch at that embarrassing revelation. He must regularly have sex orgies in his living room and be totally cool with it.

"Oh, yeah, I remember that now, it's all coming back to me," Jess said. "And then I ripped it open with my teeth…"

"You ripped it open with your teeth?" Mr Jackson said. "That's how you break them!"

"Oh!" Jess said, laying the surprise on thick. "I never knew!"

"You did know!" Noah squealed. "You attended sex ed classes! It's the only class where you've ever scored full marks on a pop quiz!"

Jess shrugged and batted her eyelids at her father. "He's trying to blame me!" she said.

"It's amazing," Mr Jackson said, stepping closer towards a quivering Noah. "We've gone from nothing happening, to clothes being removed, sex scores and condoms in under a minute!" Mr Jackson shook his head. "You know how people in this town talk! How do you think it'll look if people find out my daughter is pregnant with an illegitimate child? I'm president of the Rotary club! People look to me as a person of good standing. *Respectability* equals *good business.*" He sighed and looked down at his tasselled loafers. "Not that I'd expect people like you to understand any of that."

"Hold on a sec," his mum said, taking charge. "When did this supposedly happen?"

"It did *not* happen two days ago," Noah babbled.

Mr Jackson looked up, sharply. "Two days ago? Oh no, these two have been seeing each other for *months*, haven't you, Jess?"

"Yep!" Jess said, brightly.

"Oh, God!" Noah howled. "Seriously? You're seriously saying that? Ha! She hated me before the other night!"

"Are you going to do the right thing by my daughter?" Mr Jackson said.

Noah blinked at him. "What? Like, marry her?"

Mr Jackson gave a dismissive little snort. "No. Are you going to accept responsibility? Help pay for the child? It's about damage limitation. This sordid little accident's far from ideal, but at least if there's a willing father who's doing his best to make it work, it looks a little less appalling."

"But I'm not the father!" Noah pleaded.

Mr Jackson shook his head. "Don't make me involve my lawyers."

"Right, that's enough," his mum said. "*You –*" she pointed at Jess "– are a lying little bitch with no future. And *you –*" she pointed at her dad "– are a gullible twat who looks like a pig in a suit."

Yay, get in, Mum!

And she wasn't done yet: "I know damn well there is no way my son, who is better, brighter and kinder than all your awful, common, new-money family put together, would ever make a girl pregnant in these circumstances. And when we get a DNA test done, the proof will be there for all to see. And then never mind *your* lawyers, *we'll* sue your skanky little asses for defamation. So, why don't you slime your way back to your pathetic bling-bling house and shove your little heads that contain no brains up your massive fat arses?"

She slammed the door in their faces and waited until

255

she heard the doors of their BMW slam and the car drive off. "And that's how you deal with scumbags," she said.

Noah looked at her, wide-eyed. His mum had been bloody brilliant. Right now, he totally loved her. She was epic. "I love you, Mum," he grinned.

"Sure. But you're gonna need to *prove* she's lying, Noah. If she really is pregnant, she and her pig father are clearly going to cause you grief."

"Yes. But you do believe me, right?"

She cocked her head. "Hmm. You get back late two nights ago and I find you burning your clothes in the garden. Nothing remotely suspicious about that, is there?"

"No, but—"

She put her hand up. "S'fine. I believe you. That's what mothers are for."

There was a forceful knock at the door. "Bloody hell!" his mum said, flinging it open, "Why can't you just—" She stopped dead, seeing the two policeman standing there. "Oh my God, they've actually called the police too!"

"It wasn't me!" Noah told them. "Jess is lying. I didn't even push her, she just ran towards my hands and recoiled with the force – simple physics will tell you for every action there's an equal and opposite *reaction*. That's all."

"He didn't sleep with her," his mum added.

Noah nodded. "I did not."

"He's not really into all that sex stuff yet anyway."

"MUM!"

"Well, it's true," his mum said.

The policemen looked back at them. "That's … very informative, but we're actually making enquiries about a missing boy."

Noah rolled his eyes. *God's sake.*

"Oh?" said his mum.

"You look about his age," one said, smiling at Noah. "Not been home since yesterday afternoon, hasn't been at school and hasn't made any contact. We need to know who might have seen him last. His name's Eric Smith."

"Eric Smith?" Noah repeated, trying to sound as neutral as possible whilst every atom of his being was screaming omigod! Omigod! OMIGOD!

"Do you know him? Have you seen him at all?"

"He's… I mean, yes, he's in my year…"

"We have a witness who says they saw a lad fitting Eric's description walking down this street at about four p.m. yesterday. We just need to know why he might have been here. He lives across town, see, so he must have been here visiting someone or meeting someone… Any clues could help us find him."

Noah shrugged while his heart raced. What could he possibly say? That he'd brought Eric here to pay him eighty quid for some dodgy video footage? According to Eric, that footage had under-eighteens on it, *doing stuff.* How could Noah have been so stupid? If there was any nudity on that memory stick, any sex, it would land Noah in a whole heap of trouble. What the hell had he done? No way could he admit this. No way. It would all unravel and then ... prison, probably. Branded a sex offender. He couldn't breathe. He couldn't swallow. Why hadn't he listened to Harry?

And, that aside, where the hell was Eric?

"Is there anything you can tell us?" the second policeman said, breaking into Noah's storm of thoughts.

He glanced at his mum, who was tight-lipped and silent. "Er, no. There isn't."

The policeman considered him for a few seconds. "OK. Thanks for your time."

Noah closed the door and leaned against it, weakly. His mum looked at him. "He was here, so why are you lying?"

"It's OK, Mum. It wasn't anything bad. It's fine. It's not ... relevant. I'm sure he's ... fine."

"He had better be." She went into the lounge.

It felt like some sort of net was closing in on Noah. And, just when he thought things couldn't get any worse ... they could.

CHAPTER THIRTY

"Heard you got with my girlfriend," the lad said, cornering Noah against the prickly hedge that ran along the pavement by the back entrance to the school. "Heard she's havin' yer kid."

"No."

"Calling her a liar?"

"No..."

"Calling *me* a liar?"

"It's Kirk, isn't it?"

"That's me," Kirk said, his voice indicating a beating so imminent it was DEFCON 1. Noah noted with increasing panic that Kirk not only had fully developed muscles that bulged out of his Nike T-shirt (a T-shirt! It was *December*!), he also had a smattering of facial hair — like, stubbly stuff, not the pathetic fuzz that occasionally grew on Noah's top lip. Noah was dealing with a fully grown man. A grown man with several tattoos ... one of which was in the shape of a heart with the word "Jess" underneath it. It was not a promising set of circumstances.

"She said you'd split up," Noah squeaked, edging backwards and wincing as the holly prickles penetrated his trousers. "That's what she said."

"We have."

"Oh." Noah was bricking it. He was definitely going to die.

"But first of all, it's not OK to move in and bag another lad's girl so soon."

"No. No, I agree, it's not good form." He would agree to anything Kirk said; this was not the time to argue a point. "I mean, you can have her back... She's all yours."

"Think I want your sloppy seconds?"

"Well ... technically, thirds now, 'cause..."

"Shut your face."

"OK."

"You've made me a laughing stock."

"I am ... so sorry. I'm so sorry."

"I said, *shut yer face*!"

"Yes! Sorry. Yes. It's shut."

"Thing is," Kirk said, suddenly clasping his thick hand around Noah's throat, "you two have apparently been seeing each other behind my back for months, and I don't like sneaky shits who think they can get one over on me..."

"Aaaarrrh … don't … think … that…" Noah croaked, standing on tiptoes as Kirk lifted him off the ground.

"I could kill you right now. D'ya know that?"

"Uh-huh…"

"Could snap your puny little neck…"

"PUT HIM DOWN!" shouted a voice from behind him. "And piss off while you're at it."

Noah clattered to the ground as Kirk spun round to confront Noah's saviour, his James Bond, his Jason Bourne. Josh Lewis – his *Superman*.

"Who are you, giving me orders?" Kirk swaggered up to him aggressively. "Fancy a trip to A&E, do ya?"

"Now, come on, Kirk," Josh smiled, not the least bit perturbed, "just because you're covered in crap tattoos and wanker-branded sportswear doesn't mean you have to be the douche you look like."

Holy shit, Josh was brave, but he was surely heading for an almighty beating.

"Are you havin' a laugh?"

"No, I'm having a conversation with a guy who can't handle the fact his girlfriend would rather shag geeky little Noah than him!"

Noah wasn't sure how he felt about being called "geeky" and "little" but it didn't matter because it was all over incredibly quickly. Kirk had barely swung his arm back to launch the first punch before Josh had already got in there with his ace reflexes and landed a brilliant right hook on Kirk's jaw. Noah had never seen a proper fight involving an actual punch before, and he was surprised at how quickly and easily Kirk dropped to the ground, clutching his mouth as blood poured out.

"Want some more?!" Josh shouted, ready to kick him in the bollocks.

"Stop!" Kirk squealed. "You can't! I had blood cancer when I was ten!"

Noah gasped and looked worriedly at Josh. Of course! The stories in the papers. Kirk's brave fight. The fundraising coffee mornings and sponsored walks to pay for the pioneering treatment in Germany. Josh had just hit a cancer patient! That was bad. If the local paper found out, what would they say? *Cancer survivor assaulted by two healthy boys!* There would be a picture of Kirk, his face bloodied and swollen, with the caption "The cancer came back after the vicious attack." Oh God. They were done for now!

"Presumably you've made a full recovery?" Josh replied, patiently.

Kirk shrugged. "What do you care?"

"I'm sorry for what happened to you when you were *ten*, Kirk, but it doesn't make you any less of a dick *now*."

Kirk didn't argue. He scrambled to his feet and hobbled off down the pavement, muttering vague words of vengeance, leaving Noah wide-eyed in awe at Josh's majestic bravery. Josh had done all this, for him! No one had ever done anything like that before, not Harry, not anyone. Josh was shaping up to be an excellent replacement friend. In fact, Noah had possibly upgraded to a better model.

"Thank you," he said, stopping short of swooning into Josh's strong arms whilst whimpering "My hero!"

"All in a day's work." Josh shrugged, casually yawning and stretching his arms so his shirt rode up his body, revealing rock-hard abs and the waistband of his boxers, which read "100% British Beef".

Those abs. Noah couldn't stop staring. Josh must work out a lot ... in the gym ... getting all hot...

"Er, listen," Noah said, snapping himself back to reality. "Jess came round with her dad last night. She's actually pursuing this nonsense about me having impregnated her. And there's no way I'm taking that. Imagine! A dad at fifteen! I can't wait for a DNA test to prove her wrong. And if she is pregnant, it's obvious who the father really is!"

"Who?"

"Kirk! She's just split up with him, and he doesn't want anything to do with her, and I reckon she found out she was having his baby. So she needs someone to take the blame. And that's where I come in. I shall go full Poirot and get to the bottom of the whole damn thing! I'm going to find the truth! Going to prove it!"

Josh nodded. "Wow! A man of action! I like it. So, bet her dad was pissed?"

"Oh, yes, *pissed*. Totally *pissed*." He was delighted he knew that Josh meant pissed *off*. They were both so cool! He would use it again. "He was really, really *pissed*."

"If there's anything I can do, you know, to help, just let me know, yeah?"

Noah wanted to throw his arms around Josh's toned, tanned body and lose himself in the heavenly scent of his musky eau de toilette. He didn't. That might be a bit gay. So instead he just said, "Thank you *so very* much, I'm forever in your debt, Josh," and did a little curtsy.

"Good man. Could you get me a bacon butty from the canteen while I go and have a quick fag?"

"Oh. Um, sure."

"You're my main man. I like you!"

"I like you too!" Noah beamed. "Do you want ketchup?"

"Brown sauce, bro. Brown sauce. And make sure they cook it crispy, in a white bap."

"Brown sauce, white bap, crispy!" Noah nodded eagerly. "I won't be long!" and he scampered off in the direction of the canteen with a bounce in his step. He didn't mind being Josh's bitch on this occasion. Josh had just saved him from being mauled by Kirk. Getting him a bacon butty was the least Noah could do.

CHAPTER THIRTY-ONE

Thursday evening. Forty-eight hours since Eric was last seen, but no one seemed particularly worried. The word on the street was that he'd either run away, sick to death of his chaotic home life, or he'd had to go into hiding because he'd blackmailed the wrong person with something he'd found on them. Noah still hated Eric's guts for the position he'd put Noah in, but even so, he couldn't help but feel a bit sorry for Eric. Literally *no one* seemed to care.

He knocked on Gran's bedroom door, as the sound of Madonna's "Like a Virgin" blared from within. He hoped she was in the mood – and had the clarity of mind – for a sensible chat, peppered with sound advice.

"Piss off!" she shouted from the other side.

"It's Noah, Gran!"

There was a moment's pause before the music was turned off and the door opened. His gran's face was a picture of disappointment.

"You. I want words with you!" she said, pulling him into the room by his school tie and slamming the door shut again.

"Gran, can I just say—"

"What did I tell you?! Keep it in your pants, that's what!"

"Gran, I—"

"And what have you done?! You've not only gone and got the damn thing out of your pants, you've gone and put it straight into the first available girl, and now look!"

"I didn't, though!" How the hell did she know about this?

"Peanut, if I had a shiny pound coin for every boy who's ever claimed they didn't do anything when a girl gets pregnant, I would not be held prisoner in a council-run care home. I would be luxuriating somewhere *private*."

"Gran, I absolutely one-hundred-per-cent guarantee to you that I kept it in my pants!"

"Then why is your hanky-panky with this girl all over social media?"

Bloody hell. What had Jess done? "What's it say, Gran?"

"Pictures, Peanut! Tagged with you and her! Some scan of a baby. And phrases like 'Me and Bae' and 'Someone's gonna be a daddy!' Explain yourself!"

Noah sighed. Jess wasn't going to give up easily. "Look, I took your advice and said nothing, including when this rumour that I might have ... *done things* with Jess got started. But then they all *assumed*. And it seemed like an OK thing for them to assume because it made me popular, so I didn't deny it. But I didn't say it was true either! So now it looks like I really did do it, and to make it worse, I gave her a score for..."

"A score for what?"

Awkward. "For when ... like, when a man and woman love each other very much and they get very close and then the man gets very excited and puts a *seed* inside the woman so they can grow a baby? Like a score for that."

"Jesus wept."

Noah flopped down on the single bed and sat on something uncomfortable. He reached under the thin duvet and pulled out Gran's passport and a roll of euros. "What the hell's this?" he asked.

"Nothing," she said, whipping them off him, throwing them in one of her drawers and slamming it shut. "Er, what else is happening? How's Harry? Any news on your father?"

"Whatever you're up to, it's not going to work and it's not a good idea."

"No idea what you mean."

Noah sighed. "OK, so Dad's living in Spain and he's been writing letters the whole time that Mum has been keeping from me."

Gran stared at him, dumbfounded. "So he really is in Spain?"

"What do you mean *'really'*? That suggests you—"

"I tell you when I get my hands on him!"

"Who told you he was in Spain?"

Gran stared at him. "What are we talking about again?"

Noah bit the inside of his lip and weighed her up. "Also, I apparently have some sort of secret sibling. Who's in my year at school. And I want answers, so ... over to you, Gran."

She looked at him blankly. "Who's got a secret sibling?"

"Me!"

"And who is it?"

"Well, that's the point! I don't know!"

"And he's in Spain?"

"No, Little Fobbing!"

"Who is?"

"My... Oh, forget it. It's fine. I'll find out."

"What would Jessica Fletcher do?" Gran said.

Noah sighed and crossed his arms. He'd just told her that her missing son was alive and that he had a secret half-sibling – and she didn't seem remotely surprised or, indeed, interested in discussing it further. Was that her condition? Was that the dementia? Or was it because she already knew?

But if she already knew, then who had told her?

One thing was certain: he couldn't really press the

point. In between the lucid moments, she spent a lot of time confused. It wasn't fair to make matters worse, get stressed and frustrated, and make her feel bad.

Besides, she'd already let one very important clue slip, without even realizing it.

"How's Harry? You sorted things out?"

"Fine. He's fine." Noah nodded, looking directly at her because it was DEFINITELY ALL TRUE.

"What's happened?" she asked, grimly.

"OK, well, he thinks I'm seriously awful as a human being, and it's all over and we're no longer friends."

She shook her head. "You bloody idiot."

Noah looked down at the floor. He missed Harry. What was Harry doing right now? he wondered. Was he laughing about Noah's problems with his new best mate? No, he wouldn't be. Harry just wasn't that sort of boy. He didn't take delight in other people's misfortune. He wasn't mean. And that made Noah all the more sad.

"Do not let him get away," Gran said. "He's special. And you know it."

"Sometimes people drift apart, though."

"Not people like you and Harry. You can get over this. You have to."

"Why?"

"Because in one lifetime, you won't find anyone else like him. This is wisdom, Noah, from a wizened old hag who has seen it all. You know I'm right. I always am."

He felt his heart get heavy again. Of course she was right. But it was too late now.

He slouched against the pillows and stared out of the window, engulfed by the enormity of everything that needed sorting out.

"This girl," said Gran, "the one you got pregnant?"

"Except I didn't," Noah said, turning back to face her.

"But *someone* did."

"Yeah, her ex-boyfriend, Kirk."

"So, all you need is some proof that she and Kirk –" Gran winked at him "– *you know.*"

The pieces in his mind started connecting.

How could he have been so stupid?

He'd been totally hung up about his stupid kiss with Harry being on the memory stick. *But what else was on it?*

The other events of the party that night.

Events that might save Noah's arse.

His heart was racing like it might explode out of his chest. He jumped up. "Gran, I have to go. There's something I gotta do!"

CHAPTER
THIRTY-TWO

Breathless, Noah flopped down in front of the computer in his bedroom, fished the little memory stick out of its hiding place and rammed it in the USB port. The memory stick contained footage of everything that happened in that bedroom the night of the party. Who knew what shenanigans went on there, who else Eric had been blackmailing?

Jess Jackson and her boyfriend, Kirk, were at the party. If they got up to anything in that room, Noah would be exonerated and this whole pregnancy thing would be shown for the sham it was.

He didn't want people talking about him, not like that. *He didn't want people to think he was like his father.* His life was going to be different. And Jess Jackson was not going to derail everything.

The stick finally showed up in the menu bar. A double click revealed its contents, and he double clicked again on the video file. It began to play.

Close-up on Eric. His grinning face as he set the camcorder up. Looked straight down the lens. "Project Adios is go..."

Noah felt a cold tingle down his spine. What the hell was "Project Adios"? Eric *was* up to something. Something bad enough for Eric to need to disappear. Or bad enough to have someone else want to disappear him.

The frame shook randomly as Eric clambered up on to a chair and positioned the video camera on top of the wardrobe, leaving a wide shot of an empty bedroom.

Noah skipped through the footage until the first unwitting occupants entered the room. Three lads he recognized from Year Nine. One pulled a bottle of something from his bag that they clearly didn't want to share with the people downstairs. They took turns chugging it whilst talking about whom they wanted to get with...

Noah continued skipping through...

Ella and James. They almost fell into the room. Drunk. Lustful. She pushed him back against the door and they started tonguing, greedy hands all over each other...

Not what he needed...

Four girls gossiping. Giggling. Running out...

Harry.

Stormed in. Punched the wardrobe so the camera

shook. Connor came in and tried to talk to him. Harry ripped the head off a Barbie...

Noah didn't need to be reminded of what happened next, and in high definition. He skipped through until the room was empty again.

A boy ran in. Frantic. Opened the window and was sick out of it. Wiped his mouth and went back out...

Jess Jackson...

Oh please ... oh please... Noah resumed normal play.

Jess Jackson ... led a male figure into the room...

Oh please... Please... YES! OH YES! Kirk. Her "boyfriend" Kirk...

Kirk wedged a chair against the bedroom door. Like something out of a film. Who knew that really worked? And then...

They were kissing ... and then...

And then something strange happened. Jess stopped him. Sat him down on the bed. "Kirk? I've got something to tell you."

"What's up, babe?"

And she took a deep breath...

"I'm pregnant. You're going to be a dad."

And she did this hopeful little smile, like she wasn't exactly sure how he'd feel, but maybe he'd get over the shock and be OK with it.

And he just stared at her.

And he breathed.

And he stared.

And breathed.

And then he shook his head and walked out without looking at her, like it was all too much.

She was left sitting on the bed. Alone.

Noah pressed pause and took it in.

She'd admitted it on video. Noah was a free man.

He felt a bit sorry for her, but also, WHAT THE HELL?! How dare she try to ruin Noah's life, just because hers was a shambles? Maybe if she'd been a bit more honest and kind, Noah would have taken pity on her. Organized a charity event to raise money for the baby or whatever. Instead, she'd made an enemy of him. An enemy with all the proof he needed to TAKE THE LYING BITCH DOWN!

Laughing, he ran down the stairs in joyous abandon and flew into the lounge, completely forgetting it was Thursday evening and he was meant to be staying in his room because − "Mum! Mum! Guess what?! It isn't mine! The baby isn't..."

He stopped dead. Looking back at him in frozen horror was his mother and...

Noah gulped. *Mystery Man*.

But...

Noah blinked as he tried to comprehend it.

"You?" he finally muttered, not wanting to believe it. "What are *you* doing here?!"

CHAPTER THIRTY-THREE

The image that would forever be etched on Noah's mind from the incident was of a male figure whose shirt was riding up, revealing his boxers as he leaned over Noah's mother on the sofa. A pair of boxers that had a distinctive waistband... One that bore the slogan "100% British Beef".

"Josh?" He was barely able to think, let alone speak. *"Josh Lewis?!"*

"Hiya, mate!" Josh replied, like this was all a pleasant surprise.

"Mum?!"

"Noah, I gave you express instructions not to barge in here unannounced when I'm entertaining – and now look!"

"Mum! Are you and Josh... You and Josh... You and Josh are... Oh God, you're... You and Josh are..."

Shaking, he turned and ran out the front door as he heard Josh tell his mum, "Just stay there, I'll sort it, man to man!"

Noah hotfooted it down the street, not knowing where he was going, but knowing there was no way he was staying in that house ever again.

"Noah? Mate? Bro?!" Josh called, running up behind him.

Screw that. Noah sped up even more. But it didn't take long for a guy who played sport *at county level* to catch up with an asthmatic kid who normally avoided PE with a note from his mum.

"Noah? Mate! Wait up!" Josh jogged up, skipping round in front of him to block his feeble, wheezy path. "Don't run off, mate! We gotta talk this out!"

Noah glared at him, furious. How dare Josh make this sound like *Noah* was the one who was behaving unreasonably? Noah's breathing was short and erratic. The blood coursed through his veins, adrenaline pumping, anger rising. Josh was gonna get it, and he was gonna get it good!

"You," Noah snarled, voice quivering with unmitigated hatred, "are an *arse cactus*!"

Noah let his words hit home, the full force of them doubtless cutting Josh like a really big sharp knife. No, a *spear*. A bloody great *spear*. No, a machine gun. A great, big, nasty machine gun, pummelling his pathetic, vein body with his powerful *word* bullets.

Josh gave him an unimpressed look. "Bro, *really*?! That the best you can do?"

"This is, basically, *the worst* thing one guy can do to another guy. Have sex with his mum! His friend's own mum! All this time… Has it been you, all this time?"

Josh screwed his face up. "Just a couple of months, bro, no biggie."

"No 'biggie'? It's … illegal!" Noah squealed.

"Mate, it's not. I'm nineteen! I can do what I like. Shag who I want." Noah felt bile rise into his mouth. "Even teachers at school, if I want, it's all basically cool with the cops!"

"POLICE! It's the POLICE! This isn't sodding AMERICA!" Noah screamed.

"All right! *Police!* Whatevs, bro. Don't sweat the small stuff."

"How did you meet?" Noah demanded. He wanted to know. He wanted to know everything.

"Down the pub." Josh shrugged. "She sang a Beyoncé song at the karaoke. Man, it sucked, but you gotta give her points for trying." He gave a little chuckle, like he remembered it fondly. "Told her she shouldn't give up the day job and she laughed and bought me a drink."

Noah looked up at Josh with tears in his eyes. "I thought you liked me. I thought we were mates."

"Yeah…"

"No." Noah shook his head as he pieced it together. The

"'chance" encounter in the canteen. The quick friendship. "No, someone like you would never be friends with someone like me. It was never about me and Jess. Mum put you up to it, didn't she? She asked you to be my friend, didn't she?"

"Mate, she was worried that you… She was just worried that you were … kinda unpopular and maybe … you know, acting a bit weird and stuff, so, you know…"

He stared at Josh. "I'm not a charity case."

"Hey, *totally*, I know! And once we got chatting, well, I saw that you're a pretty cool guy…"

"We both know that's not true," Noah muttered. *"Why?* Why would you want to do stuff with my mum?"

"What can I say?" Josh shrugged. "We have a connection. And sure, she's a bit older, and some people might think that's weird, but attraction doesn't always fit into society's expectations, you get me?"

Noah looked up at him sharply. Josh didn't care what other people thought, he just did what made him happy. For all the other idiotic things Josh had said, he sure picked his moment to come out with the one thing that maybe Noah could just a little bit understand.

But he wasn't going to give him any credit for that. That "older" woman was his *mum*.

And how could *she* do this to him? What the hell was wrong with her? She was *forty*. Why couldn't she date some other sad fucker her own age? God forbid Noah should have a *normal* family life with *normal* parents who actually cared about him. He clenched his fists as a flash of heat surged through his body. "Tell Mum I hope she has a nice life!" he said.

"Mate!"

"No! Screw you! *And everyone knows the only reason you're still at school is because you failed all your A levels and couldn't even get into London Met to do Leisure Management!*" he screamed, turning and walking, *really fast*, away from Josh and away from everything.

On autopilot, he instinctively set off for Harry's house ... stopping himself two streets later when he realized: no way Harry would talk to him, not after their fight that afternoon. He stood in the middle of the pavement. No, Harry would just make out this was somehow all Noah's fault, presumably for not being gay enough.

He couldn't go to Gran's, they wouldn't let him in after hours.

The tears bubbled up inside him. He had nowhere to go. Nowhere except ... *unless...*

She'd said he could visit any time. She'd said she wasn't even starting at her new school until next week. So, maybe ... Sophie?

There was a bus that stopped along the main road on its way to Grimsby. If he was quick, he could catch the next one. From Grimsby, he could get a train to Milton Keynes. Sophie would understand. She was nice and kind and she would take pity on him and might even give him cuddles and stuff. She would be everything Harry was no longer willing to be. He would definitely have enough money to get there. Beyond that, in a longer-term sense, he didn't know and didn't really care. All that mattered now was that he got the hell out of Little Fobbing, with its slutty mothers, duplicitous "friends" and lying girls who made out you'd got them pregnant when you actually hadn't.

Up the road he saw headlights loom into view as an ancient double-decker wheezed its way along, holding up a queue of infuriated cars behind. Noah had never seen a more beautiful and welcome sight. That old bus represented his freedom. His fresh start. His escape.

The bus pulled into the stop, releasing a gigantic fart of diesel fumes as it shuddered to a halt and opened its doors. Noah swallowed hard. This was it. He was really going to do it. He held his three-pound fare tightly in his sweaty hand and waited patiently as a lone passenger disembarked. He took a deep breath and lifted his foot, ready to embark on the first stage of his new life, and—

"Noah?"

He spun round. It was the lone passenger, standing on the pavement, looking at him. A man in a baseball cap and overcoat with the collar turned up, carrying a small sports holdall.

The cogs in Noah's brain took a moment or two to turn.

A Google search…
An apartment complex…
A Ralph Lauren sweater…
And then his eyes nearly popped out.
"Dad?!"

CHAPTER
THIRTY-FOUR

"Are you getting on, mate??" shouted the driver as Noah stood gawping, half on the bus and half on the pavement.

He was totally confused. "Dad? What you doing here?"

"Thought I'd come back, didn't I? Thought I'd come see my boy!" his dad said, glancing up and down the road before settling his eyes on Noah and smiling.

"Mate? Off or on?" shouted the driver. "We've all got homes to get to!"

"You off somewhere?" his dad asked.

"I... I'm not sure, I..." Was this even real? What the hell was going on?

"I think you should get off," his dad suggested, pulling Noah away as the pneumatic doors started to close on him.

Their weedy teenage impediment removed, the doors snapped shut and the bus pulled away, leaving a plume of noxious exhaust gas in its wake. Noah wiped the soot from his eyes and looked at the slightly dishevelled bloke standing in front of him.

Dad.

But he looked nothing like the photographs Noah had seen on Google. Where was the tan? The bright white teeth? The confident swagger?

This "top businessman" apparently liked to wear baggy Adidas sweat tops with trackie bottoms – and quite evidently not because he'd just been to the gym. His face was pale and drawn, with a heavy smoker's yellowish cast to it. There were bags under his eyes and a dark shadow of unkempt stubble. And, most disappointing of all, he was shorter than Noah remembered. If these were the genes he was working from, Noah knew there really was little hope for a growth spurt.

It was a bit disappointing, yes, but still, his dad was here! Should Noah hug him or something? He had seen television programmes where long-lost relatives were reunited and they always hugged and cried and stuff.

But Noah didn't feel like hugging this man. He didn't know what he felt.

And then he did feel something, and it surged up inside him. It was a mad destructive rage, the like of which he'd never felt before, and he was screaming, "Fuck you, fuck you, fuck you, fuck you!" and pummelling his feeble fists into any and every part of his dad he could find, to hurt him just a fraction of what Noah had been feeling all this time.

And when it was over, Noah staggered back to the little bench, collapsed down and started crying, huge gulps of engulfing tears that made it sound like he was choking to death.

"Nice to see you too, mate," his dad said, coming to sit next to him.

"Where have you been all this time?!"

"Spain."

"I know that!"

"Why ask me, then?"

Noah urgently wiped his streaming eyes with the palms of his hands, doing his best to man up, only for his dad to gently put his arm around him and the uncontrollable tears to start all over again.

He fought valiantly against the gentle pressure being applied to draw him closer, unwilling to so easily give in and make it seem like everything was cool. He wanted his dad to know he was angry. He wanted him to know he hated him, because everything that was bad about life, everything that was wrong, it was *all* his fault.

But Noah's resistance broke down far quicker than he would have liked, and it wasn't long before he was nestled into his dad's shoulder, sobs gently subsiding with each whiff of comforting aftershave.

"I'm sorry, Noah. I'll make it up to you. I'll make it all up to you."

"It's OK." It really wasn't. It was going to take a lot more than a single apology to make up for *six years* of misery.

"I promise you, everything I've done ... it's only because I wanted to make life better for you. That's all I've ever wanted."

"I know." He really didn't. What sort of man just abandoned his kid, with no explanation?

"We've got a lot of catching up to do."

"You've no idea," Noah said, grimly, sniffing to clear his nose. He pulled away and sat more upright, remembering he was nearly sixteen, not six, and cuddling up to your dad wasn't really the done thing any more, even if you hadn't seen him for six years.

Catching up. How about we start with a little *truth*, then? "Tell me about my secret sibling." Noah stared his dad down and crossed his arms. His father owed him that much, at least.

"Your *what?*"

"Come on, who is it?"

"...I've no idea what you're talking about!" His dad shrugged. "Is that some crap your mother fed you?"

Noah dropped his eyes. *It possibly was.* Another lie, designed to cover her back. She'd probably spent the money on herself and her inappropriate choice of *men.* She'd probably used it to buy stupid boxer shorts that said "100%

British Beef", whilst poor old Noah had to make do with virtually wearing bin liners and old sacks, bashing out essays on an old-fashioned typewriter ... practically... OK, a PC from three years ago, which was basically the same thing. God! Noah had been so *gullible*.

Probably sensing his realization, his dad kindly changed the subject. "Did I just catch you running away from home?"

"Oh. No. No... I was just... I just fancied a trip out."

His dad grinned. "Mum pissing you off, then?"

"Mum is ... she is a very bad person ... a liar and a... She said you were *dead*, by the way ... and I hate her and never want to see her again."

"But you've been writing me letters every other month."

"What?" Noah spluttered.

"Letters. From you... Or..."

They both realized at the same time. "Unbelievable!" they chorused.

"Mum's been pretending to be me!" Noah squealed.

"I should have known. Of course you didn't demand to take Food Technology as an extra GCSE option."

"No, that's true."

"Oh. Oh well. But the bit where you say you're taking an active interest in your mum's career and do I think she should diversify into doing Elvis, Michael Jackson and Eminem?"

"What? No, that's not something... *As if?!*" Noah spluttered. "And how would that even work? Ridiculous!"

"Can't believe it. Can't believe I fell for it."

"I wrote you a real letter, though! The other day. I guess you didn't get it yet..."

"Must have arrived after I left."

"Why don't we both go to live in Spain?!" Noah said, suddenly having the best idea he'd ever had. Everything that was wrong here would be better there. He didn't have any best mate at all now, so he could make a new Spanish best mate. Called *Javier*, maybe. He would be tanned and toned, and have carefree, tousled hair. It would be lovely. "Take me with you when you go back!"

"That's a..."

"Come on! It's an ace idea!"

"That's a... It's not that simple. There's school ... and shit."

"Shit" just about summed it up. "Have you got a pool?"

"...Yeah."

"Amazing. And it's hot? All year round?"

"Not all year. There are still seasons, like anywhere."

"Take me!"

"We'll talk about it, OK?"

"Yeah, all right." Noah was fine with that. It wasn't a no, it was a "talk about", which was full of possibility. "Where are you staying?"

"Well, I was thinking..."

"Not at home. You can't stay at home."

"Oh."

"It's just... Mum and stuff... It wouldn't be good."

"She seeing someone?"

Noah grimaced.

"Who is he?" his dad smiled.

"No one. It's not serious. Just some no-hoper, really. I've only met him once or twice. Thinks he's some sort of *Adonis* or something, but he's just an idiot." Noah shrugged it off like it meant nothing, but in his head he was APPLYING A BLACK AND DECKER SANDER TO JOSH'S BALLS.

"Well, I can't say I blame your mum. We didn't leave on great terms, and it has been a long while. I haven't got anywhere else to go, though."

"What about the bed and breakfast?"

"I don't wanna spend money on that!"

"Have you got any mates you could crash with?"

"Been away six years, Noah! Doubt any of them will remember me now!"

Something about this didn't seem right. Noah couldn't quite put his finger on it, but it felt wrong. "You're not in trouble, are you?"

"'Course not! Jeez!"

"Huh. OK."

"Just thought, be good to spend some time with my boy. Be there for him, for once."

Noah nodded. *Maybe.* He thought through the highly limited options. "The shed? You could stay in the shed?"

CHAPTER
THIRTY-FIVE

Noah gave his dad strict instructions to quietly sneak into the back garden and wait inside the dilapidated and rotting wooden structure that could, at a stretch, be labelled a "shed". Then, after checking his father had reached safety across the garden, Noah steeled himself and confidently opened the front door to the house.

"I've returned," Noah declared, walking into the lounge and massively swallowing his pride.

"Noah, I'm glad you've seen sense," his mum said, putting down her glass of wine (wine!) and balancing her cigarette (that his father had doubtless paid for!) on the side of the ashtray. "Josh and I would *love* to talk this through with you."

"No need!" he chirped. "I've already thought about

everything and it's all cool with me!" He walked straight through to the kitchen, turned and silently flicked through a rapid sequence of obscene gestures at the door that had closed behind him. She clearly hadn't even called the police, even though her emotionally distraught fifteen-year-old son had just run away and could have been in terrible danger. "You do as you please, it's no bother to me!" he sang, quickly setting about his task.

"Sweetheart," she said, appearing in the kitchen like she was all sweetness and light, "I'm glad we can have a grown-up conversation about this."

"Me too!" *It's just acting, Noah! It's revision for GCSE Drama, that's all.*

"And you mean it? You're really OK with all this?"

Noah nodded. "Absolutely." *You lying, evil MOTHER FROM HELL!*

"I'm so proud of you for being so mature about this."

"Uh-huh!" *Unlike you!*

"Thank you, Noah," she said, pecking him on the cheek. "This means so much, and I promise you..." She leaned in and whispered too loudly in his ear. "I promise you that you will always come first. You'll always be my number-one man!" She winked and sauntered back through to the lounge.

Good. She had fallen for Noah's acting skills and was clueless as to his real motives. She had no way of knowing that concealed in his pocket were two custard creams and five rich tea biscuits, procured by stealth from the plate of biscuits – *where in this godforsaken house is that woman hiding the stash?!* – she had laid out on the counter, presumably for *Josh*. The plan was very much in motion.

"Mum? I'm just popping outside to get some air…"

But she was already giggling with Josh in the lounge and didn't register he was talking. Suited him just *fine*.

"It'll keep you going for a bit," Noah explained, as he pulled the broken biscuits from his pockets.

"Cuppa would be great too," his dad said, looking up from his open holdall as he pulled out a jumper.

"Would it?"

"And if there's any leftovers from dinner…?"

"Yeah, OK." He hadn't bargained on his dad being so demanding. Parents weren't meant to be needy and ask things of their kids until they were really old. "Do you need a blanket or something too?"

"Yeah. Couple of blankets and a pillow. I'll need other stuff too."

"What sort of stuff?!"

"I've only got the basics with me, Noah…"

Noah thought that seemed odd. Why embark on travel without the stuff you needed?

"They lost me luggage at the airport, didn't they?" his dad said, looking right at him.

"Oh. That's *terrible*." A sense of dread started creeping

through his body. Direct eye contact like that meant LYING. He knew because he did it himself.

"Yeah ... probably ended up in Timbuktu, or God knows where!"

Noah nodded. *Timbuktu.* The precise place Noah had thought of when he first lied about his dad being kidnapped. "What do you need, then?"

"A mobile. Pay as you go. With thirty quid credit on it."

Noah pointed at his dad's iPhone in his open bag. "But you've got a phone."

"Sure. But I like to keep one for business, one for pleasure."

Great, Noah thought. Just like a drug dealer or some other shady underworld guttersnipe.

"And I'll need some more clothes," his dad continued. "Only got enough for a couple of days with me. Maybe some stuff to wash with, a razor, that sort of thing."

"Where are you going to wash, though? It's not a good idea to come in the house!"

"I'll sneak in whenever your mum goes out. Just leave me a key."

This was turning into a nightmare. "OK. Have you got some..."

"What?"

"Money?" Noah asked, holding out his hand.

His dad smiled quizzically like the request was the most bizarre thing in the world. "Ah, matey, I wasn't gonna

292

say, but I got pickpocketed, didn't I? In Madrid, on the way to the airport, I reckon. Didn't have my wits about me, see? Thinking about other stuff. Thinking about seeing you! My silly fault for being so excited to see my boy!"

"Oh, so..." Noah felt his throat tighten. He knew bullshit when he heard it, and this was grade A.

"They took the lot!"

"Oh. Then what..."

"Clever, resourceful lad like you – you can get some money, can't you?"

Noah hesitated. This felt wrong. He'd thought he would be comforted by his dad's return. But this wasn't right. And he'd had enough of lies.

"Dad, will you just tell me the truth? Don't you owe me that, at least?"

His dad sighed. "Sure. Sure, you're right. I owe you that, at least." He flopped down on the floor and leaned against the side of the shed, whilst Noah remained standing in the doorway, watching for any little body-language giveaways to suggest this was anything less than honest. "A few things didn't go well in Spain. Some deals went bad. I owe some money over there. So ... I've had to come back here."

"And you had to leave in a hurry?"

"Yeah, well, some people get pretty mad when you owe them. Like, lose-your-kneecaps mad. So, it's the best thing."

"Well, that's just *brilliant, Dad*," Noah said. "And what about the people you owe money to here?"

"They'll get it."

"How?!"

His dad shrugged. "Give me a chance, I only just got back here! I've got contacts. Cut some deals, duck and dive, pull in some moolah. You'll see."

Noah looked away. He was sounding like Eric. And look where that had led. Conmen always ended up disappearing.

"What would be *great*, though, Dad, is... See, the situation is that I didn't know where you'd been all these years, and so what I told people was that you'd been held hostage. By pirates. Now, I took a lot of stick for that. Lots of people called me crazy. So I was thinking, maybe you could tell everyone it was true?"

"You want me to say I've returned from being kidnapped?"

"Basically, yes."

"Mate, I need to be keeping a low profile right now. Get me? I don't need no media attention. People chatting."

"I see."

"Else there'll be a queue of people at the door demanding their cash back, right now. And I ain't got it *right now*."

"No, of course, silly me. I just thought... It's fine. *Fine*."

His dad looked him up and down – a sensation that

made Noah feel like a second-hand car that his dad was thinking of buying. "You've not turned out too shabby," he smiled.

"Oh, *thanks*," Noah said, furious that was the best he could manage.

"I guess you might grow another inch or two."

"Or *five*, hopefully."

"You seeing anyone? A special friend?"

Noah flicked his eyes down to the floor. "Special friend"? Was that his dad's way of suggesting Noah might be gay? "No," he muttered. "But I have been hanging out with this *girl* called Sophie. Yeah, she's cool and everything, but we'll see, we'll see."

His dad smiled. "Sounds good."

"Yeah, well, I think she'd like to take things to the next level, but I'm like, Whoa! Hold on a sec! What's the rush? You know?"

His dad nodded. "I guess."

"She lives in Milton Keynes now, so it's this complicated long-distance relationship thing, but absence makes the heart grow fonder, and she is pretty damn *fond* of me, let me tell you. Very *fond*. She is *fond*."

"Your mum mentioned some guy called Harry in her letters."

Noah's eyes widened. "*What* did she mention about Harry?"

"Just that you were good mates."

"Well, that news is out of date," Noah said.

His dad nodded again. "Anyway, can you get me the stuff I need?"

"Yes! Fine. I'll ... I'll do your bidding."

"Tonight would be good."

"Now? You want all these things *now*?" Noah ran his hands through his hair. "You do know this is Little Fobbing? Everything closes at six. What do you think I'm going to do?"

"Borrow from a mate?" His dad shrugged.

A hysterical little laugh bubbled up inside Noah. A mate? Like who? The only mate he could *ever* trust this information about his dad coming back with would be Harry. The only mate he *wanted* to talk to about any of this was Harry. Everything, every *little* thing, came back to Harry. But Harry wasn't...

Gran's words bounced around his head: *In one lifetime, you won't find anyone else like him.*

Harry wasn't...

Do not let him get away!

But he couldn't...

You can get over this. You have to.

Yes. He did. He *had* to.

"I'll see what I can do," Noah said, backing out of the shed, his mind made up.

CHAPTER THIRTY-SIX

Noah hurried along the pavement towards Harry's house, not wanting to waste another second not being friends. He needed Harry. He needed his kindness and his humour and his way of making Noah feel like nobody else mattered, just them. Only them. And when the rest of world had proved themselves to be liars – unreliable, useless or just plain *criminal* – he needed Harry in his life. And that's just what he was going to tell him.

"Oi, dickhead!" said the voice.

Noah looked up and came face-to-face with Kirk. *Shit.* He desperately looked around. *No one.*

"Haven't got your boyfriend to rescue you now, have you?" Kirk said.

"Josh is not my boyfriend—"

"You're gonna die this time. You know that, right?"

Noah crossed his arms and cocked his head to the side. "No, I don't think so. I don't think so one little bit!"

"What?!" Kirk snorted.

"I know about you and Jess. She told you she was pregnant at Melissa's party. *She told you.* The baby is yours. I've got it all on video, thanks to Eric Smith." He felt about ten feet tall, towering over Kirk with his brilliant revelation. "The baby is yours!" he said again, laughing. "*You're the daddy!*"

"No, *you're* the daddy!" Kirk said, jabbing a finger at Noah's chest.

"*You're the daddy!*"

"I'm *not* the daddy!"

Noah gave a mocking laugh. "Did you honestly both think you'd get away with this? You're an idiot. Now, if you'll excuse me—"

"No," Kirk said, ashen-faced. "You're wrong, Noah."

"No, I'm not," Noah said, and then, since he was feeling particularly powerful, he added, "You *cock cheese.*"

Kirk grabbed him by the throat and hurled him up against the wall. "What did you call me?"

"No!" Noah wailed. "No! I'm sorry! I didn't say anything!"

"I want that video. You give it to me."

"But it's evidence! In court, it's what I'll use to prove my innocence!"

"Give it!" Kirk tightened his grip on Noah's throat.

"Aarrggh – huh – that video … aaah … s'mine… and no way … huh!"

Kirk let go and dropped him down.

Noah brushed himself off. "You can kill me if you want," he said. "But I'm not giving you that video."

"You will!"

"No! No, I won't. And if you even try to make me, I'll go straight to the police! I'll tell them everything! And then they'll probably think you killed Eric! He's missing, after all – well, what if he's dead? What if he's dead and you killed him because he knew secrets about you?"

"Eric? You think… Oh, shit." Kirk considered him. "You are such a bitch squealer."

"And proud of it!" said Noah.

"Fine. Then I'll tell you why that video doesn't show jack shit. Why it won't help you showing it to anyone. And then you promise me that you won't do anything with it, 'cause most people don't know about this, and no one's gonna know. Yeah?"

Noah shrugged. "What do you mean?"

Kirk shook his head. "I had cancer when I was a kid."

Noah squinted at him. *This again.* What had this got to do with anything?

Kirk shuffled towards him, pulled out his phone, tapped away at the screen, then handed it to Noah: a Google page, about how certain kinds of cancer treatment, when administered to young men and boys, can leave them unable to conceive children later in life.

Noah scrolled through the article, realizing with horror that if this was true, if this was what happened to Kirk, there was *no way* he could be the father. He looked back up at Kirk, who was kicking his feet against the brick wall. "So, you mean..."

Kirk nodded. "I can't have kids. Jess didn't know that. No one knew that. It's not the sort of thing you spread about, right?"

Noah stared at him, breathing hard.

"So when she told me she was pregnant that night, I knew the kid couldn't be mine. I knew she'd cheated on me. And worse, I knew she was prepared to lie about it."

"Then ... who's the father?" Noah said, trying to swallow back the sour taste in his mouth. "It's not me, I promise you that!" He wanted to run, hide, get far away from there. He'd thought he had the solution to his problems – but no. That memory stick had brought nothing but trouble.

Kirk shrugged. "I dunno. But if that video gets out, I'm gonna have to tell everyone why it ain't true. And I don't want everyone round here knowing my business like that. You with me?"

"I'm sorry."

"Don't worry about it. I'm used to being dealt the shitty cards. Had them all my life." He looked up at Noah. "But you go back on your word, you die. I'm not messin' about. *You die.*" Then Kirk seemed to remember himself. "Oh, um, but that doesn't mean I killed Eric or anything like that. I didn't."

Noah nodded and Kirk trudged off down the road, while he remained frozen to the spot. So that was it, then. Noah was screwed. He'd got the clues all wrong, misinterpreted them...

He needed someone on his side.

He needed someone to help.

Harry was his only hope.

CHAPTER THIRTY—SEVEN

Noah kept his finger on the doorbell until Harry's mum opened the door. He'd seen people do that on TV. It was the best way of getting a speedy response. It said, *This is urgent.*

"Hello, Noah," she said, opening the door a crack and peering round.

"Is Harry in?"

"Well, yes, but—"

Noah slithered through the gap in the door. "I need to see him." He hurried through the hall, pulling his trainers off as he went – Harry's mum had a thing about shoes in the house – up the stairs, across the landing, a polite knock on Harry's door and a three-second wait just in case he was, *you know*, and then opened the door, walked in and—

"Noah!" Harry said, wide-eyed. "Me and Connor were just doing the history homework."

Connor gave a half-hearted wave from where he sat, next to Harry on the edge of the bed.

"I should've phoned, but I ... didn't," Noah explained.

"Sure," Harry agreed.

Noah turned to Connor. Harry's new best friend situation was really inconvenient. Especially now that Noah didn't have a friend at all. "Um, look, sorry and all, but this is *really* important and I *really* need to talk to Harry, you know, *alone*. No offence."

Connor held his hands up. "I'm out. Catch you later, Harry." He collected his school bag, turned to Noah and gave him a nod. Noah nodded back, and Connor left, closing the door gently behind him.

"What's up?" Harry said.

"So, I found out who my mum is seeing, and it's Josh Lewis."

"Ouch," Harry said, flinching.

"And I found out I'm still in the frame with Jess Jackson because Kirk was my prime paternity suspect and it turns out he... Well, there's solid evidence he's not the father."

"Uh-huh..."

"And Dad's come back."

Harry looked at him agog. "He's—?"

"He's come back, Harry. He's here. Well, he's in the shed. But, yeah. He's here."

Harry took a step towards him. "And ... well, how do you feel?"

Trust Harry to cut to what mattered. Where other people might be full of questions about the whys and wherefores, the "where's he beens" and the "what's he been doings", what Harry cared about was how Noah felt.

And Noah didn't really know how he felt. The tears that suddenly bubbled up out of him were ones of relief, confusion, anger and feeling totally overwhelmed by every single thing in his life right now.

"Come on, it's OK," Harry said, standing up and putting his arms around him.

It felt so good. Harry holding him like that. The bad words between them melting away. Everything could be fine. Everything OK. He wiped his eyes with his palms, blinked away the tears, looked at the bed where Harry had just got up from. "Where are all your books?"

"What?"

"You said you'd just been doing history with Connor, but ... no books."

"We'd finished. We'd packed up."

Noah broke away and stepped back. "You're in the other top set for history. Connor's set two. You don't even have history together, so..."

Harry sighed. "Trust you to know what bloody *set* everyone is in for any subject." He shook his head. "Look, I know we've been through some *stuff* this last week, and I did spring things on you that I maybe shouldn't have done, and for that I'm sorry, but also, you've done stuff that maybe you're sorry about too..."

"Yeah, I am, I totally am—"

"Right, yeah. And so I hope I'm right in saying that after all that, and after doing a lot of thinking, we still basically like each other and I think we're always going to be friends. Right?"

"Well, yes," Noah said.

"OK. So, that's fine. That's good. Because I've missed you. But you know, I'm still gay, and that's kind of part of me. And a pretty important part in some ways, you know? I suppose what I'm trying to say is, in terms of that, in terms of the gay stuff, and I think this'll be a relief to you, I guess I've kind of moved on."

The words hung in the air. "What..." Noah swallowed hard, his mouth dry. "What do you mean? How? Moved on, how?"

"Oh, come on, I think you've guessed, right? *Connor.* We like each other. We're kinda seeing each other."

Noah stared at him. "You and Connor? But I thought ... you were just mates?"

"Well, we were. That's how it started. That's how this sort of thing usually starts, isn't it? Being friends? Having stuff in common, making each other laugh."

"He makes you laugh?" Noah said, feeling his chest tighten.

"He's funny, yeah. We got chatting at Melissa's party, before I freaked out, and then ... things went from there."

Noah nodded and took a couple of shallow breaths. "OK, right. And so ... have you kissed?"

Harry snorted. "Noah, come on! Seriously?"

"No, I just wondered. Just wondered if you'd..." He felt his heart beating hard, his throat tight, strained. "Was it good? Good kiss?"

Harry took a step towards him. "If there's anything you feel like you want to say to me, Noah, anything at all, now would be a good time."

Noah stared down hard at the floor. *Focus*, he told himself. *Don't lose it.*

"Noah? *Tell me.*"

He looked up. "Nothing to tell," he said. "I'm pleased for you. I'm happy. It's a surprise, but I hope... I hope it all works out well and everything."

Harry tried to touch his arm, but Noah backed away.

"I really gotta go... You know, my dad and everything, and ... it was nice to chat, Harry. Nice to... I'm glad we're friends again because I ... I really like you. Right? I really, really do. OK? There's no one else like you, and I like you the best. OK. Bye, then."

Out the room.

Clattered down the stairs.

Grabbed shoes.

Out the front door.

Ran down street in socks.

Right turn into alleyway.

Crumpled down against fence.

"Oh, fucking hell," Noah sobbed, head in hands.

CHAPTER THIRTY-EIGHT

He didn't want to go home.

He didn't want to be anywhere near this whole shit town.

What was the point? What was really here for him? A father who owed everyone money and was basically in hiding (great role model, way to go, *Dad*); a mother who was *engaged in the most inappropriate of relations* with the dumbest – albeit most beautiful – lad in school; a girl who claimed she was having Noah's baby; and a best friend who...

Well, whatever Harry'd actually done. It was awful, anyway. Now Harry wouldn't have time for him any more. Sure, he'd *said* they would be friends, but in reality he would be busy doing boyfriend things with Connor from now on.

They would be looking through catalogues and choosing curtains together, staring at each other over Caramel Macchiatos in Starbucks, running through meadows of flowers or taking autumnal walks and kicking the leaves with their feet and not caring that it was a bit nippy because *the warm embrace of young gay love was keeping them warm.*

He'd managed to catch the last bus to Grimsby, then spent the night walking the streets, trying to keep a low profile, waiting for the first train of the morning, but now, here he was, speeding along the West Coast Main Line, eyes glazed, staring forward.

It was all fine because he wasn't gay anyway and he was going to see Sophie and maybe even propose that she should be his girlfriend and then *he* would be choosing curtains and enjoying the warm embrace of *young straight love* and everything would be BLOODY WONDERFUL.

Unless she said no, of course. Which she probably would. Because that was exactly his luck.

He glanced across the carriage, where a young man was sitting, watching videos on his mobile without headphones, legs stretched out under the table and muddy shoes resting on the seats opposite. It was everything that was wrong with society in one single human being, but Noah just turned the other way and looked blankly out of the window instead. What did it even matter? Who even cared?

He got a cab to Sophie's house. He remembered her

telling him that she wasn't starting her new school until next week, but still, he should probably have phoned. It's just he hadn't been able to. He didn't know how to explain things, where to even start. And he didn't want to bring all that baggage with him. This could be a fresh start. This could be him and her picking up where they left off, and he wanted it to be perfect and fun and easy and light. So he would act like he'd deliberately set out to surprise her. And she would be happy and glad to see him and then … well, only think about *now*. *It's only* now *that matters,* he told himself.

"Noah!" she said, a smile creeping across her face after the initial shock of seeing him on opening the door. "What a lovely surprise!"

"Surprise!"

"Yes."

"If you've got a boyfriend or anything, it doesn't matter!" He hadn't meant to say that. Not right then, anyway. He had all these things he wanted to say, but the sequence he had planned so carefully on the train had vanished.

She gave him a wry smile. "I haven't. Thanks for asking."

Awesome. "Me neither," he assured her. He wanted her to know they were both very much still single.

"Come in, then."

He grinned and followed her inside. Just seeing her,

just exchanging a few words with her – it was the best thing that had happened to him in ages. *Sophie.*

The house smelt brand new, even though Sophie's mum had been living there for a few years. The carpets were an immaculate cream. It was all very minimalist and trendy – definitely the sort of place you would see in *Ideal Home* magazine. Harry would like it here. It was just his sort of style. He'd often talked about interior design with Harry (like he was sure plenty of lads their age regularly did), and this was right up Harry's street. If they had an integrated coffee machine in the kitchen, Harry would totally go crazy.

But, of course, Harry wasn't here and this was nothing, *nothing*, to do with him.

Noah pulled his trainers off by reflex. "Nice place."

"It's starting to feel like home," she said. "Why didn't you call to let me know?"

"Sorry. Are you busy?"

"No. . ."

"Will your mum mind?"

"She's out with friends till tonight. . ."

Noah nodded. "Cool."

"So, what's the matter?"

Noah looked at her. "Nothing! Just came to see you! Just thought I'd hang out in Milton Keynes for a bit!" He did a completely unnecessary yawn and stretch. "It's nice here. Very relaxing."

Sophie crossed her arms. "Any news?"

Noah blew his cheeks out, trying to think of something that wasn't going to tip him over the edge into uncontrollable tears. "News? News, you say? Let me think … news, news, news … er, well! Here's a thing! I thought my mum was dating Mr Baxter."

Sophie's eyebrows rose. "Why?"

"Because she was dating a mysterious stranger and he started acting all concerned about me, like he cared and was my stepdad or something."

"He probably does care. You know he's gay, right?"

Noah gawped at her. "No way! Gay? Mr Baxter? So he…" Noah gasped. "He likes me? He's got a thing for teenage boys?"

Sophie rolled her eyes. "No! He obviously saw the bullying and wanted to offer support. A sympathetic ear. Someone to talk to. Now, *what's the matter?*"

"But how did Mr Baxter know I like Agatha Christie so much?"

"Noah, everyone knows that. The presentation you gave in Year Ten, in English? An entire hour of Agatha Christie, including PowerPoint slides and staged scenes from ten of the books. I'm sure he heard about it."

Noah nodded, pleased. "You think Mrs West told the rest of the staff about how impressive it was?"

"I'm sure she told all the staff, yes," Sophie said, trying not to smile.

"You know, I made the costumes myself."

"Yes. Now, *what's the matter?*"

He attempted a look of mild confusion. "Matter? Nothing's the matter!"

"Only you look wrecked and your eyes are all red, like you've been crying." She moved towards him and gently touched his upper arm. "What's up?"

He panicked as he felt his defences start melting away with her tenderness. Why did she have to be so sensitive and intuitive? He had spent the journey shutting everything terrible away behind lead-lined walls and steel doors with a billion locks. "Nothing's up!" he whimpered, his throat tightening as the tears welled up inside him. "Everything's fine... Everything's great... Life couldn't be... It..."

He collapsed into her in a wet, snotty mess of uncontrollable sobbing. *Damn it.* In spite of his best efforts to be a confident and capable *man*, of the type a typical girl or woman might find attractive, he had once again revealed himself to be a snivelling little boy. When would he learn? Now she would undoubtedly treat him like the *child* he clearly was and—

"Do you want a biscuit, Noah? Choccy biccy?"

...*Yep!* There it was!

Although, in point of fact, he was quite peckish and this sounded like a promising offer. "What sort?" He sniffed back the tears and wiped his eyes.

"KitKat?"

Yes! Not just a biscuit, but technically a full-on chocolate bar! "OK, then."

"And a nice cup of tea?"

"Have you got squash?"

"Fine. We'll have a KitKat and some squash and you can tell me all about it, OK?"

That sounded nice. He had always known it, but this just confirmed it. Sophie would clearly make an excellent girlfriend. "OK, then," he smiled. "Thanks."

By the time he'd finished the story, they had got through two KitKats and three glasses of tropical fruit squash *each*. He had told her *everything*. In a quest to get everything out in the open and just tell it like it was for once, he had omitted no detail, however gruesome. The money from his absent father, Eric's secret video, Jess Jackson's pregnancy accusation, the revelation about his secret sibling, Eric going missing, possibly *murdered*. His dad coming back but having to lie low. Josh and his mum. Kirk not being the father of the baby. It was all there. Every horrible, vile little detail.

"And you know what makes it all the worse?" He was keen to wrap it up because he needed a wee now. "That it's Little Fobbing. If I lived in London, all of this would be perfectly normal. Happens all the time in *London* because everyone there is into debauchery and general deviancy, and no one would have the energy to care about every little bit of it. But it's the fact that everyone in Little Fobbing just *loves* gossip so much. They can't wait to chat about it all and stare and point and I've just had enough, Soph. I've had enough now."

Her face was a picture of flabbergasted incomprehension. "Oh my *God...*" she muttered.

"Yeah," he said, glad she appreciated the appalling horror of his plight, "I've had it pretty tough, you've no idea."

"You have somehow managed to get yourself into the mother of all pickles," she said.

"Huh, yeah," he said, shifting uncomfortably on the sofa because he REALLY NEEDED A WEE. "Sophie? Is it OK if I just go to the—"

"And you've had no one to fight your corner, have you?" she interrupted him.

"Not really. Actually, not at all. Thing is, we can definitely keep talking about this, but first I need to—"

"But what about Harry? He fought for you – literally."

"What? What do you mean?"

"The black eye? Apparently some stupid jerks were saying stuff about you..." Sophie looked away, shaking her head.

"Oh. I see." Harry had got into that fistfight to defend Noah's honour? Why didn't he say anything? Noah felt his heart sink even further. "Well ... we stopped talking for a bit, but now we're talking again and he's seeing Connor in an about-to-do-*bow-chicka-wah-wah* sort of way."

"What? Why?"

Noah shrugged. "I don't know. I think Connor's a poor choice too. He's got stupid hair. Must require an inordinate amount of product to keep it up. It's fake, fake, fake."

"I don't mean that. I mean, you and Harry are *so* right for each other."

Noah laughed and wiped his sweaty hands on his trousers. "Yeah, well, about that. I'm… This whole *gay* thing… I mean, *am I gay?* That's the question, right?"

Sophie narrowed her eyes at him. "And what's the answer?"

"Ha! What indeed!" Noah said, crossing his legs so he didn't wet himself. "Anyway, more of this in a moment, after I've—"

"But you fancy him, don't you?"

"Look, I *like* him, yes I do. But I could like girls too." He looked at her, hoping she might take the hint. "I mean, I'll be honest, I've only ever kissed Harry. I've never even kissed a girl. So how do I know if I like kissing girls or not? Maybe I'll love it."

"Maybe."

"I could … for example, this is just an example, but what if I … kissed *you*, for example, say? What if I did?"

Sophie gave a cautious smile. "Uh-huh?"

"So, say we had a kiss, and I was like, *wow, yeah, I really liked that!* You know, that could happen."

Sophie gave a frustrated little sigh. "Right, we've had

enough of this nonsense, so let's get it over and done with. You can kiss me if you want."

"Say what?"

"Kiss me. You can kiss me. I don't mind."

Noah cleared his throat. "Huh? What? Kiss? Me and you? A kiss? What?"

"This is so that you *realize*, idiot. I bet you ten pounds you won't enjoy it. Not really. Up to you. Offer's there."

"Right. OK." He geared himself up for it. This was it, then. This was the moment. He wanted it to be a good kiss, so he could compare it to the one with Harry. He moistened his lips a little, since the cold winter air had chafed them somewhat.

"Why are you licking your lips?"

"Um—"

"That's not an appealing thing to do before kissing someone, just FYI."

"OK, sure. *Sorry.* Um – what if your mum comes back?"

"She's not due back until tonight."

"What if she comes back early? And she finds us kissing and thinks I'm taking advantage of you and hits me?"

"If you don't want to kiss me, you don't have to."

"No, I do! I certainly do! Shall I start doing it now?"

"If you want."

"OK. *Initiating kissing sequence!*" he said, in a jokey computer voice.

"Shut up and kiss me."

"You can start," he told her. That would be better. She would know what to do.

God, he needed a wee. He sort of hoped she would back out of it, so he could go and have one. As it was, she just smiled and leaned in towards him until their lips gently touched. This was actually happening ... *to him*! She was kissing him! He was kissing her! They were *kissing*.

And it was just typical. The first time he was kissing a girl, *the first ever time*, and he couldn't properly enjoy it because he was having to concentrate more on not wetting himself. Bloody brilliant. This was how he was going to remember his first kiss – *bladder agony*.

"See?" she said, breaking off. "You didn't feel anything, did you?"

"Er—"

"I knew it! Now you owe me a tenner."

"Now, you hang on a second!" Noah said. "We were just getting into it. I demand a rematch! You can't just do an experiment once and then say *here are the results*! You've got to test a theory!"

"Fine!" she muttered, going in again. It wasn't like electricity, as he'd been led to believe it would be, but it wasn't awful. As such. The kissing was OK. It was going quite well, wasn't it? It wasn't *amazing*... Should it be amazing? Wasn't it *meant* to be amazing? Or was that just a lie? Another media *lie*? It had been pretty amazing when it had been Harry he was kissing. But that didn't mean he was gay. That must have just been … the alcohol! Drunk kissing was different. Maybe he should suggest they down several shots of Baileys to liven things up a bit? He liked Baileys. Gran used to always give him a little to drink at Christmas. It was smooth, silky, sweet and luxurious … a nice sort of drink … oh, the kissing was still happening; it was not going well… Did her mum have any Baileys? No! *Stop thinking of liquids when you need to pee. Think of … desert and sand…*

"OK?" She broke away again and crossed her arms. "What did you think?"

He badly needed to pee, that was his only thought. Literally no other thoughts were possible right now because all his brainpower was taken up with instructions to *not piss himself.* The experiment would have to be done again once he'd—

"Look, you don't have to work it all out now. That's what growing up is all about. Don't pressure yourself if you don't feel ready…"

Oh my God, she was making him out to be an immature little kid. She probably thought he didn't have pubes or something. "Ready?!" His voice did the range-of-octaves thing. On *one* word! Sometimes he wanted to take puberty by the throat and throttle the living daylights out of it. "Sophie, I am sixteen in just a *few* weeks and I am absolutely, I can assure you, *mature* and everything, it's just … I am *literally* going to wet my pants any second now because I really need the toilet."

She burst out laughing. "Oh, Noah! You're *so* funny!"

"Yes, but I'm serious, though."

"Top of the stairs and it's right in front of you."

"Cool."

He left her giggling in the lounge and flew up the stairs. It wasn't ideal, and it *had* broken the moment somewhat, but it was better than him ending up weeing all over her.

He stood at the toilet, noisily peeing into the bowl. After this it would be better because he would be able to properly concentrate on the kissing. He hadn't been able to before and that must have been why he wasn't enjoying it much. Kissing Sophie should be the best thing ever. It *should* be all his dreams coming true, and it *should* be awesome and *sexy*. It must have been because of needing to pee. A normal boy would find kissing Sophie to be an act of staggering sexiness. It would make a normal boy really damn *horny*. He zipped up, moved to the sink, gently turned on the tap and water burst forth with extraordinary pressure, splashing absolutely everywhere. He glanced down.

Horror.

Noah had a massive wet patch all over the front of his chinos. It looked like he'd had a toilet accident. Brilliant. He had literally said, "I'm literally going to wet my pants" – and here it was! And Sophie knew all about the London Dungeon incident in Year Eight too, so she would naturally assume the worst, however much he protested his innocence. He grabbed a fluffy hand towel and tried to blot the wetness away, but to no avail. He needed a hairdryer or something. The radiator! He could press the wet patch against it, and the heat would hopefully dry it off in no time. He didn't want to sustain burns to any particularly valuable and much-loved areas, so he pulled his chinos off and knelt down, pressing the trousers against the heat. If she came upstairs and wondered what was taking so long he would have to lie and say was suffering from diarrhoea or something. That would be fine and they could carry on kissing in a bit.

There was a tapping at the bathroom door. *Damn*. Sophie was up here! "Er, Noah? There's two policemen at the door for you."

"What?" he said, assuming he must have misheard.

"Police, Noah. They want to speak to you."

He looked towards the locked bathroom door in horror. What did they want? Was it because of his dad? Had they found him in the shed and assumed Noah was some sort of accessory to his petty crimes? Or maybe Eric? Had they found out he'd lied about Eric visiting him at home? Or was it the memory stick? Or...

No. No way.

He wasn't going to stand for this. He had to get away. No one would understand. No one would believe him. Why should he carry on taking the blame for everyone else's actions?

"Tell them I'll be with them in a minute!" he said, trying to sound as normal as possible.

He darted over to the bathroom window, quietly opened it and leaned out. There was a drainpipe down to the garden below. Beyond that, lawn to a fence and to fields beyond. He needed to shimmy down and sprint to freedom.

He threw his trousers out of the window. There would be time to put those on when he was good and hidden. He scrambled up on to the loo and placed a foot on the windowsill, then backed himself out bottom first, clenching the drainpipe between his sock feet and lowering himself down, hand by hand.

His feet kept slipping. They didn't have any grip, his socks sliding about against the smooth pipe.

If he let go of the windowsill he would fall straight down. His arms weren't strong enough to take his weight, or pull himself back up.

Below, a carnivorous bush awaited his arrival, its treacherous spikes hungry for fresh boy meat. It was like a massive Venus flytrap or something. *Oh God!*

The muscles in his arms and legs started trembling as the drainpipe started to come loose from its fixtures.

It was a long way down. Definitely enough to kill a person. Or paralyze them for life.

At best he would end up in a coma for evermore.

His mouth was dry, chest tight, eyes popping out of their sockets as he tried to hold on.

"HELP!" he screamed. "HELP ME, PLEASE!"

CHAPTER THIRTY-NINE

Noah sat on the lawn, huddled under a blanket, as the firemen took away their ladders and the ambulance crew packed up their first-aid kit and stretcher.

"Dare we ask what you were doing climbing out of the bathroom window in your underwear?" asked one of the policemen.

Noah fiddled with the blanket and looked at the lawn. "My, er – trousers fell out the window after I... So, yeah."

"These ones?" said a policewoman, holding up the offending item so you couldn't miss the massive wet patch.

"Ahh!" said the policeman. "Had a little accident, did you? Bit embarrassed in front of your lady friend?"

Noah looked in horror at Sophie. "No! No, I didn't wet myself! Check my boxers if you like, they're—"

The policeman put his hand up. "I've no desire to inspect the boxer shorts of a thirteen-year-old boy, but thanks for the offer."

"Fifteen!" Noah squealed. "Nearly sixteen!"

"Really," the policeman said. "Anyway, we're glad we've found you, your mother's been extremely worried—"

"I didn't do it!" Noah wailed. "I'm innocent! I need a lawyer!"

"Calm down, son, you're not in any trouble. We just thought she might be with you, that's all – since you both went missing at more or less the same time."

Noah looked at him and screwed his face up. "Mum's missing? What are you talking about?"

"No, your gran. She seems to have escaped from the Willows. No sign of her, except a short note that read 'Adios, suckers'. We've no idea how she did it; all we know is she couldn't have acted alone. We've searched the immediate vicinity and there's no sign of her. Plus, we have a witness who thinks they may have seen her driving a motor vehicle – a 1970s Reliant Robin, to be precise. With a lad in the passenger seat who fits your description. When you were reported missing too, we just assumed it was you."

Noah put his head in his hands. "Oh dear God. She's got dementia; she could have gone anywhere!"

"I know. Hence why we're trying to find her. Look, give us a minute while we finish up here and we'll take you back over to Little Fobbing – you can help with the search."

324

Noah looked up at Sophie. "Soph, I know we're courting and everything, but I'm going to need to get back to Little Fobbing. I gotta help find her."

"Of course. That's fine. And about this 'courting' thing, I mean—"

"I liked the kiss, so I can't be gay!"

"No, you didn't, and yes, you are."

Noah stood up and pulled the blanket around him. "Look, we will need to discuss this fully another time. Thank you for your hospitality."

"Noah, just one thing." She stopped him. "What you were saying about Jess and the pregnancy, it got me thinking, and I remembered something."

"What?"

"I was at a party at Jess's house, maybe six or seven weeks ago, and there was this big fuss at one point because Jordan Scott had apparently walked into one of the bedrooms and stumbled upon two people who really shouldn't have been getting with each other."

Noah thought back to the night when Jordan Scott had walked in on him and Harry. *I'm always walking in on people I shouldn't*, he'd said. "Who did he walk in on?" Noah asked.

"Well, that's the strange thing," Sophie said. "I was wanting to go home and my coat was in that bedroom, so I was heading up that way when the drama happened. One of the people was definitely Jess, but when I got in there, there was no sign of the person she'd been with; whoever it was had jumped out the window, climbed down on to the garage roof, got down into the garden and run away – and that's no mean feat; escaping out of high windows is tricky, isn't it, Noah?"

Noah gave her a look that said *not funny.*

"And Jordan was saying nothing either, which means he was either bribed, scared or being loyal to someone he considered a friend or looked up to."

Noah sighed. "That's a lot of variables. I'm not sure it really tells us anything."

"But I did find this, on the bed," Sophie said, placing a small object in Noah's palm. "I picked it up thinking someone would put on Facebook that they'd lost it, but no one ever did. I'm guessing because it might connect them to being in the room with Jess."

Noah held the item between his fingers. "Well, well, well," he said. "I know exactly whom this belongs to."

He was sitting in the back of the police car as they headed towards Little Fobbing, lost in thought. What Sophie had found was a strong clue, but he needed something more. Something that wasn't circumstantial.

In any case, this wasn't really what mattered. What mattered, *really* mattered, was Gran. He never in a million years thought Gran would go through with her plan. It had seemed so implausible. Impossible. Surely the Willows had security against this type of thing? How the hell had it happened?

"So my mum reported me missing, then?" he asked.

"That's not quite how it happened," said the policewoman, twisting round in the front passenger seat to look at him.

"How *did* it happen?" he said, grimly.

"So, basically, we turned up at your mum's house after your gran was found missing, and your mum decides to help with the search because we thought she might have been close by. So, your mum goes out into the garden to get her flashlight from the shed and—"

Noah flinched.

"There's this almighty scream from the garden," the policewoman continued, "so we rush round, to find your mother beating a man – who transpires to be your father – with a sweeping brush. He was living rough in the shed."

Noah looked down at the floor of the car.

"Of course your father is wanted in connection with a number of low-level thefts and cons spanning the last ten years, so we've taken him in for questioning. Mainly for his own protection, really. Seems he owes a lot of locals money, and if they knew his whereabouts, I'm pretty sure they'd all be round with the pitchforks and flaming torches." She chuckled, like this was somehow a hilarious tale.

Brilliant. At least on the plus side, his dad hadn't dobbed him in to the police.

"He told us you'd helped him hide there," the policeman

said, looking at him in the rear-view mirror.

Noah took a deep breath. "No comment."

He glanced up at the mirror to see the policeman grinning at him. "It's fine," the policeman added. "You didn't know he was a wanted man. Did you?"

"No, of course not!" Noah said. "I'm very honest and truthful. Ask the school. I'm top set for everything."

God, his dad was completely selfish and only out for himself.

"Your dad very kindly told us you'd probably be in Milton Keynes. He said you had some crazy crush on a girl who'd just moved there called Sophie. So, we tracked down her dad and got the address."

Noah grimaced. *Crazy crush?* And what the hell had the police told Sophie's dad? *Brilliant.* Why couldn't Noah's dad just keep his mouth shut? Was he trying to get a reduced sentence by being cooperative?

There was some static from one of the radios and some talking that Noah couldn't make out. "Copy that," said the policewoman, "we'll get over there now." She twisted round in the seat again and looked at Noah. "OK, she's been found—"

"OK..."

"But ... she's been involved in an RTA; that's road traffic accident."

"But she's all right?"

"She's in an ambulance heading to Lincoln County

Hospital. Apparently she's awake and talking. We'll get you over there as soon as we can."

He felt his shoulders relax a bit and he sat back in the seat, comforted by the fact that Gran was apparently uninjured. They were about thirty minutes away. Thirty minutes to go through it all and join the dots.

Noah kept his eyes front as a tall, gym-toned (and very sensitive) male nurse led him down a corridor. He always felt particularly comforted around healthcare professionals like this one. It was probably just the knowledge that, should Noah be stricken with a choking episode, heart attack, or even just a verruca, they would know exactly what to do in order to save him. Also, nurses like him were not just in excellent physical form, they were notoriously kind people, who would give warm and gentle sponge baths when necessary, and stroke your fevered brow whilst whispering tender, soft words in your ear...

"Are you OK?" the tall, gym-toned (and very sensitive) male nurse asked.

"Yes?" Noah said.

"Only you were making a sort of ... a sort of *groaning* noise."

"Tummy troubles," Noah said, patting his stomach, and wondering what the hell was wrong with him. *Your gran is in hospital! She may be fine, but nevertheless, focus!*

"Can I get you anything to help?"

Noah looked at the tall, gym-toned (and very sensitive) male nurse and wondered, *How do you get to be this nice?* The man couldn't be any more loving and perfect if he tried. Also, he was Australian.

"You're groaning again."

"I'll be just fine," Noah assured him.

"You can wait in here," the nurse said, opening the door into a family waiting room. "As soon as we've done our initial tests, I'll come and find you. The lad who was in the car with her is in there too. He won't say anything to us, but maybe you can get him to tell you what happened?"

Noah muttered his thanks and took a deep breath. He knew exactly what he'd find the other side of that door. Or more accurately, *whom.* He pushed it open.

"Well, well, well," Noah said, "My half-brother, I presume?"

"Hi, Noah."

"Hello, *Eric.*"

CHAPTER FORTY

Eric gave him a slow handclap. "Well done, Noah, you got there in the end."

"Oh shut up, you stupid *anus*," Noah said, slamming the door behind him and standing with his hands on his hips in the middle of the room. "What the hell have you done?"

"I did what I had to do, my friend, I did what I had to do."

Noah took an unsteady breath, barely able to control the rage inside him. "Really? Well, you'd better start talking, else I'm going to do what *I* have to do!"

"Yeah? And what's that?"

Noah glared at him. "I shall refrain from a physical attack at the present time," he sniffed, "so you may count yourself lucky. But we all know the pen is mightier than the sword. So! Beware!"

"What you gonna do, write a devastating poem about me?" Eric chuckled. "Who blew my cover, then?"

"I'm the one asking the questions!" Noah declared, triumphantly, like he was the main cop in a TV police drama.

Eric shrugged, refusing to meet Noah's stare. Then he actually got his phone out like all this was totally casual, totally relaxed, and nothing out of the ordinary was happening.

"Er! You just put that away right now, mister!" Noah hissed. "You put that right away!"

Eric chuckled again and slid the phone back into his pocket. "No one blew my cover, did they? This is all a sweet surprise for you!"

"That is grade-A bullock poop, Eric," Noah said. "Or as coarse people like yourself would say, *bullshit*. I knew, all right. Clue one – Mum accidentally told me my secret sibling is in my year at school. Clue two – Gran accidentally referred to the sibling as 'he' in conversation. Clue three, when you came back to my house to trade the memory stick, my mum knew who you were, when she doesn't know who anyone in my year is. So why did she know *your* name? Clue four, you mentioned 'Project Adios' at the start of your illicit video recording, and Gran left a note reading '*Adios*, suckers!' at the Willows. *Adios* being *Spanish*, of course – and Spain happens to be where Dad was. That's a hell of a lot of coincidences! Clue five, Dad speaks in exactly the same way you do, ducking and diving and all that crooked 'geezer' shit. Clue six –" Noah cleared his throat and looked out of the window "– there is some mild and unconvincing argument for saying we look alike in some vague way."

"Yeah, a lot of people say that," Eric said.

"Do they?!" *This was mortifying!*

Eric shrugged. "Well, we're both quite short—"

"I am still growing!" Noah said. "I didn't hit puberty until the middle of Year Nine, so shove that up your arse! *I'm still growing.*"

"Both got dark hair, prone to grease—"

Noah held his hand up to silence Eric. "Listen, *bucko*, I happen to use a very expensive shampoo, with extracts of tea tree and grapefruit, so *prone to grease*, as you so eloquently put it, is not something my hair could be accused of!" *The bloody nerve of the boy!*

"When I first went to see Gran, she actually thought I was you," Eric said.

"She's got dementia, Eric!"

Eric sighed and looked down at the floor.

"But anyway," Noah continued, "on a balance of probabilities, you were the most likely candidate, and when the police told me Gran had escaped with someone fitting my description, that's when I knew for sure, even though the police are wrong about that and we look nothing alike in reality. By the way, where have you been the past few days? The police have been looking for you; they even came to my house!"

Eric levelled his gaze at Noah, sphinxlike. "Sorry, bro.

I'm afraid that's none of your business."

"Well, that is simply not good enough! I'm sure the police are—"

"What part of 'none of your business' have you failed to grasp, Noah?" Eric stared at him, long and hard. "Do yourself a favour and forget about it. Yeah?"

"Okaaay," Noah said, unsettled. "Well, how long have you known about … us for?"

"Few years," Eric said, looking up. "Found out your mum was giving my mum money."

Noah nodded. "Yeah. Your mum blackmailing mine, was she? That's the sort of thing your family does, right? Threatened her with a good kneecapping if she didn't comply?"

"You have a low opinion of me," Eric said.

"Fancy that!"

"Actually, it was because of my mum's partner, the bloke I *thought* was my dad."

"You mean, Mad Dog Razor Jaws Smith?"

Eric sighed. "Yeah, otherwise known as *Colin*."

"He lost his eye in a fight!" Noah said.

"That's what he tells people. Actually, it was just a congenital deformity. He was born like that."

"Oh."

"But he *is* a crazy, violent scumbag. No doubt about it. And if he'd known the truth – if he'd known he wasn't really my dad – he would have…" Eric made a throat-slitting motion with his finger. "Get me?"

Noah nodded.

"So my real dad, *our dad*, wanted nothing to do with me or my mum, for his own personal safety," Eric continued. "Kept his distance, pretended it never happened. But I guess your mum is a soft touch, felt sorry for us, or maybe just wanted to keep the secret, so she gave my mum cash, under the radar, like, that our dad had sent her. And it wasn't much, trust me. He never sent what he should have. But it was fair enough. I mean, he did have *two* sons, after all. Couldn't just pretend I don't exist."

"More's the pity, Eric."

"So, that's when I found out the truth. Colin, the guy I thought was my dad, wasn't my dad at all. My real dad, *our* dad, lived in Spain."

"How did you find him?" Noah asked.

"Paid some peeps a bit of cash, they did the searching."

"Well, I tried Google, but—"

Eric smirked. "This was a bit more than a Google search, Noah. This was following shell companies and foreign bank accounts. This was a network of connections that was so well hidden no tax authority in the world could follow it. Clever guy, our dad."

"Well, really," Noah huffed. "You expect me to believe you hired ... *Anonymous* or some other hacker group to find Dad?"

"Not Anonymous, exactly," Eric said, "but people with

similar interests."

"Well, you needn't have bothered. His address was there for all to see on the letters he sent Mum."

Eric shook his head. "That weren't his real address. He didn't live there, it was just an office that received mail on behalf of customers."

"Well! You know it all, don't you?" Noah said. "Well, I know some stuff too, and I know what you were up to. Your plan was to raise enough money through your blackmailing antics to go and confront him! Get what was rightfully yours! The maintenance he hadn't been paying all these years! And if he didn't pay up, you'd threaten him that you'd tell Mad Dog Razor Jaws Colin everything! Oh yes, that's—"

"No."

"What?"

"I play a longer game than that, Noah." Eric grinned. "Who cares about a few hundred quid here and there? I didn't want money off him. I wanted to *join* him. I wanted in on his business schemes. Wanted to be his apprentice. The money I got off the likes of you and everyone else – that was my investment money. I wanted in as a shareholder; I didn't want no maintenance. I'm not some little kid who needs looking after."

Noah stared at him. Never in a million years did he think that would have been the case. His dad and Eric? In business together? It sounded insane.

But at the same time, Noah couldn't help but feel a tiny

bit affronted at the idea, as outlandish as it was. Why would Eric think Dad would choose *him* as a business partner? In stark contrast, Noah had excellent design and copywriting skills (evidenced by his time as editor-in-chief of the school magazine, *Fobb Off!*), financial acumen (Cub Scout treasurer), and a sharply honed sense of good customer service (tuck shop monitor in Years Eight, Nine and Ten). If anyone in their right mind had a choice of business partner, they would pick Noah.

"Why did you involve Gran if you'd got it all so sorted out?" Noah asked.

"Save money on the trip over, right?" Eric said. "Once I'd established that she wanted out of that care home, and her mate Dickie had the wheels, it seemed an obvious choice. I get to Spain cheap, she gets to escape. More dosh for my first investment, then."

"She's got dementia!" Noah shouted. "How could you have been so utterly stupid, Eric?"

Eric shrugged again like it was all water off a duck's back. "I didn't actually know about that. She talked a lot of sense ... most of the time. Well, now you mention, *some* of the time. But I didn't know about the dementia, I just thought she was old!"

"You know, I have been through *hell* these last few days—" Noah told him.

"Oh, boohoo, Noah. Boo-bloody-hoo."

"Right, fine, well, when the police come asking

questions, expect no favours from me. Brother or no brother, I hate your guts, you're a total—"

"Noah—"

"Screw you!"

"Noah—"

"Pathetic little *cockwomble*."

"Noah—"

"And in the final analysis, there's me – never been in trouble, generally a good boy,"

"Even your farts smell of roses?" Eric offered.

"Actually, Eric, I don't break wind. Breaking wind is a *choice*. I choose not to do that because it's disgusting. Like you." *Point to me*, Noah thought. *And there will be plenty more points to be had before this little meeting is over!*

"I know who the father of Jess Jackson's baby is."

Noah stopped dead. "Oh?"

Eric nodded.

"Well, I know too," Noah said, his heartbeat starting to echo round his head.

"But you ain't got actual proof."

"I have proof," Noah said.

"Not like this, you don't. This is, as they say, *incontrovertible*."

He was bluffing. Noah was sure of it. "Impossible."

"That day you were stuck up the climbing frame in PE with a boner—"

"That's not true!" Noah squealed. "I didn't have…

Nothing was going on in that department!" He cleared his throat. "But continue..."

"I was doing a little bit of filming on my phone."

"Yes, I saw you, *pervert*," Noah said.

"At one point I popped out to the corridor that leads to the sports hall reception area. Wanted to view back some of my footage..."

Noah nodded. He remembered Eric walking out.

"And that's when I saw them," Eric said. "So I hid round the corner and filmed the whole thing. A conversation no one was meant to witness."

Of course! Of course he had! It's what he always did. "Eric, I... There's actual evidence, you say? On your phone?"

"Yeah," Eric said, grinning to reveal his full set of orthodontically challenged teeth.

"May I... I wonder if you would be so kind as to show me the footage? Maybe I can have a little look? A little peek? At the footage? See what's what? Check my theory? Could I? I ... I know I've been mean to you. I have. And I am throwing myself at your mercy. I am pleading forgiveness. I've been under a great deal of pressure and I'm not thinking straight. I'm sorry. Do you hear me? I'm apologizing for calling you those mean things. You're not a cockwomble. You're ... a great guy. A nice guy. Someone I—"

Eric handed him the phone. "Get your eyes all over this."

Noah pressed play and watched, wide-eyed, as the

events played out on the screen. Ninety seconds of HD video that changed everything.

"Brilliant," Noah said, when it had finished.

CHAPTER FORTY-ONE

"What's happened? How is she? Oh God, you're both here together; you know everything, don't you?" his mother gabbled, barging into the room, breathless and frantic, with Josh following behind.

"Hello, Mother. Yes, I can confirm Eric and I now know *everything*. The lies, the deceit, the duplicity – it's all come out. *Almost* all of it, anyway."

"Well, *you* can talk, Mr Holier Than Thou!" she said. "Keeping your father hidden in the shed! See, Noah? Your no-good father's got this way of making people do things, keep secrets. He's a slimeball like that!"

Noah nodded. "It's true. Some people do have the gift of the gab. They have this way of making people do things that they wouldn't normally ever dream of. Why don't you

take a seat, Mother? Josh? Make yourselves comfortable."
He stood and began pacing up and down the room,
imagining a roaring log fire behind him and a rug made
from a dead bear.

"Noah, what's happening with your gran? Is she OK,
or...?"

"We have been assured she is fine, and we are currently
waiting for medical staff to complete routine tests. All is
well, and Gran will live to see several more years of you *not*
visiting her, so don't worry," Noah said. "In the meantime,
I've gathered you all here—"

"*What are you talking about?* Have you taken drugs?"
his mum said. "You didn't bring us anywhere; *you* ran away,
mister, we couldn't find you!"

"I just went on a minibreak," Noah hissed. "To Milton
Keynes. I don't have to inform you of my every move. *You*
certainly don't."

His mum sighed and sat down in one of the chairs.
"Just sit down, Josh. It's easier, believe me."

Noah watched as Josh smirked and sat down next to
his mum, hideously taking her hand like all this was really
distressing for her. "Ever one to milk a situation, Mother,"
Noah said.

"Actually, Noah, this has all been extremely upsetting.
I know you think I hate your gran, but I don't. I just hate
going to the Willows, that's all."

"Why's that, Mother? Does it remind you how close

death's cold embrace really is, now that you're in your forties?"

"Death will be embracing you if you don't watch it!" his mum bit back.

Noah turned on the spot, sweeping an imaginary cloak around as he went. "The mystery of Jess Jackson's pregnancy is one that has eluded some of the greatest minds, myself included," Noah began, ignoring the eyerolls in his audience. "Why would a girl like her make up such a ridiculous story? What was the real truth behind it all? *Who really was the father?*"

His mother sighed. "I need a fag."

"You'll need more than that by the time I've finished," Noah said. "But enough of that. I have in my possession – I shall not say how – video footage showing Jess Jackson telling none other than her boyfriend, Kirk, that she was pregnant and he was the father."

"I knew it!" Josh said. "That girl's got some neck! Good for you, Noah, for finding proof. So Kirk dumped her and she blamed you for the baby, just so her parents don't go mental at her!"

"Interesting that you know so much about her parents, Josh," Noah observed, turning and looking at him from the corner of his imaginary mantelpiece as he sipped a brandy.

Josh shrugged. "Yeah, I know Jess. And her parents. It's all about show. All about what other people think of them."

"The downfall of so many," Noah said with a faraway look, knowing damn well that applied to him too.

"I'd love to see her father's face when he finds out," his mother said.

"My tale is not yet done!" Noah snapped. "Now. I presented Kirk with this evidence," he continued, beginning to parade around the room again, "but, of course, Kirk wasn't the father."

"I thought you had some bloody film saying he was?" his mum said.

"I *did*. But what no one knew, not Jess, not anyone, is that Kirk... The treatment he had for cancer as a kid had the unfortunate effect of leaving him unable to have children. There was no way he could be the father."

"*Man*. That is... So, we're back to square one?" said Josh.

Noah did a theatrical sigh. "It would seem so," he said. "Oh! I almost forgot – I have something for you, Josh!"

Noah reached into his pocket and pulled out the little item that Sophie had given him.

A stud. Square and glistening. Like a diamond.

"My stud!" Josh said. "Where did you find it?"

"Someone picked it up as lost property. It is yours, right?"

"Cheers, bro," Josh said, taking it from Noah. "Love this stud. Thought I'd never see it again." He fiddled around and put it back in his ear.

Noah had to admit, it did look pretty good.

"Well, this has been really interesting," Noah's mum began.

"Oh, sorry, Mother, I still haven't finished," Noah said, a smile spreading across his face. "About a week ago, I was stuck up a climbing frame in PE with a ... with a *small* problem. Well, when I say *small*, I mean ... *average*. Or just below average. I was stuck up a climbing frame with a slightly-less-than-average *problem*. And that's when Jess Jackson ran into the sports hall clutching your stupid flyers."

"Where the hell is this leading, Noah?" his mum said.

"Jess Jackson *ran in*. She was meant to be doing gym like the rest of us, but she *ran in*. She'd clearly found your flyers in the reception area of the sports hall, but what was she doing there in the first place, when she should have been in PE?"

"Toilet?" his mum offered.

"Or was she meeting someone?" Noah said. "The best time to meet anyone in school, if you don't want other people knowing, is when everyone is in lessons. Who was she meeting that she didn't want anyone to know about?"

"Well, do tell, because we're all *gagging* to find out!" his mum mocked.

"The other person who was up to no good that day was none other than Eric," Noah continued. "He was busy filming the girls on his phone, for what purposes I can't imagine."

"Masturbation," Eric said.

"Thank you, Eric, it was a rhetorical question! I didn't ask, and no one wants to know," Noah said. "Eric slipped out of the sports hall at one point, and by the sweetest of chances, he sees Jess Jackson talking to our mysterious stranger. And Eric being Eric, he films it. Jess Jackson talks to this individual and reveals that she is pregnant. She claims she had a drunken night with the individual at a party at her house some weeks ago, but one that sadly didn't involve any form of contraceptives. 'No,' says the individual. 'It can't be me. It's almost certainly Kirk's ... and I'm not going to take the blame. If you say it's mine, I'll deny it. And you have no idea if the baby is mine or Kirk's, and you can't force someone to take a DNA paternity test, and even if you could, you'll have to test loads of guys, won't you? Think how that'll look to your parents!' That is what the individual said. Wasn't it ... *Josh*?"

Silence. Josh erupted in laughter. "You kidding me, right, bro?"

"No, *bro*, I'm not. It's all on video, isn't it, Eric?"

"Every last word," Eric said.

"What an honourable, decent guy you are, Josh," Noah said. "Shaming Jess, refusing to take responsibility for your actions, and later being quite happy for me to take the blame! When Kirk dumped her too, Jess was panicked. She just needed *someone* to be the dad, so her parents wouldn't go completely ballistic. As you say, Josh, for them it's all about what other people think of them. When I ended up at her house that night, she realized I was the perfect option. She mentioned how her parents would love it if she brought a 'boy like me' home. I was the ideal mark – uncool, vulnerable to the sweet temptations of popularity—"

"Sexually naive," Eric offered.

Noah grimaced. "If she could just make it look like we'd been seeing each other, she'd have the perfect solution. Well, for the moment, anyway. It wasn't a foolproof plan, but when you're up against it, desperately trying to hold your life together, and genuinely scared about what other people think, sometimes you don't make rational choices." He glanced away from everyone and briefly closed his eyes. *God knew he had experience of that.* Him! Mr Intelligent. Mr Top Set for Everything! Even he had fallen into that trap.

His mum extracted her hand from Josh's. "Josh?" she said. "Is this true?"

Josh laughed. "She did the same to me as she did to Noah – made shit up. Of course I haven't slept with Jess. I don't even really know the girl. Never even been to her..." He stopped dead, his fingers involuntarily touching the stud in his ear.

"Never been to her house, Josh? Was that what you were going to say?" Noah smiled. "Except that's where you lost your earring, isn't it? About six weeks ago, at the party round at hers. In your extreme sexual passion, as you doubtless ravaged one another with your greedy, hot hands, and lost yourselves in some sort of vile, sweaty, so-called bliss, the stud was ripped from your ear. Then Jordan Scott walked in on you both and you had to make a quick exit – leaving the stud to be discovered by my friend Sophie."

"Josh?" his mum said again.

"Man, I don't know. That girl's slept with everyone; anyone could be the father."

"But did *you* sleep with her?" his mum said.

"Well, *yeah*, sure I did. I'm a red-blooded teenage guy, so shoot me."

Mum's eyes blazed. "Six weeks ago? When you and I had already started seeing each other?"

Josh laughed. "Man, it was just a shag!"

"Well, I refuse to go to jail for murder or GBH, so this'll have to do," Mum said, standing up and looking back down at him. "You're a piece of shit, you really are. I'm sick of men like you – arrogant, entitled, full of crap. Think you've got the world on a plate because you've spent your whole life getting everything you've wanted. Think your good looks and your toned body mean you can say and do whatever you like. Get away with whatever." She shook her head. "And so often, you do. But where has all that got you? Nowhere! You've just turned into the biggest shithead wanker in the world. That's what you are, Josh. A shithead wanker. Plus, you give it all the urban slang, but everyone knows you're just a pathetic middle-class boy who wouldn't last two minutes in an actual city amongst people whose parents didn't have Amex cards. And you're shit in bed."

"There we go," Noah said. "And it's *prison*, Mum, not *jail*. Just to remind everyone, we're not in America. Josh? Anything to say?"

Josh glared at him. "Suppose you're going to make the videos public, are you?"

"No, Josh," Noah said. "I won't. For God's sake, have some decency. Kirk is a *cancer survivor*! I might not be ace at sport or really hunky like you, but I'm a good person, and I'm going to respect his privacy around his medical condition." *And, happily, avoid being killed.* He continued, waving his arm in a circular motion, "And now you, Josh, have the chance to be a slightly less shit person. So this is what you're going to do: talk to Jess, take responsibility for the baby."

"What? No way. What about my leisure management course at London Met?! I can't party at uni if I'm shackled to some baby!"

Noah grinned. Seeing Josh cut down to size like this was utterly blissful. "I'm sure there's a course closer to home that'll teach you how to wipe down gym equipment."

Josh stood up and shot over to Noah.

"Is this the part where you try to kill me, Josh? Just to warn you, Eric knows kung fu!"

Eric looked up, sharply. "Er..."

Noah glared at him. "Shut up, *yes, you do*! You're a black belt!"

"You're scum," Josh said.

"No, Josh," Noah's mum said, pulling Josh around, "you're scum. You should leave. Now."

Josh took one look around the room and stormed out, slamming the door behind him.

His mother slumped where she was standing, unable to meet Noah's gaze.

"Sorry you had to find out like that," Noah said.

His mum looked up at him and nodded with sad eyes. "I've been ... a bit stupid." She looked back down, shaking her head.

"Yes. You have," Noah agreed, surprised and pleased at her admission. "Very stupid." *Could it be? Could she be turning over a new leaf, finally becoming the mother he deserved?*

His mum looked back up sharply. "Well, don't be a dick about it."

Or not. "You know, Mother," Noah said, "you're so wonderfully kind and nurturing, it's a wonder someone hasn't snapped up the book rights for your guide to parenting."

She narrowed her eyes at Noah, then turned to Eric. "Has anyone checked you over properly yet?" she asked.

"I'm fine," Eric muttered.

"I tell you what, why don't we just pop on down to see a nurse and make sure? Just to be safe? And on the way, I'll buy you something nice from the vending machine."

Eric's eyes lit up. "Like a bag of Haribo?"

Mum turned to Noah and smiled, maliciously. "Yes, Eric. A bag of Haribo."

Noah rolled his eyes in response.

"Cool. Later, Noah," Eric said, getting up and heading straight out the door. "Oh, look," his mum said, pulling some coins out of her pocket as she followed after him, "I seem to have enough here for three bags. Lucky Eric!"

Noah shook his head as the door closed behind her. He didn't feel like eating anyway. He still couldn't quite believe he'd managed to piece everything together.

But what now? Eric Smith was his half-brother – what would *that* mean? Of course, no one could know about it, or Eric's mum would be in danger from Mad Dog Razor Jaws Smith. And maybe Noah would prefer not to know either: Eric was still a no-good crook who clearly felt no remorse. And he was clearly still hiding secrets – like where the hell he'd been these past few days.

And regardless of the Jess Jackson baby fiasco, there was still one huge Harry-shaped ball of sadness in his gut.

The door pushed open and the tall, gym-toned (and very sensitive) male nurse from earlier gave Noah a kind smile. "She's fine; she's asleep, but she's fine."

"Can I see her?"

"Of course; follow me, matey."

Matey. Noah liked it when the tall, gym-toned (and very sensitive) male nurse called him that. This was a *good* hospital. He would definitely give it a very favourable online review.

CHAPTER FORTY-TWO

They had put Gran in a small, private room at the end of one of the wards.

"Don't worry about the heart monitor," the nurse said, taking his cue off Noah's alarmed expression as they walked in. "It's just precautionary – her blood pressure's fine, and her heartbeat's normal. Can I get you some tea or anything?"

"Or some Haribo?"

The nurse smiled. "I'll see what I can do."

Noah pulled a chair up to the side of the bed, kissed Gran on the cheek and held her hand. "Honestly, Gran," he said. "This was not one of your better ideas."

He sighed and glanced around the room. There was a TV on the wall, a door through to an en suite, and a nice view of the park outside. It was more like a hotel room, and Noah had no doubt it would meet with Gran's full approval. She liked things to be proper.

He felt his chest tighten. *Would she still care about proper?* Perhaps the dementia was worse than he'd thought. To have actually gone through with this crazy plan of Eric's, it must have been. She was here for now, but bit by bit, piece by piece, Gran was being taken away from him.

She was the kindest, funniest, wisest person he'd ever known. She loved him. And he loved her. But all the things he hadn't said. Hadn't asked.

She was the only person who had ever called him "handsome" or "clever" ... told him how proud she was of him... She had often told him what he meant to her, but he'd never really told her what *she* meant to *him*.

She wasn't dead. But was it still too late? Too late to say stuff that would really mean anything to her? And he was struck, in this terrible moment, with how fragile and temporary life was. How we're only here for a relatively short time anyway – and how that time can be even shorter with a twist of fate, a bit of bad luck.

You shouldn't wait for tomorrow to do the things you want. You shouldn't wait for tomorrow to tell the people who matter to you how you feel about them. There's no guarantee you'll get that chance again.

And he didn't suppose anyone lay on their deathbed and thought to themselves, *You know, I've done nothing that*

I wanted to do, I did nothing controversial, I didn't wear that fabulous outfit, I didn't say what I really thought, I didn't kiss that person, but at least no one ever gossiped about me and said stuff behind my back. *I can die happy.*

Why was it that you had to be facing the very worst thing before you could see what it was that really mattered?

The door edged open. "Noah?"

He turned to see Harry poking his head round the door, wrapped up in a blue Parka jacket, cheeks red from being outside in the cold. The fur trim around Harry's hood looked warm. Looked soft. Looked puppy-dog cute. And all at once everything bubbled up inside of him and he started crying.

…Just like the last time he saw Harry. He really needed to get a grip.

"How is she?" Harry said, coming in. "Come on, it'll be OK," he murmured, as Noah got up and collapsed into his arms.

"She's fine," Noah said, gulping tears back and burying his face into Harry's shoulder. "She'll be OK. For now."

"Good."

Noah sniffed, extracted himself from Harry and wiped his eyes. "I thought… I didn't think you'd want to be here, I mean…" He pulled a tissue out of his pocket and blew his nose. "Why did you come?"

"Because my best friend's gran is in hospital and I knew he'd be totally gutted because he loves her more than anything." Harry pulled his coat off and hung it on the back of the chair. "Seriously, do you need to ask me that?"

Noah shrugged. "Sorry. I just thought you might be busy with Connor. I didn't know if... Sorry." He glanced at Harry and tried to give an apologetic smile, but what he really wanted to do was go in for another hug. There was something deeply warm and comforting about Harry's hugs. Harry's arms and shoulders felt strong, but gentle. Harry's neck was strangely attractive... Noah kind of wanted to ... nuzzle it. Was that weird? Even if it was, he still wanted to. And Harry's hoodie smelt of fabric softener – Lenor Moonlight Harmony, if Noah wasn't mistaken. *Nice choice.*

Harry held up a bag of Haribo. "A really hot nurse gave me these to give to you. Got an admirer, have you?"

Noah managed a half-hearted chuckle, sighed and blew his nose again. "Sorry, this is really unappealing, I know," he muttered, trying to fold the soggy tissue up in as dignified a fashion as possible. He snuck a glance at Harry, who was looking back, smiling a very disarming smile at him.

"What?" Noah said. "I'm sorry, OK? I know I've been a dick about lots of things."

Harry shrugged. "Yeah? Like what?"

"Everything, *you know.* I am sorry, truly."

Harry nodded. "Cool."

"Cool."

Noah looked back at Gran. Then back at Harry. Harry was still looking at him with those deep brown eyes of his.

What more did Harry want? He looked back at Gran again, then gave Harry a bit of subtle side-eye to see if he was still looking at him *and he was*, so what the hell?!

"All right," said Harry eventually. "This is crazy. I'm going to say something, and I want you stay completely silent. Like, not a word. OK?"

Noah nodded, tight-lipped.

"OK," said Harry. "So here's some stuff that I *know*, and some stuff that I *think*. Let's start with the stuff I know, because that's the easy bit. I know there's no one else in the world I enjoy spending time with as much as you. I know you get me like no one else gets me, and I know I definitely get you, and not being rude, I think that's probably a pretty rare thing. For example, I know you're very fussy about bread-roll-and-butter etiquette, like when I buttered *the whole roll* at that Pizza Express, rather than breaking bits off and buttering individually."

"Like some sort of *caveman*!" Noah said. "Practically picking up hunks of meat with your bare hands and hurling the bones over your shoulder."

Harry blinked at him.

"Sorry, that was ... very rude of me," Noah said.

"I had some other funny 'things I know', but I'm not going to say them now—"

"Oh no! Go on, say them! Say them! I won't speak," Noah said, putting his finger to his lips.

Harry wavered a moment before clearing his throat

357

and continuing. "I know I'll really annoy you if I adopt an upward inflection at the end of a sentence when it's not a question. Like this? Like, this is about the worst thing I could do?"

"GAAHHHH!"

"You said you wouldn't speak."

Noah took a deep breath. "Intolerable."

Harry reached out and put his hand on Noah's shoulder. "I know we've been friends for ever. I know I feel like being more than friends. I know I don't just like you; it's so much bigger and more powerful and out-of-this-world-amazing than that. I know I don't want to be without you. I know I want to kiss you. I know I want to do more than just kiss. I know you're scared, and I know this came out of the blue, and I know you sometimes care what people think way too much.

"But I *think* you feel the same. I think you like me too, but I think you have a hard time saying it out loud because you're nervous about what that means and you're quite shy, really, and I think that's cute."

Harry's hand dropped away. "So, here's what I'm proposing. Connor does like me, and, you know, he's a nice guy. But he's not *my* guy. My guy is *you*, Noah Grimes. And I told Connor that. And he's cool, he gets it. I don't want to be with Connor; I want to be with you. And I think you want to be with me. And you don't need to say anything. It's hard for you, I get that, so don't say anything. Unless I'm wrong.

Unless I've got it all wrong and I'm an idiot, then you should say something. You should tell me."

Noah looked him in the eyes. "No."

"No?"

"No, Harry. I *want* to say something."

Harry nodded and swallowed. "OK."

"So, I know and think some stuff too. And being silent about it is no good because I think you've got to tell people these things. Because you never know when. . ." He indicated Gran. "Right? When it's gonna be too late."

Harry nodded.

"And also, Gran's advice was to shut up and let people do and say what they like. And to an extent, I agree. Let them. Who cares? But then another part of me thinks you shouldn't hide who you are. You should be proud of it."

Harry raised an eyebrow.

"So, I *think* everything you just said was a pretty . . . accurate description of the way things are. But I'm going to say it. I'm going to say –" he swallowed "– I think you spent most of last night writing that speech, didn't you?"

"Maybe," Harry said.

"Because, I mean, if that was spontaneous, then I doff my cap to you, sir."

Harry shrugged. "I gave it a bit of thought."

"That time in sick bay, when you came in with the black eye? Why didn't you tell me you'd got into a fight because of me?"

"Because you'd told me you didn't need protecting, so I thought you'd be annoyed."

"I may have slightly changed my mind about that," Noah said.

"Yeah?"

Noah smiled. "I love you."

"Really?"

"Really. I don't know if that means I'm gay. I'm not sure I really know much, the more I think about things. And maybe I need to stop thinking about things and just... I guess, what I feel about you..." Noah swallowed and looked Harry straight in the eyes. "Will you be my boyfriend?"

Harry's eyes nearly popped out. "Did you actually just ... say that? Like, so completely plainly?"

"I did, I did," Noah said. "Don't leave me hanging now."

"You're OK with people knowing?"

Noah shrugged. "People can think and say what they like. They will anyway. And who cares?"

"Oh my God..."

"I know," Noah agreed, "it's a brave new policy. But it's right. There's something else I know too."

"Yeah?"

"I know I want to kiss you. Like, *now.*"

Harry smiled and wrapped his arms around him, pushing their bodies together, and it felt so right. So totally right. He felt like the luckiest boy in the world. On top of the world. King of the world! Harry's lips soft against his own,

their cheeks brushing, him tasting sweet … like Haribo…
Had Harry already opened the bag that the hot nurse had given him?

Oh well … it didn't matter. Now they were boyfriends, they would share everything … everything that Harry had would be half Noah's by law…

"Oh, *get a room!*"

Noah broke off and turned round. "Gran?!"

"I'm wired up to every machine on the planet, drips in my arms, on death's door, and you two are standing there, sucking face!"

"Gran!" Noah said, taking her hand. "You're not on death's door, you're going to be OK. And this machine, it's just precautionary. And the drip … well, I'm not sure what that is, to be honest; the nurse didn't say, but I'm sure it's harmless."

"How's Eric?" she muttered, averting her eyes from Noah's.

"Yes! About that! What did you think you were doing?!"

Gran shrugged. "Going to see George."

"Gran! George is dead. He died, Gran!"

"You look like him…"

"Well, yes, maybe I do, we're all related after all, but I'm—"

"George?"

He sighed and gave her a smile. "I'm Noah, your

grandson. Your grandson who loves you very much. Who you've taught so much to, who has listened to everything you have ever told him, and who will always eat with the correct cutlery, be able to tell a sherry glass from a port glass and will abide by the laws of good English grammar. So, thank you, Gran. You mean the world to me."

Gran smiled back at him, for once at a loss for words.

"But if you ever try something like this again, I swear to God, I'll go feral, just to spite you! I'll get everything pierced – and I mean *everything*. I'll get unverified Chinese letters tattooed on my arm, I'll play music out of my phone on public transport ... *I will put my feet on the seats!* But worst of all, I will use the spelling T-H-E-R-E *for the pronoun*. Get it?"

Gran nodded. "Fair enough."

"Eric's fine, but next time I've got a secret half-sibling, you tell me, OK?! It's ridiculous."

Harry perched on the edge of Gran's bed. "Eric?"

Noah sighed. "OK, so there is a *lot* of stuff to tell you, and some of it you're probably going to find surprising, and possibly hate, but you're my boyfriend now, so you're obliged to love me anyway, no matter how bad it is. Yes?"

Harry smiled. "Hit me with it."

"Eric's my secret half-brother; he blackmailed us both to get money so he could become a business associate of my dad. Who is also *his* dad. And Josh, who *isn't* dating my mum any more, is the father of Jess Jackson's baby."

"Your family is a screw-up. It's a good job you're pretty."

Noah giggled and gave Harry a playful push.

"So ... I'm assuming you two have sorted things out, then?" Gran said.

"Yes," said Noah. "You, Gran, can be the first to know. Harry and I are ... we're boyfriends!" Noah grinned.

Gran looked at them both. "Right. Well, the good thing about boys is you can't get them pregnant. That's a big part of their charm. But! I have one word for you both, and it's very important. Condoms!"

Noah groaned. "Gran!"

"Don't you 'gran' me! Do you want a nice bout of syphilis? Is that what you want?"

"Gran, obviously not." He felt his cheeks start to redden. "But—"

"HERPES!" Gran shouted.

"Don't worry, Mrs Grimes," Harry said. "We'll exercise the utmost care in that regard."

Noah couldn't even look at Harry. Talking about *this*. About *sex* stuff. He hadn't even thought about any of that.

Gran looked between them both like she didn't believe anything anyone was saying. "Well, you're a very cute couple. Gonorrhea! Now, one of you get your phone out – chlamydia! – and find me some good old eighties tunes – *genital warts!* – to get me some of my energy back."

"I've got just the thing," Harry said, tapping his

screen as "Alive and Kicking" by Simple Minds started playing.

Noah leaned over and gave Gran a kiss on the cheek, then gave Harry another, somewhat more lingering one, on the lips. Everyone gets a moment. A moment when everything, everything, is just *right*. When *they* are the ones having the best time in the whole world. And this was his. This was *theirs*. Because this was where he wanted to be. This was who he wanted to be with. This was his life. And starting now, he was going to live it.

His mother poked her head round the door. "Noah – exciting news! I've just heard from your father. He used his one phone call to ring me."

"Wants you to pay for a good lawyer, does he?"

"*Au contraire*," his mum said, alarmingly using French, which meant she was feeling smug about something. "Your father has been doing a lot of thinking whilst 'doing time'..."

"He's only been in the cell at the police station for a few hours!"

"And he's realized a lot of things," his mum said. "And of course, I've been doing a lot of thinking myself lately. I mean, what was I thinking, running around with a nineteen-year-old? That's not me. So I'll cut to the chase, Noah. Your dad has asked me to reaffirm our marriage vows."

Noah's blood ran cold. He stared at his mum, long and hard. "What did you say, Mother?"

His mum smiled sweetly. "I said yes, of course! Oh,

Noah! We're going to get him out of jail and he's going to move back in. We're going to all be a family again!" She looked across at Gran. "Looking *great*, Millie. Love the ... hospital gown and the ... drip. Good news, huh?"

With that, his mum disappeared and left Noah staring at the door.

Life did not wrap itself neatly into pleasing episodes. There was no such thing as a "happy ending". No sooner had everything gone right than Noah's life was about to plummet into a brand-new circle of hell...

Oh *God*...

ACKNOWLEDGEMENTS

It might be my name on the front cover, but you wouldn't be reading this book if it wasn't for a lot of very talented (and very lovely) people who have helped me along the way. So, in no particular order...

Thanks to Sam Mills and Catherine Coe, who both read early drafts of the book and gave me such insightful editorial feedback.

I owe an awful lot to everyone at the Golden Egg Academy, especially Imogen Cooper for all her help and support, and my wonderful Golden Egg editor,

Jenny Glencross, who helped me hone and shape the manuscript and gave me the confidence to get it "out there".

Huge thanks to Sara Grant and the whole team at SCBWI Undiscovered Voices. The first two chapters of this book were selected for the 2016 anthology and within a year I had an agent and a publishing deal – thank you.

I'm lucky to have the most wonderful agent ever – Joanna Moult at Skylark Literary, who has held my hand through the whole process, been brilliant at working on the manuscript with me and is generally all-round fantastic. Thanks, Jo! Jo runs Skylark with the equally lovely and supportive Amber Caraveo, and they really are the bee's knees!

To Linas Alsenas, my awesome editor at Scholastic: I couldn't have wished for a better, more talented, funny or lovely person to work with on bringing Noah into the world. Thank you for championing me, and the book, for all your brilliant notes and ideas, and for your endless support. You. Are. Wonderful.

Massive thanks also to the rest of the team at Scholastic – especially my publicist, Olivia Horrox, Roisin O'Shea and the marketing team, Lauren Fortune, Sam Smith, all the other fab editors, the sales team, copy-editors, and the amazing Liam Drane, who designed the brilliant cover.

Travis – thank you for your feedback and comments. It's been great being able to run this by a real teenager!

Thank you to all my friends, fellow writers from SCBWI and Golden Egg, book bloggers and Twitter pals for your support, humour and, where appropriate, gin.

Mum, thank you for believing in me and supporting me from the start – right from when I wrote Toxic Danger! on Gran's typewriter, through to now actually being able to pick up a real book. You're the best. And to Jonathan, Alfie, Liz, Tricia and the rest of the family; I think Dad, Granddad and Gran would have been very pleased about Noah … even if some of the content might raise the odd eyebrow! Thanks for everything.

Sue and Peter Counsell – thank you for your support and generosity and for the perfect excuse to come down to Devon and spend time writing!

Finally, there is one incredibly special person, who has been so kind, generous and supportive. So, to Sarah

Counsell, who has read the manuscript about a million times, who has been on this rollercoaster journey with me from the start, and who turned back on the motorway at Bristol when it transpired I had left my laptop (and the entire novel) in a barn in Devon – thank you. You've always believed in me and Noah, and that means the world to me. This book would not have happened without you. And now you can go through it all again with the next one!

SIMON X

ABOUT THE AUTHOR

Simon James Green grew up in a small town in Lincolnshire that definitely wasn't the inspiration for Little Fobbing – so no one from there can be mad with him, OK? He enjoyed a classic British education of assorted humiliations and barbaric PE lessons before reading Law at Queens' College, Cambridge, where he further embarrassed himself by accidentally joining the rowing team despite having no upper body strength and not being able swim. When it turned out that being a lawyer was nothing like how it looks in *Suits* or *The Good Wife*, and buoyed by the success of his late night comedy show that involved an inflatable sheep, he travelled to London to pursue a glamorous career in show business. Within weeks he was working in a call centre, had been mugged and had racked up thousands of pounds worth of debt. Finding strength and inspiration in the lyrics of "Tubthumping" by Chumbawumba, he eventually ended up working on a range of West End shows and UK tours, co-writing a feature-length rom-com for the BBC and directing *Hollyoaks* for C4 / Lime Pictures. After trying really, really hard, he also managed to write *Noah Can't Even*. If you are interested in stalking him, he still lives in London, where he spends a lot of time telling people that *Noah Can't Even* is only partly autobiographical, and his mum has definitely never done a Beyoncé tribute act.

You can follow Simon on Twitter and Instagram @simonjamesgreen.

For bonus content, breaking news and awkward pictures of Simon trying to act like he's some sort of cool author, visit www.simonjamesgreen.com.